The Rogue of
Islay Isle

Highland Isles Series

The Rogue of
Islay Isle

Highland Isles Series

HEATHER
McCOLLUM

Entangled Publishing, LLC
2614 South Timberline Road
Suite 109
Fort Collins, CO 80525
Visit our website at www.entangledpublishing.com.

Scandalous is an imprint of Entangled Publishing, LLC.

Edited by Alethea Spiridon
Cover design by Erin Dameron-Hill
Cover art from Period Images and Shutterstock

Manufactured in the United States of America

First Edition May 2017

SCANDALOUS

This book is dedicated to my tea buddy, Pamela.

And to all the women who act with courage.
May we always be our true selves, not who we've been told we must be.

Gilded lace, woven into a glittering cage.
Sugared pears on gold plates,
Sweet wine to numb the spirit and muffle the refusals.
The bird throws her breast against the bars,
Her heart tattered but her wings strong.
Fly, bird! Fly before the gilded cage becomes a golden coffin.

Chapter One

Cullen Duffie crossed his legs at the ankle before the hearth fire and took a long pull off his tankard to wash the dust from his mouth. Hair still ruffled from the winter wind, Cullen welcomed the heat from the flames, prickling against his chilled skin. The hearth sat centered along the far wall of Dunyvaig Castle's great hall. He could almost stand his six-foot-four-inch frame within its stony maw. If he jumped in the flames he wouldn't have to listen to the continued lecture coming from his two uncles standing before him. Hmmm... burning to death or dealing with these jackanapes? It was proving to be a difficult choice.

"Ye can't leave Islay like that," Uncle Farlan MacDonald said, his jowls shaking with the snapping of his words. The man's bulbous nose seemed rosier than usual. Either he'd been drinking whisky or tugging on the appendage in his agitation. "Ye're the chief now, The MacDonald," he stressed, and crossed his thick arms over his chest.

As if Cullen didn't know that. Over the last five months, Cullen's life had been turned upside down when his dying grandfather, Gerard MacDonald, the chief of the mighty MacDonald clan of Islay Isle, named him his successor over his own two sons.

Uncle William MacDonald glared down at Cullen and shook his bald head. What hair he was missing on his noggin bushed out from his jawline in a full white beard. The two brothers were only a year apart in age, but vastly different in rendering a lethal stare. Uncle Farlan was loud and brash, but compassion made him feed stray cats in the barn. Uncle William, on the other hand, would quietly feed the kittens to English soldiers if he thought that would keep them off Islay Isle.

"A leader must remain at the helm, not dance off to make merry, Cullen," William said. "One raised to lead would know that."

Cullen's gaze rested momentarily on his mother, Charlotte, where she gripped her hands in a chair beside him, her lips pinched in a tight line. Cullen swung back to the ornery pair. "Do ye two lie in wait for me to walk through the door?" He rubbed the back of his skull where a dull throb reminded him how tired he was. He'd just returned from Aros Castle on the Isle of Mull, where his friend Tor Maclean had wed an English lass. At Aros Castle the mood was joyous and hopeful, while Dunyvaig remained dismal and damp.

Farlan swore. "Making light. Exactly like your irresponsible father. I don't know what my da was thinking, naming ye The MacDonald."

Cullen ignored the slander of his dead father. He'd grown up hearing how Anderson Duffie had gambled away his mother's dowry. He was a foolish Duffie and not one of the serious MacDonalds.

Cullen inhaled deeply through his nose. "The Macleans, and now the MacInneses, are our allies because of my trip off Islay. I returned as soon as possible, but helping our neighbors creates a stronger alliance against the English. Grandfather would agree."

William tugged his beard. "'Tis best we stay far from the English. Our young lad of a king and his French regent won't be helping us if King Henry's troops overrun Islay. Already, they've infiltrated the mainland up to Oban, hunting for French conspirators against England. I hear they hauled Will Campbell and his wife down to London for trial just for serving a French meal last Christmastide."

"The English are like black taint creeping up a leg," Farlan said. "Closer and closer, without notice, until ye're dead."

A dry slice of peat crackled and spit in the hearth, making the flames brighten. Shadows from the iron grate slid against the walls, dancing like witches casting spells. Wind whistled about the corners of the stone castle that perched on a small peninsula jutting out into the sea, adding an ominous symphony to their dire predictions.

"I have no intention of inviting the French to Islay for dinner or attacking the English," Cullen said. At least not unprovoked.

Had his uncles ever made merry in their lives? His mother swore they were young once. William had even been kind to her as a lass. But anger over their father's choice for the next chief, and his hate of Cullen's da, made William, especially, a bitter nuisance. How could Cullen prove his worth to them? Become a leader they could trust?

Farlan craned his thick neck back and inhaled, filling his barrel chest like a stretched wine bladder, which could only mean another lecture. "There's much to do, Cullen. The harvest—"

"Came in with bountiful results," Cullen finished. "I

left Broc and Errol to make sure everything continued to run smoothly." He nodded to the openmouthed man. "And I thank ye and Uncle William for keeping the island free of English while I was away strengthening our alliances."

Cullen uncrossed his ankles, planted his boots with a *thud* on the woven rug, and stood, stretching tall. His father may not have left him much, but Anderson Duffie had given his son great height and a carefree smile. Unfortunately, his uncles thought that his casual, slow-to-anger attitude made him a poor chief and constantly pointed out that he hadn't been born, nor raised, to be the leader of the huge MacDonald clan of Islay.

"Now I will find my bed." He bent to kiss his mother's cheek.

"But we should run down the accounts with ye," Farlan said.

"In the morning," Cullen answered, knowing his uncles would painstakingly go through every sheep sheared, fish caught, and candle dipped.

The fire flickered with a gust of wind down the chimney, and thunder cracked outside. "Ye best find your warm homes," Cullen said. It was December and winter storms battered Islay from the Atlantic.

Charlotte stood, the top of her head coming only to his shoulder. "I will find my bed as well." Cullen offered her his arm and led her toward the dark corridor at the back of the hall. They reached the stairs, leaving the grumbling uncles behind.

Charlotte's face softened. "I'm glad ye're home. My brothers…" She shook her head, sliding her long braid off her shoulder. "They are tiresome."

"Aye, but I'm sorry to be gone so often."

She patted his hand. "A necessity."

He followed her up the winding stone steps, lit by oil

sconces set in the stone, their little flames undisturbed behind glass shields. His mother's fingers trailed along the rough wall. Was she happy here? Living in her father's huge, frigid castle instead of the cozy cottage Cullen's father built? She and Cullen had moved in right after Gerard died, before the uncles could do so. Perhaps they didn't belong here.

They reached the top of the stairs. "We can move back out to Da's cottage," he said, causing Charlotte to spin toward him. "And I could come to the keep for council—"

"Nay," she said. "Ye can't." Her gaze flashed toward the dark stairs. "They will swoop in here before the beds are cold."

"I will still be The MacDonald."

"Dunyvaig Castle is the home of The MacDonald, Cullen. My father thought ye to be the best leader for the clan. The one to guard us against unneeded war."

"Grandfather liked me for dancing with Grandmother and complimenting her white teeth." The woman had told everyone about her young grandson's comments to her one festival, and the teasing began. To a ten-year-old Cullen, a pretty smile, with a bounty of white teeth, meant healthy and happy. Since he couldn't live the comment down, he'd embraced it.

"'Tis more than that." His mother tapped his chest. "I have great faith in ye. Ye are clever and honorable. Ye have the best qualities from your father and none of his excesses. Ye are a leader, and no matter what anyone says, my father named ye The MacDonald."

He leaned against the wall, its silent strength reminding him of his grandfather. "But does a title make a man into something he wasn't before?" A year ago he would have been called warrior, grandson, Highlander, rogue. Now, he was called chief. Could he live up to the title? He was a warrior, fighting with ease on the battlefield, but he needed to be more, much more, to keep his people safe as their leader.

Charlotte's tapping turned into a jab in the chest. "Before doesn't matter. Now ye are the protector of Dunyvaig and Islay. Ignore those two old fools." Her glare crackled with suppressed ire.

"Why do I suddenly worry about my uncles' longevity?"

She patted her thigh through her skirts. "I do carry a blade."

They stopped outside his inherited bedchamber. "Cullen," she said, resting her palm on his door. "I went by your room earlier, and I thought I heard someone in the secret stairway."

Grandfather's secret stairway wasn't a secret. Gerard's father, before him, had renovated the small birthing chamber into an antechamber that hid an ancient set of steps he'd found behind the hearth. His wife, Cullen's grandmother, had been so excited by the discovery that she'd told the whole village about the chief's secret stairs, which led out beyond the wall around the castle.

"Not to worry," Cullen said. "It's probably one of the lasses who saw me return." Maybe the buxom twins or the raven-haired young widow who had a sinfully talented mouth.

"That's what I'm afraid of," she muttered. "Foolish chits." She pointed a finger at him. "They're hoping to get with child, Cullen, so they can make ye wed them."

Och. He surely didn't need more titles: father, husband, bastard-maker. A well-known MacDonald look crossed her fine features. "Mark my words," she continued. "The first one ye get with a bairn in her stomach will be the next Lady MacDonald."

"Wise words," Cullen said. He'd always attracted the lasses, from which he'd benefitted immensely. But since he'd been named the new chief, they'd become brazen, their desires stemming less from the power beneath his kilt and more from the power his title brought with it.

His mother tugged absently on her braid. "Ye should

marry anyway and start a family now that ye're chief. 'Tis part of your duty."

He was only too aware of all the responsibilities recently thrust upon him, including a need to further his family line. "I might wed an English lass like Tor Maclean did. It could keep Captain Taylor's soldiers on their side of the strait." Captain Taylor and Captain Thompson patrolled the mainland for King Henry and were always looking for a reason to attack the Scots, taking away their land and moneys for England.

Charlotte huffed. "I suppose, though I hate the idea of some English ninny."

Cullen moved his hand to the latch but stopped. "Ye know of no bairns already, do ye?" he asked. He was always careful with the lasses he bedded, making certain to withdraw before conclusion. 'Twas risky, but he was controlled, never losing his head on the battlefield or between a lass's legs.

Charlotte shook her head, and Cullen felt the tight knot in his stomach relax. She glanced toward the door. "Do ye want me to chase off whatever trull is in the tunnel?"

The poor lass would have her ear tugged off if Charlotte MacDonald got ahold of her. "Nay," he said with as much seriousness as he could muster. "I will give her a sound talking to about honor and virtue."

His mother's tight face said quite plainly that she didn't believe him. After all, she knew his reputation. He bent to kiss her cheek and strode into the large bedchamber. His mother slept in one of the moderate rooms down the corridor, far enough away that a lusty lass in his bed wouldn't wake her.

Cullen released a long exhale, deflating his chest, and looked about the heavily furnished room. It still felt like his grandfather's abode since Cullen hadn't had time to change out the hanging tapestries depicting serious, bloody victories from MacDonald history. It was a wonder his grandmother had been able to sleep in here with the walls draped in death.

The large bed sat in the middle of hanging velvet curtains that still clutched his grandfather's tangy, old-devil smell. The heaviness of the room weighed on him. The only part of the room he'd leave unmolested would be his grandfather's whisky decanter and glasses.

Och, that was what he needed, some of his Aunt Maggie's fine Duffie brew. Cullen shucked his boots, setting them together to the side of the hearth. He poured a glass of the whisky, swirling it in the pewter cup, and took a sip. Smooth. It trailed a hot path down his throat.

Now to discover what delights awaited him on the other side of the door to the secret stairs. Padding silently over, he stood and listened. Nothing. The lass may have tired of waiting. Lightning flashed, followed immediately by a clap of thunder outside the windows. He used the cover of the thunder to lift and drop the heavy bar, jerking open the door with his free hand.

"Bloody hell," the woman squeaked from the shadows. "Cull, ye scared the life out of me."

Not the widow or the twins. Mild disappointment turned his smile into a crooked grin. Cullen inhaled deeply and took a step back to let Beatrice MacDonald out of the dark closet. She wore a woven shawl over a sleeping smock.

"What are ye doing sneaking up here?" he asked. Beatrice had grown up with him, their cottages next to each other. He thought of her more as a sister than a bedmate. She'd seemed to agree, but lately she'd been hinting that she wanted much more than a friendship. Hence showing up in his bedroom in her smock.

Beatrice fluttered her lashes. "I saw ye ride home and thought I'd come see to yer…comfort." Her face flushed red, but she held her mouth in a smile as if it were painted there.

"In yer smock?" he asked, one brow raising.

She stepped close enough for her breasts to press against

him, making her pale skin swell up over the low neckline. "There's quite a bit of comfort a lass can give wearing nothing but her smock."

He stared down into her bonny, blushing face. "Hell, Bea, ye need this more than I do." Stepping back, he thrust the whisky into her hand. With only a slight hesitation, she threw it back. Did she know it was whisky?

Her eyes widened, but she swallowed it down. "Thank ye."

Cullen crossed to the hearth, throwing a block of peat onto coals that someone had kindled earlier when he'd arrived. "So ye've joined the pack of lasses trying to drag me before the kirk."

"Cull," she whispered, and he realized she'd followed. He planted his hands on her shoulders to keep her from pressing into him. "Ye've known me since I was born," she said. "We grew up together. I've always been fond of ye, even when everyone talked bad of yer da. Ye didn't take on his foolish bent, or your grandda wouldn't have named ye chief." Her gaze traveled up and down his frame, an eyebrow raised. She drew her one hand across her bosom, petting herself.

Cullen exhaled and turned, walking over to pour himself some watered-down ale. One of them better stay sober or Beatrice's plans to get him into bed would be successful. *Would that be a terrible thing?* He watched her as she spun around like a leaf in an eddy, skipping to the decanter to pour herself some more.

"Our mothers have practically planned our wedding, Cull." She took two gulps of the fiery liquid and breathed out the smooth fumes in between each. She poured a third cup, plopping down on the end of his bed. Cupping the drink in her palms and dangling her slippered feet, she looked too young for a seduction even if she was reaching a score in age.

Cullen sighed. Aye, Beatrice was bonny and womanly,

but she was often condescending and sharp-tongued, like her mother. To tangle with her would cause more trouble than a romp in bed was worth.

Lightning flashed outside the windows, followed by a crack of thunder. "Ye should get home, Bea, before the clouds open up." He watched out the window as a splinter of light crossed the sky through the clouds, as if cleaving them open with a blade. Another streak lit the billowing mass, illuminating the sea below like midday. In the flash he saw angry waves rising up to beat against the rocky shore, and…was that a…?

Rain pelted the thick glass panes his grandfather had set in the window openings. Cullen rubbed a hand across the cold glass and watched lightning zigzag down. Aye, he was right. There *was* a ship tossing in the swells, halfway to the horizon. Keeping himself from blinking, he waited, knowing exactly where it battled to stay above the waves.

Flash. The large ship bobbed sideways, her tall masts like limbless trees reaching up to the angry clouds. The sails were collapsed, probably tied down by anxious sailors who prayed and ran about while their captain steered into each swallowing wave. Would it hold together through the night or break up in the brutal smash of wind and water?

Cullen's nose brushed the glass as he stared, waiting for another lightning strike. When it came, he didn't see the ship. Could it be lost in a swell or sinking to the bottom of the icy black sea? For long minutes he watched, occasionally spying the tips of masts still pointed toward the angry heavens. He turned, shaking his head.

"There's a wretched ship being tossed…" His words trailed off as his gaze fell on Beatrice, flopped back across his bed, eyes closed and mouth open, the empty cup clutched to her bosom. Sound asleep. Aye, the lass couldn't hold her whisky.

Cullen slid his hands down his face as if to scrape his skin from his skull. He could carry her home to her mother, Agnes MacDonald, but the lass might get a beating, and she'd be soaked through. He sighed, resigned.

Beatrice mumbled as he lifted and settled her into his bed. He pulled the covers up to her chin. He'd sleep in the empty chamber next door. *Och*, she'd have a headache in the morn.

Cullen returned to the window, but the lightning had ebbed, leaving a world swallowed by inky black. His reflection stared back at him from the glass, splashed in an intricate rain pattern, and he said a brief prayer for the souls caught in the freezing waters of the North Atlantic.

Chapter Two

A dull ache pulsed and ebbed like a wave across the back of the woman's head. Eyes shut, she listened to the breeze and lapping ripples of the now calm sea. Freezing. Wet through. *I am dead.* But why was there such pain? Was she in hell? It was too cold for a fiery pit.

She tried to move within the confines of…she didn't know. Her back ached, a bar of some kind wedged against it, but she was too weak to roll away.

Where was she? Long minutes blended together as she concentrated on breathing, trying to hold on to wisps of consciousness. The caw of sea birds gave her a focus. As she followed their sorrowful song, the darkness behind her eyes began to brighten to red, the warmth of dawn touching her cheeks.

Her hand slid from her stomach down next to her body. Water splashed as her fingers hit a puddle by her side. Was her whole body lying in water?

The crunch of heavy footsteps on pebbles and breaking shells shot panic through her. She must get up. She must run, escape. But the puddle surrounded her, hugging her in its cold embrace. She was a hostage of her own exhaustion. Betrayal slid like poison through her blood, burning tears behind her eyes. Something besides her own body had betrayed her once. Someone. Who?

A deep voice jarred her with fear, pulsing frantically with each heartbeat. She pried against the seal of her eyelids. *Open.*

Warmth slid against her cheek to her neck. A hand. Touching her. Pulse pounding, she forced her eyes open, her fists balling up. A man. He cursed, his face contorted in fury.

Non! She threw her fists upward, her weak muscles straining in a rapid volley, her knuckles striking hard.

"Stad!" he yelled, catching her flailing wrists. She struggled, but he was too strong, and she was pathetically weak. The man held her easily with one hand as his other grabbed his nose. Exhaustion swamped her again, dragging her under to where she hovered along the edge of half alive. Only pain and cold existed here. Her throat burned with fire while the rest of her surrendered to numbness.

The man spoke again, guttural sounds she couldn't comprehend. He moved her hair, working at her battered neck. Her body shifted as he lifted under her shoulders, liberating her from the suck of the wet coffin. She pried her eyes open and licked her parched lips. Where was she? But the pain in her throat was thick, giving rise to a whimper instead of a question.

The man's face blocked the sky above as he looked down at her. Dark hair framed brown eyes, one of which he squinted. His full mouth formed a frown over a neat beard, trimmed close to his strong jawline. Blood trickled from his nose.

She watched his lips move, but his words didn't make sense to her ears. A tremor of panic rattled her sore head. Had she lost all reason?

He walked. Long, powerful strides. "No Gaelic? Do ye

speak English, then?" he asked, looking ahead as he climbed the embankment. She stared up at a lock of dark hair, which curled behind the ear she could see. His gaze met hers as his face swam in and out of focus. She tried to keep sight of the golden flecks in his one good eye.

"English? Do ye understand me?"

The accent was strange, but the words reached her sluggish mind. She nodded, the ache in her head threatening tears. She opened her mouth to speak, fingers rising to her injured throat.

"Ye can't talk with your throat so bruised," he said and adjusted her in his arms. "Hold on, lass."

The man trudged up an incline until the rocky crunch of his boots softened as he tread across grass. Shouts came, more words her mind couldn't catch.

"I found her in a small boat on the shore," the man holding her said in English. "Must have come from that ship tossing last night in the storm."

Ship? Yes. She plainly remembered the thrashing tilt of a ship beneath her feet, the crashing waves and tall masts. Sea spray cold against her skin. She stiffened as a cruel leer, in a rat-like face, flashed through her memory.

"Cullen, what the hell happened to ye?" another man asked, taking up position on his side. He shouted away from them.

"No need to call the men," the one carrying her said. "I didn't see anyone else."

"But who…? Ye mean the lass did that to your face?" a third man asked.

A low rumble of laughter floated around her as she rocked with the man's steady stride. "So a wee, near-drowned lass beat Cullen Duffie bloody?" the first asked with obvious mirth. "Retribution for the hearts ye've broken."

"Was she wielding a mace?"

The man holding her, Cullen Duffie, rattled off a series of words she didn't understand, causing the others to chuckle.

More footfalls thudded closer. "Who is she? And what the bloody hell happened to your face?"

"The lass beat him bloody."

"She hasn't said her name," Cullen said. She tried to follow the words floating around her like fish in a pond, but most swam out of reach.

"The lass blackened your eye and broke your nose? Ye jest?"

"It isn't broken," Cullen said, annoyance heavy in his accent. He sniffed, shifting her in his hold. "Get the damn door."

"Is she English?"

"There're roses on her dress." One man whistled softly. "'Tis a rich costume, from the English court maybe."

"Take Errol out with ye, and a few more, to search the shore for wreckage," Cullen ordered. "I'll come down as soon as I can."

The echo of steps, and the sudden cessation of wind, told her she was inside. A woman gasped, speaking in little rushes of strange words.

"I think she's English," Cullen said. He carried her up steps. Limp in his arms, she felt her toes brush against a wall. Her sopping skirts weighed her down, dripping.

"What happened to ye?" the woman asked.

"'Tis nothing. I startled her."

"She punched ye? God's teeth, Cull. She looks about as dangerous as a newborn lamb."

"A newborn lamb with sharp knuckles and bloody good aim."

She pried her eyes open, and the woman's face filled her view. Lines feathered out from her round eyes, showing her age and surprise. She felt the woman take her hand. "Broke the skin on her knuckles too." She *tsk*ed.

"Take her to the room next to yours," the woman continued in English. As they strode along a corridor encased in crude stone, a door opened, followed by another gasp. A young woman in a white chemise stood at the door. She spoke the unknown language, and the older woman glared at Cullen while speaking to the girl. "Send your ma, Beatrice, with her tinctures and poultices."

The girl ran down the hall.

"I can't believe ye, Cullen," the older woman chided, her tone both deflated and full of checked fury. "Send her home with a good talking to, indeed."

"Not now." He pushed past her into a cold room with rumpled blankets on the bed. "The lass is soaked through and frozen," he said and laid her down. "I'll start a fire and send up water. Ellen must know of some clothing available."

The older woman began to unlace her sodden sleeves, moving wet, matted hair from her shoulder. The feel of the clinging fabric rasped across her icy-raw skin, but she remained too weak to pull away. The tugging stopped, and the woman swore softly. "*Och*, Cullen, did ye see her neck?"

Eyes closed, she listened to the two of them. Their words were thick with a tumbling accent, their sentences like water bubbling in a swollen stream. Some words were English, but others were definitely foreign. And the dialect was so unlike… She wasn't sure, couldn't remember what accent she was accustomed to hearing, what language she knew.

"Aye, I cut it from her neck at the shore."

"Do ye think she was being hanged?" the woman whispered.

Hanged? The half-drowned woman almost reached for her neck. A rope tied around it, chafing into her skin, bruising her windpipe. She swallowed at the memory and cringed with the pain. A small flame of anger ignited in her middle. How dare she be tethered like a dog. The fury grew inside her, renewing her strength to stir.

The older woman clucked her tongue. "Agnes will have a poultice to help the skin and a brew to reduce the swelling. It's a wonder the lass can breathe."

Behind them another woman's voice called out. Confusion beat at the girl, weighing her down, as the two women spoke quickly back and forth like hens clucking. The man dipped close to her face, wiping a cloth over her lips. He drizzled a bit of water into her mouth, which she swallowed past the pain.

"Ye're safe, lass." His words were smooth with gentle encouragement, his breath warm against her cheek. Everything about him was warm, but her heart pounded at his closeness.

You are special. Let no man come near you. A memory of a woman speaking to her floated into her mind and back out like vapor, but the fear remained.

"Who is she?" the second woman asked. She rounded the bed with hard strides, much like her voice.

"We don't know," the first lady said as they rolled her gently to unlace the stays of her stomacher.

"Call her Rose for now," the man replied from far away, probably near the door. "The flower is embroidered all over her gown."

• • •

"Agnes said the woman was being hanged." Farlan's voice boomed from the shadows in the keep's entryway. Cullen strode past his uncle into the great hall. He'd just returned from searching the shoreline several miles up from Dunyvaig but had found nothing more. Rose and her small boat were the only things to wash ashore. The ship either sank to the bottom of the sea or left her behind. Had they realized she'd gone overboard and given up trying to find her in the dark waves?

"She's dangerous," his uncle William said from his usual station at the long table, running the length of the hall. "Practically blinded ye." William stood up, his heavy chair scraping the wood floor. "Wealthy and being hanged, perhaps by one of the other clans or the English. Maybe she's a spy. She could be from Spain or France under English guard. We should hand her over to Captain Taylor in Oban."

His uncles were already plotting the best way to use the poor woman. Cullen met their stares with a sharp, direct glare past his swollen eye. "The lass will heal in safety here at Dunyvaig Castle."

"If Captain Taylor and the other one—" Farlan started.

"Thompson," William said. "Captain Thompson."

"If they find her here…" Farlan pointed his finger at Cullen in sharp pokes. "And she's a spy, they will bring their combined forces against us. The English are always looking for a good reason to seize Scottish lands, especially with King Henry declaring war on Scotland this past spring!" Both Scotland and France were on King Henry's war list, as the crafty monarch lied and ingratiated himself into Spain and Germany.

"Ye will bring doom for Clan MacDonald," William added without a pause, giving his brother time to take a breath and continue their volley.

"Ye must think of what is best for the clan, Cullen," Farlan said, raising his arms wide as if the whole clan stood behind him instead of a wall of dusty tapestries. "Ye can't be selfish like your da."

The words prickled up inside Cullen, grazing the barely healed wounds from his youth. Nothing good had been expected of Cullen's father, and the man had nearly lived up to the names he'd been called. Except that he'd loved his wife and son with as much wild abandon as he'd craved whisky and gambling. And they had loved him.

"Strength and prudence must be employed as a leader," William said, his mouth opening even before Farlan's closed. Did they rehearse their bombardments? When Cullen's grandfather was chief, Cullen barely heard his uncles speak. Now they never shut up.

"Self-sacrifice and wisdom," Farlan said.

William took a step closer. "Honor to the clan above all others."

"Duty and justice," Farlan said.

William brought his fingers together. "Pious devotion to God and a serious nature."

Cullen strode to the hearth as his uncles continued to throw out words that barely had anything to do with the situation. Characteristics that, if Cullen displayed them all to his uncles' approval, he would be a priest, a judge, or God himself. By now his grandfather would have either thrown the two into the dungeons below or run them through with his sword. Maybe not in a mortal area, since they were his sons, but somewhere that would require Agnes's healing poultices for months.

Cullen kicked the clump of peat over in the hearth so the flames could catch and turned to stand with his back to it, arms across his chest. His uncles hadn't mentioned the virtue of patience even though Cullen's vast personal supply of it was currently saving their skins.

Cullen leveled his gaze on his uncles. "I understand the duties of chief, and I swore to uphold them. I also know better than to react before understanding a situation. For all we know the lass is English royalty, and King Henry himself will thank us for her safe return." Doubtful, but a reason his uncles were more likely to understand than the fact that Cullen was snared by the mystery surrounding the beautiful woman.

Cullen met their stony gazes. "Until we find out who she is, Rose is a guest—"

"Who the bloody hell is Rose?" William asked.

"Rose? Rose who? The woman?" Farlan followed.

Cullen pinched the top of his nose between his eyebrows. "Aye. She had roses on her gown, so until we know her true name, she is called Rose." People were less likely to sacrifice something with a name, which was why cattle were never given them. Although his uncles didn't look like they cared. They'd throw the lass to the wolves if they thought she'd delay an English invasion.

Cullen pivoted toward the sound of light footsteps. His mother emerged from the dark alcove into the great hall. "How is she?" he asked.

Charlotte wiped her hands on her apron. "Sleeping. We managed to get some broth in her and a honey brew with chamomile. And Agnes and I washed the sea from her skin. She's dry and warm. Bruised, but nothing seems broken, thank the good Lord."

"Any way of knowing who she is?" Farlan asked.

Charlotte shook her head. "And the poor thing can't speak, but she seems to understand when I talk in English. Her clothes are rich and…" She pulled her hand from the apron, a white necklace coiled in her palm. "She had these pearls sewn into the edge of her bodice, hidden. Careful, the strand is broken."

Charlotte tumbled them into Cullen's hand. Heavy, real, worth gold coin. He pinched one large pearl that nestled in the middle. "It's gray."

"A black pearl," Charlotte said. "Rare and valuable."

"Stolen," Farlan said.

"A spy and a thief," William said. The man scattered judgment on people like salt on stew.

"Right now, she's a nearly drowned waif of a lass,"

Charlotte retorted. She raked William with an icy gaze. "She's under my and Agnes's care, so don't ye think of pestering her." She pointed to Farlan. "You either."

Farlan threw his arms up in the air and snorted. William scowled, his gaze shifting to Cullen with the usual condescending, slow head shake.

Cullen slipped the pearls into a leather pouch he wore at his waist and turned as the outer doors to the keep banged shut. Errol MacDonald and Broc Duffie, Cullen's cousins and best friends, traipsed into the hall. They were both tall with dark hair and finely tuned warrior instincts. But where Errol had the serious countenance of his father, William, Broc's overly long hair framed an infectious grin from the Duffie side of the family.

Broc rolled his eyes to the rafters when he saw Farlan and William pacing before Cullen. Errol nodded to his father. It must gall William that his son favored Cullen, even though Errol had never said as much. Childhood days of splashing in Loch Gorm and plotting how to steal tarts from the kitchens had created a bond that even his father's grousing hadn't severed.

"Not so much as a splinter from a mast along the coast," Broc said. "And no sign of a ship."

"It must have sailed on without her," Errol said.

"Perhaps they hanged her over the side and figured she drowned," Farlan said, making even Broc lose his grin.

Charlotte shook her head. "They'd have sent her overboard in her smock, not in a court costume. 'Tis too rich to forfeit, even without the pearls sewn into it."

"I will send word to Tor Maclean and our other allies," Cullen said. "They might have seen a ship sailing off the western shores."

"How is Tor?" Broc asked. "All ox-eyed and panting after his bride?"

"I think Tor Maclean is feeling like a very lucky man," Cullen said and found his first real smile of the day. "She's already with child. *And* she has the prettiest white teeth."

Broc laughed out loud.

"Wasn't there some deceit about who she was?" Errol asked.

"She's English, ain't she," William scoffed. "Of course, there was deceit."

"English and the daughter of a countess," Cullen said, standing to find some parchment his grandfather kept in a cupboard along the wall. "Making Aros safer from English encroachment."

Errol looked to his father, his eyebrow rising. "With that rich costume on the lass, she might be titled or better."

William kept his frown. "Once Agnes has the woman's voice working again, we'll see exactly who she is."

"She's a lady, that's for sure," Agnes MacDonald called as she walked regally into the room, tucking her hair behind her ears. Agnes was Beatrice's widowed mother and a talented healer in the village. She paused, waiting for all attention to rest on her. "Her hands are soft and pale, probably from wearing gloves. A lady, no doubt. Young still. No wedding band. Rich gown." She shrugged slightly. "I'd say she was captured by pirates and tethered about the neck. Maybe she escaped."

"Cullen's eye can attest to her feistiness," Broc said with a sideways grin.

Farlan rubbed his full beard. "There could be a reward for her."

Cullen looked back at the letter he penned to send out first to Tor Maclean of Mull. Someone else must know of the ship. For now, he'd keep the lass a secret.

"A reward if she survives," William said, frowning. "If she dies, we could be blamed." Did the man ever think of anyone or anything other than keeping Dunyvaig free of English condemnation? Cullen would rather fight the English than continue to bow to their insolence, trying to blend into the Atlantic fog so as not to bring notice to themselves. "The woman is a danger to Dunyvaig, Islay, and the MacDonald clan," William said, punctuating his statement by slamming his tankard on the table with a *crack*.

Cullen poured sand over the parchment to seal the ink. He set it aside and rested his knuckles on the small desk. "Rose," he said, his voice breaking through the speculation that fouled the very air of the room. "Rose is under the protection of Dunyvaig."

Face hard, he met first Farlan's blustery sputtering and William's stony glare. "I will not throw a half-drowned woman to English wolves. She is under the protection of The MacDonald," he continued. The title still felt odd on his tongue, but he stood with confidence, like he did in battle. "Anyone who schemes or strategizes to bring harm to the lass…" He paused to make certain they were listening.

"Will be guilty of committing treason against the MacDonalds of Islay."

Chapter Three

A bear, black and lumbering, rounded the corner. The woman gasped, trying to scream, but the sound was muffled by the pain in her throat. She swung around, her hand sliding along the printed paper glued to the walls.

Sinister shadows fell around her as she yanked up her skirts to run. Heavy rumbles of breathing panted in her ears, and she fled along the dark corridor. Doors flanked her, but she knew they would be locked. No one would help her. Except... Where was he? The man who'd pulled her from the water. Cullen. She tried to call his name, but again, the pain in her throat crippled the sound.

The corner up ahead teased her, seeming within reach only to extend away. Her legs slapped against the heaviness of her skirts, and she realized they dripped with water, slowing her. Cold and drenched, she fled. Grasping the edge of the corner, she yanked herself around. No! She stopped. For there, before her, was the bear.

The woman jerked, tightening her hands into fists. The sting on her knuckles reminded her where she was, and she breathed deeply against the panic as she opened her eyes. She sucked in a breath and grimaced at the rawness of her throat.

"All is well, lass." The deep voice brought her gaze immediately to the door where the man stood. Cullen. Not the bear. She peered into the shadows, but no one else seemed to be in the room. Alone? Her heart thumped deeply. She mustn't be alone with a man. They were dangerous, strong, and usually without honor.

He held a globed oil lamp. "I didn't mean to wake ye." His steps were silent as he walked on bare feet. He set the lamp down on the small table next to her bed. "Can I get ye anything? A drink?"

The word pulled a deep thirst to the surface. She tried to wet her lips, but her tongue seemed swollen and dry. She nodded, which sent him striding to a pitcher near a narrow window.

He was tall, his shoulders straight and broad, and his legs were bare from the knees down. No hose on him at all. Only a wide swath of fabric wrapped around his waist, one end thrown over a shoulder. She'd seen the costume before in pictures. The rolling accent, the strange clothing… She let her gaze wander upon the undecorated walls of the room. Plain stone, no plaster or paint. Scotland?

He turned toward her as he poured from a pitcher. She shouldn't be alone in the room with him, especially in such a weakened state. *A woman's weapons are her mind and words.* She'd learned that somewhere, but her thoughts were still muddled, and she couldn't talk. She was completely at his mercy. But the lamplight revealed a gentle smile, and she tried to take smooth, even breaths. What other weapons could she use? Her fingers slid under the pillow, but there was no dagger.

"Fresh water from the inland falls," he said, returning with a pewter cup.

She pushed against the mattress with the heels of her palms. Despite the soreness of her muscles, she lifted herself to lean against the wooden headboard. Her knuckles were wrapped in strips of cloth, and she glanced at Cullen's face. The firelight showed his injured eye, surrounded by a dark bruise, the lid swollen.

"Here," Cullen murmured, reaching around her to grab another pillow. As he leaned over, she smelled fresh air on him. Not the stagnant, perfumed smells of… The thought pinched out, and she frowned.

She took the cup when he tried to hold it to her lips, letting the sweet, cool water fill her cheeks. Little by little, she allowed sips until she could take in another mouthful. The refreshment was worth the pain in her throat.

He carried a padded chair from the hearth to her bed to sit in. "There's plenty more water if ye need it." She set the cup on the bedside table.

Dark hair framed merry eyes, at least the one she hadn't pummeled. A charmer, certainly. He had a neatly trimmed beard, and his hair looked clean and given to curl. A quick grin turned up the corners of his sensuous mouth. It was a kissable mouth, full, but not wet, nor chapped. She raised her gaze from it to meet his eyes.

"Ye don't need to be afraid. Ye're at Dunyvaig Castle on Islay Isle of Scotland. We are the MacDonald clan, and I am Cullen Duffie."

She nodded once to show she understood. He bowed his head. "Nice to meet ye." His brows rose. "Now your turn. Who are ye?"

She shook her head with a slight wobble.

"I know ye can't speak." His mouth turned downward as his gaze dropped to her neck. "Who did that to ye?"

If only she knew. A man perhaps. Someone associated with the ship, the ship she barely remembered. She ran a fingertip over the line of fire crossing her throat, smeared with a salve. Shaking her head, she exhaled in frustration and raised her hand to tap the side of her head with one finger.

"Your head? It hurts?"

A dull throb still threatened each time she moved, but that wasn't what she needed him to know. She pointed to him with a jabbing motion.

"Cullen Duffie," he said, and she nodded, smiling encouragingly. Then she jabbed the same finger at her own chest. "And ye are…?" he asked.

Slowly she raised her shoulders in a shrug, tapped her temple, and shook her head.

His brows rose. "Ye don't know who ye are?"

She released her breath and nodded slowly, feeling her shoulders relax. She sank into the pillows.

"Your name?" he asked.

She shook her head with a shrug.

"Where ye've come from?"

She repeated the movement.

He leaned back in his chair, and his mouth formed an *O*. "Well…that's…bloody difficult."

Difficult and maddening, especially because the only thing she did know was that she'd been betrayed, betrayed and thrown into peril.

"Do you remember anything? Anything at all?"

She moved her hand as if following the waves of the sea.

"The ship?" he asked. "Ye remember being on the ship."

She remembered that the ship had been dank and confining below. That she'd been in the wind and rain above, too, but nothing else except a sickening feeling in her stomach and…yes, a tether held by a man. She pinched her fingers close to indicate a small amount.

"Anything else?"

She thought, looking down at her hand that remained

free of the bandage. It was soft, several fingernails broken from her ordeal, but no callouses. She flipped her palm over, showing him.

"Aye, ye're a lady. Your dress is rich, too." He fished around in a leather pouch and pulled out a pile of pearls attached to a frayed thread.

The sound of them tinkling against one another in his palm shot through her, straight to her heart. It galloped like it was struck with a whip, and she pressed backward into the pillows.

"It was sewn into your bodice," he said, tilting his head. "Are they yours?"

They were, weren't they? So why didn't she want to touch them? The large dark pearl in the center reminded her of an eye watching her. She shrugged and kept her fingers clenched tightly in the bedding. When she wouldn't take them, Cullen slid them back into the leather pouch. "I'll keep them safe for ye."

She met his gaze, and even though she knew that, in fact, everything was wrong, his calm nature gave her hope. And hope was something she was pretty sure she'd been without for a very long time. It made her want to trust him. *Trust will lead to ruin.*

They sat quietly for a minute, the only sound the hiss from the dying fire. She could almost hear the rapid beat of her pulse as her thoughts churned around ways to protect herself if his demeanor changed. She glanced toward the dark windowpanes. Windows were often too high and narrow to allow escape. The room was made of grayish stone walls, thick and impenetrable, heavy wooden beams lining the ceiling, and a simple hearth sat at one end. Primitive. Certainly not a palace. A palace? Had she visited a palace?

"I should let ye sleep, Rose," he said. "It's late."

Rose? She mouthed the name, her brows lowered in

confusion.

"I can't just call ye lass. Ye had roses on your gown, hence the name. Do ye mind?"

Rose? It wasn't her name. That she knew, but when Cullen said it with his rolling accent, his strong mouth forming the word, it was beautiful. She shook her head.

"Good," he said and stood, his gaze friendly. "Ellen will be up at dawn with some breakfast. Try to sleep." For a moment, they stared at each other without moving, though Rose swore she felt a pull toward him. His eyes were dark as if desire was surfacing. She'd seen desire before, and it was dangerous.

"Well, then," he said, breaking the tether of their gaze. He walked to the doorway, pausing to look back. A golden splash of firelight cast him in honeyed tones like a bright flame. Was he as dangerous as a flame? *All men are dangerous.* The whisper shuddered through her like a forgotten nightmare.

He nodded and closed the door. Rose held her breath, waiting, but no key turned a lock; no bar lowered from the outside. So, she was not a prisoner of Dunyvaig. She sank into the warm blankets, her eyes resting on the fire. But she'd definitely been a prisoner somewhere else.

• • •

Cullen delivered a downward blow, striking Broc's long sword in the middle. Broc grunted, letting the force swing his own sword toward the ground, gaining momentum to arc upward. But before he could bring it all the way around, Cullen raised his knee and thrust the sole of his boot into Broc's bare gut. His friend flew backward onto his arse, sword hitting the packed dirt, still clutched in his fist.

Broc growled, angry with himself, and rolled to his side to spring up in a fluid motion.

"A long sword takes too much time to swing a full arc

unless your opponent is tired," Cullen said and wiped his arm across the sweat on his forehead. Even in the crisp winter air, they'd removed their shirts in the heat of training. Steam rose from their skin.

"And Cullen never gets tired," Errol said from where he stood, arms crossed, legs spread in a warrior's stance.

Cullen snorted but didn't disagree. He'd spent his whole life excelling on the battlefield. Proving to the clan that he was not his weak father, in muscle or character. Now, more than ever, he needed to remain strong, a leader of men and clan. He must prove that he was The MacDonald of Islay. "Ye should have used my own force against me," Cullen said and held out his sword. "Block and then drop it, throwing me off-balance."

Broc nodded and took a pull of water off the bladder he carried with him.

Cullen drank from his own and tossed it by a pile of stones as Errol approached, his sword drawn. Behind him, Cullen heard the babble of lasses walking into the bailey through the gates. He kept his gaze on his opponent, circling. Despite sparring for the better part of an hour, Cullen still held his arms wide, giving Errol a false opening to strike. Would his friend fall for it?

A small grin ghosted over Errol, showing that, no, he remembered Cullen's trick. But Errol lunged anyway, enacting their old routine to impress the girls as the three cousins were growing up. Were they still foolish boys? Apparently, Errol was. Cullen barely retained his laughter. Which one would be the winner this time? It used to depend on which lass was walking by.

Cullen blocked the thrust, sliding Errol's blade down his in a rasp of steel. He spun away, his gaze flashing upon three women, Beatrice in the middle of the twins, Bonnie and Blair. They stood with baskets on their arms, watching. When he clashed again with Errol, swords smashed together to form a lethal X between them, Errol's lips pulled back from his teeth. "My turn to win," he hissed softly, apparently looking to impress one of the three.

"Win, Cull!" Beatrice yelled, and the other two giggled.

With an internal groan, Cullen decided that he'd feign losing one last time, anything to turn Bea's interest from him.

Errol twisted, bringing his sword in an arc, and Cullen met it, though took a small stagger back. He turned again and thrust at Errol, who knew precisely where the tip of Cullen's sword would be and struck it away easily. Cullen grunted, pretending the impact was sorely felt up his arm. For several minutes, they battled, Cullen giving a good performance of tiring until they faced each other several steps apart.

Errol opened his arms wide like Cullen had done at the beginning. For the farce, he should lunge while Errol sidestepped, throwing Cullen to the ground to give Errol the victory.

The wind blew cool against Cullen's sweaty skin, making him consider a dip in the ice-edged lake. Best to end this now. A movement near the keep caught his gaze. Rose.

It had been five days since he'd found her on the shore, four since he'd sat with her at night, and over an hour since he'd forced his thoughts to turn away from the mystery of her. She stood before the keep doors like a radiant queen. A smooth, heart-shaped face turned outward, surveying the bailey with large, almond-shaped eyes. They were a deep gray-green, he remembered. She raised an arm to tuck away an errant strand of long, dark hair. Such fluid grace. Had she been raised to walk the halls of the English court?

"Come, Cull!" Errol yelled. "Or do ye forfeit?"

His focus returned to his cousin. Broc stood apart, grinning like a fool as he looked purposely between them and Rose. Broc knew something that Errol did not. The farce was over.

Cullen took a refreshing breath. Strength filled him, and he gave a little head shake to Errol. Hopefully his friend was paying attention. He strode into the circle again, his sword by his side. Errol frowned in confusion and swung his sword, missing as Cullen spun around, slamming his sword down on Errol's blade. It wobbled in the warrior's hand as the shock splintered up his arm. Still, Errol held on to the weapon, spinning to face him in time to block his advance. Their swords clanged together, left, right, left. Cullen pushed him back with what must look like a sudden resurgence of energy to Beatrice and the twins. But he cared nothing about what they thought.

Errol parried back Cullen's assault, his lips hitched to show gritted teeth. With a quick squat and turn, Cullen eluded Errol's push, throwing the man off-balance. Another slam of his sword on Errol's blade sent the weapon flying from his cousin's hand, throwing him facedown in the dirt. Cullen stabbed the tip of his blade into the pebbled earth and reached down to help him rise.

"What the bloody hell?" Errol spat but took Cullen's hand.

Broc clapped Errol on his dusty shoulder. "The drowned waif has dried out." He leaned closer to Errol's ear. "Ye didn't stand a chance with Cull putting on a show."

"How in hell was I supposed to know that?" Errol grumbled, glancing up to the steps where Rose still stood. He cursed low.

The three lasses finished their applauding. "Brawn as ever," Bonnie called out.

"All of ye," Blair said. She stared sweetly at Broc.

Beatrice tugged the twins to follow her onto the practice field where Cullen grabbed his shirt off a fence post, his gaze going back to Rose.

"I hear she's a criminal who was being hanged," Beatrice said as they approached the men, her face scrunched like she'd stepped in dung.

"And I heard ye're carrying Errol's babe," Broc said without a moment's hesitation. Errol coughed, his wide-eyed fury falling on his grinning cousin.

"What?" Beatrice screeched, her gaze flipping between Errol and Cullen.

Broc shrugged. "It's amazing how someone can take bits of nothing and talk them up into something huge." He opened his arms wide.

Blair looked over her shoulder at Rose. "And she doesn't speak or know who she is."

"Mute and dumb," Bonnie added.

"Mistreated and injured," Cullen retorted and left them to their ridicule. He strode purposely across the bailey toward Rose.

Chapter Four

Rose watched Cullen, her heart tapping faster as he approached. He was bare chested with a sheen on his tan skin. The edge of the plaid, wrapped around his waist, rode low on his taut abdomen. Muscles lay in perfect order under a thin sprinkling of hair across his chest. Here and there, scars puckered along the lines of his upper arms and chest, evidence of battles past. It was as if he were made for war. War or making ravenous love to a woman. She felt her cheeks warm and slid the borrowed shawl higher to hide the chafed skin that encircled her neck like a macabre necklace.

Cullen reached the bottom of the stairs and smiled up. "Hello."

Her throat remained swollen, her speech less than a whisper, so she nodded in return. She clutched the skirts of the blue day gown and stepped down slowly. "Ye are feeling better?" he asked as she reached the bottom.

She nodded, but worry tightened her face as her fingers touched the sores around her neck. The bruises had faded somewhat, but the broken skin looked worse with the dark scabs.

"They'll heal," he said.

She knew that, but even if they didn't scar her skin, she'd always carry the scars inside. Why had she been tied about the neck? Had she been a slave, tied like a dog? Or nearly hanged like Charlotte had whispered? Was she wicked? A criminal deserving of such punishment?

Rose pushed down the festering worry and pointed to his eye.

"It's healed faster than my pride."

Her face pinched in a look of apology. He shrugged with a half grin. "I learned an important lesson. Even beautiful mermaids can be dangerous."

Mermaid? Their gazes connected, and she allowed a grin. Cullen Duffie was definitely a charmer. She moved her focus to the sword Cullen had used to knock down the other warrior. The twisted cherrywood handle rested easily in his palm, an extension of his arm. The steel blade reflected the muted sun, giving it a lethal gleam, and a large oval ruby sat embedded where the handle formed a cross.

"'Tis a claymore," he said, hefting it higher. The weight made his bicep bulge. What would it feel like to be surrounded by such strength?

With a flip of his hand, he grabbed the wooden handle below the cross so that he held the sword out to her, tip down. He moved closer, making Rose's heart pound. "It belonged to my grandfather, and his father before him, and his before him."

Purposely moving her gaze from the man to his weapon, she ran one finger over the ruby. Cold and hard, and exceedingly coveted. She pulled back her finger, as if the edge of her memory burned it. She'd seen other gems before.

"There's a legend," Cullen said. "That my great-great-grandda cut the bloody eye from a cyclops as it tried to make its way onto our island. He mounted it in his sword."

Rose raised one eyebrow, and he laughed. "It seemed more believable when I was a lad of six." He took her hand, the knuckles mostly healed. Her first instinct was to snatch it back, but his palm was warm, and his touch made her feel more awake and alive than she had these past days. "Here, try to hold it," he said.

Turning her palm, he laid the handle of the magnificent sword in the center. The twisted wood, rubbed smooth from generations of battle and practice, held Cullen's heat. Rose grabbed the hilt with both hands as the heaviness threatened to drag her grip down. "Aye, there ye go," he said, backing up so she could hold the sword outward.

The weight pulled her off-balance as she tried to keep the tip even with Cullen's chest. Her weaker arm muscles strained, tugging at a faint memory. She'd held a sword like this once, pointed at a man's chest. It made her stomach roll with nausea, and she let the tip drop to the packed dirt.

One of the other warriors whistled as he and the third followed Cullen over. "Less than five minutes, and the lass has ye disarmed, Cull." He had longer hair and a teasing grin. He elbowed the serious-faced warrior walking next to him. "She's better than ye, Errol." Behind the men walked the three women, their gazes assessing.

Rose tipped the hilt to Cullen for him to reclaim it. Gesturing toward his men, he said, "This is Broc Duffie and Errol MacDonald, my two cousins and second-in-command."

"I'm second," Errol corrected. "Broc's third." He took Rose's hand and bowed slightly, stopping shy of kissing it. A gentleman.

Broc took her hand and bowed his head, his lips leaving a feathered touch over the backs of her uninjured knuckles. Still bent, his gaze raised up to meet hers. "Third-in-command but first in masculine beauty." His eyes shone with humor and the glint of sexual prowess.

"Let off, Broc," Cullen said, his voice low.

One of the ladies whispered in another's ear, making her snort. She slapped a hand to her mouth, trying to catch the sound before it escaped. The two women on the outside of their little trio looked alike, both wearing condescending grins. But it was the voluptuous one in the middle, smiling sweetly, who seemed to be the leader.

Rose nodded to her, and the woman nodded back. Friend or foe? It was obvious that the woman didn't like the attention Rose was receiving. Since she'd staked her ground in the middle of the small group, she preferred to be the center of attention.

The woman tipped her head side to side. "This is Blair and Bonnie McDougal. They're sisters, twins."

"I'm the bonnier one, even though her name is Bonnie," Blair said.

Bonnie frowned at her sister. "I'm the talented one. I weave cloth, the loveliest in the isles."

The middle woman studied Rose. "And I am Beatrice MacDonald. My mother is Agnes MacDonald, the woman caring for ye."

Rose could see Agnes's sharp features in the woman's long face. She remembered Beatrice from the hallway when Cullen had first carried her up into Dunyvaig Castle from the shore. Beatrice had been in her chemise, exiting what Rose knew now to be Cullen's bedroom. Were they lovers? The thought left a hollow feel in Rose's stomach. If they were, Cullen's attention made Beatrice even more dangerous. For jealous women were a deadly poison, sometimes fast-acting and sometimes working slowly to bring down the mightiest rival.

Rose nodded her head in greeting, her face grateful and one palm against her heart. She was thankful to Beatrice's mother for her help, despite the jealousy obvious in her daughter's narrowed gaze.

"Ye seem to be feeling better," Beatrice said. "Although your poor neck." She *tsk*ed, shaking her head.

"It's sure to scar," Blair said.

"Scars show a warrior's heart," Cullen said. His relaxed features had soured into an uncomfortable frown.

"A battle scar," Bonnie retorted, looking down her nose. "Not a…" She gestured toward Rose's neck. "A hanging scar."

"Well, I suppose a hanging scar could show a person's heart," Blair added, her eyes wide like she was helping, instead of insinuating that Rose was a criminal with a black heart.

Rose's fingers curled as the heat rose in her cheeks. Her lips parted on a retort, a sly comment to knock the woman down a peg, something brief and knowing, delivered with a coquettish bend to her lips. But Rose had nothing. She physically couldn't utter a word without further damage, and for all she knew, she *had* been sentenced to the gallows. All three women gave Rose a pitying look that fed the blush in her cheeks and the subdued anger in her blood.

"Many an innocent lass and lad have suffered hanging these days," Cullen said, his words washing the clever glances away. He shrugged into the linen shirt he held and offered Rose his arm. "Would ye like a tour of the village?"

"Not strong enough yet for a walk beyond the walls," came a voice from the doors of the keep. Agnes MacDonald stepped out, her lips tight. "I've heated some more of my honey tincture for your throat." She looked pointedly at Rose. "We need to get ye talking as soon as possible. Don't ye think?" Her comment was completely appropriate, but the tone questioned if Rose was feigning illness despite the obvious injury.

"Another time," Cullen said, disappointment in the quirk of his lips.

"Ye three need to bathe anyway," Bonnie said and wrinkled her nose.

"We'd be happy to help," Blair added, making her twin giggle and nod ferociously.

Agnes tugged Rose behind her. "Silly chits. Let's get ye inside out of this cold breeze." She led her from the fresh air into the dark keep. Although the wind couldn't reach her, the castle still felt icy, like a crypt with the heavy stone surrounding her. Rose walked directly toward the hearth where a fire leaped about the grate.

Charlotte stood holding a clay pot. "We have some more of Agnes's throat tincture for ye. And salve for the rope burns."

Rose returned Charlotte's smile and sat in the chair that Cullen's mother tapped to take the warm cup of soothing brewed herbs. She sipped at it and let the heat slide against the soreness. Slowly the muscles in her throat relaxed.

Agnes came forward, her gaze on Rose's neck. "The scabs could scar." She shook her head. "But this will hopefully make them less noticeable." She indicated the little pot.

Cullen's two uncles stomped into the great hall from the entryway. "Is she talking yet?" the round one with the darker beard asked.

"Not yet, Farlan," Charlotte said. "But we have the swelling down, and she's healing nicely."

"Has she communicated who she is or where she's from?" asked the thinner one with a bald head and full, but combed, white beard. She thought his name was William, Charlotte's other brother.

"No, I don't think she can remember," Charlotte said.

Farlan snorted, and William glared at Rose, like he wished to crawl inside her mind. If he could coax her memories out, she'd let him. Whatever her mind was keeping secret was very important to her.

"Her nature is obstinate," William said.

"How so?" Charlotte asked, hands going to her hips.

"She doesn't look away from my stare. Willful," William said.

"Obstinate, richly dressed, being hanged," Farlan ticked off on his sausage-like fingers.

Rose opened her mouth to defend herself, but only a breath came out. A mere whisper that couldn't be heard above the snapping conjecture of the two elderly men.

"Possible thief," William added. "Of pearls."

"One pearl being a black variety, highly valued," Agnes said. She tapped her pinched lips.

"Abandoned by a ship during a storm, with a noose around her neck," Farlan said. "They could have wished to get rid of her. Did she have signs of disease?" He glanced her way, paling.

If only she could sneeze at that precise moment. She sniffed but no tickle was evident.

"None." Charlotte shook her head. "Only bruises, scrapes, and the rope burn."

"We certainly don't need a plague in our midst," Agnes murmured.

"She certainly is a beauty," Charlotte said. "Who would want to hurt a sweet lass?"

"Ye don't know she's sweet," William said without looking at her. "Maybe she's bewitched someone."

"Or even killed someone," Farlan said, his bushy eyebrows going high on his broad forehead. "I feel in my bones that she's a danger."

A danger?

Charlotte planted hands on her hips. "She's a wee thing. How could she kill someone?"

"Poison?" Agnes said.

Rose sat while the four of them stood. No one looked

at her now, just talked about her as if she wasn't present. The uncles switched to their foreign tongue while Charlotte continued in English.

"Well, I wouldn't know that," Charlotte said, her cheeks growing red. "I'm not planning to do that thorough an examination either."

Examination? Were they discussing her maidenhead? The men continued to say things, and Charlotte answered, switching to their language. But Rose could tell they were all discussing her, intimate details about her, like she was a horse to breed.

Rose's pulse thrummed in her neck as her anger grew. Even Charlotte had turned away from her now, tossing retorts back at the uncles. Rose stood, but no one noticed. She was merely a new fixture in the castle, and they couldn't figure out where to put her or how best to use her.

"She is under the protection of Dunyvaig Castle and Cullen," Charlotte said, switching back to English.

"But ye don't know her background," Farlan insisted. "Traitor, thief, harlot, witch…"

Imbécile. Rose felt tears press behind her eyelids and forced them away with her anger. This feeling of being only an object, ridiculed and discussed, was all too familiar. The memories sat on the edge of her mind, frustrating her like an itch she couldn't reach. Was the whole world full of cruelty?

Rose strode to the prominent table near the entryway. Grabbing her skirts, she stepped on the seat of a chair and onto the table. With her ire licking through her like a flame, she turned toward them and stomped her feet, her borrowed boots banging on the hard oak planks.

All four turned to stare, and for the moment, they were silent. She held out her hands at them, palms outward to signal that they should stop and wait.

"God's teeth! She's daft," Farlan said.

"Come down from there," William said.

Rose stomped her foot, pointed a finger at him, and raised her palm to stop him. He crossed his arms in tight defiance. She flapped her hands before her, making both her hands look like ducks quacking in imitation of their continuous bickering. She shook her head, pointed a finger toward herself, and stomped her foot.

"What does that mean?" William asked.

Farlan lowered his bushy brows. "I tell ye, she's daft. Does she have a weapon on her? We could be in danger."

"She's trying to tell us something," Charlotte said and nodded encouragingly. "Go ahead, Rose."

"Rose," William scoffed. "It's not even her name. Her name could be traitor for all we know."

"Her name could be princess," Charlotte volleyed back.

Rose stomped her foot and made her hands into squawking ducks again.

"I think she means that ye are talking a lot," Agnes said. Her bored glance plainly excluded herself from the group.

Rose nodded. Behind her, the door banged open, but she wasn't giving up the stage yet. She moved her hands in a circle to encompass them and made the squawking sign. Then pointed to herself and to the space under her feet. *I am here.* They should talk with her, not about her.

"I missed that," Charlotte said.

"Completely lost her mind," Farlan grumbled and gestured toward her. "She's bloody standing on the table."

"What are ye trying to say to us?" Agnes asked, though her voice was terse. Rose went through the hand motions again. Pointed at herself and drew a line in a circle around them all, turning to include herself.

In mid turn, she stopped, her stomach dropping. Standing with his two friends, and the waspish Beatrice, was Culler Duffie.

He watched her from the entryway arch. Beatrice wore a comical expression while Errol and Broc studied Rose's signals. Only Cullen kept a neutral look, as if seeing a woman stomping on a table was the most natural sight in the world.

"Cullen, carry her down from there," William said.

Rose braced herself as Cullen strode across toward her. Would he grab her, drag her from her perch in front of Beatrice and his terrible uncles who asked questions that made Charlotte blush?

Cullen stopped at the chair she'd used as a ladder and planted his own boot on the seat. Swiftly he propelled himself up onto the surface of the table to stand next to Rose. He didn't try to touch her but turned out to look upon her audience.

"She's trying to tell ye to stop talking about her, without her." He made the duck motion with his one hand. "Ye squawk without including her in the discussion." He drew a circle in the air with his finger, imitating Rose. "She doesn't want ye to talk about her as if she wasn't in the room."

Rose pulled in a full breath of air and nodded. She looked outward and pointed to the ground.

"Oh, I don't know," Cullen said, taking her arm to lay along his. "I rather like it up here." He grinned. His touch shot like hot wine through Rose, both relaxing her and making her pulse speed.

"Ye look foolish," Beatrice chided, her face growing hard like her mother's.

Cullen surveyed their audience. "Aye, but if it gets their attention, the foolishness is worth the profit."

Broc came over as Cullen helped Rose down. "I'd like to see the view from the table, too."

Charlotte slapped his shoulder. "No more boots on my table."

"Have ye seen the kitchen garden yet?" Cullen asked

Rose.

She shook her head, and Cullen led her toward the back. Beatrice began to follow.

"Are ye here for something, Beatrice?" Charlotte asked.

"Aye…to pick some tansy from your herb garden."

"I'd be happy to take ye," Errol said.

Rose glanced over her shoulder and saw him take Beatrice's hand, although the woman's eyes were narrowed on Rose. If she had been Cullen's lover, his attention seemed to have moved on, making her even more dangerous to those she considered a rival. It hadn't even been a week since she was in his bed. Rose must guard herself. Surely she was drawn to him only because he rescued her from the rocky beach.

Cullen led Rose down a narrow corridor out into the crisp winter air. They stepped down into a sunken garden where the tiny leaves of herbs had shriveled. Cullen leaned toward her ear. "Apologies for my uncles. They are trying, and obsessed with protecting the clan, so their intentions are good even if their tactics are infuriating."

Trying to ignore how the feel of his breath on her ear teased her, she huffed, noticing the vibration in her throat. Could she speak? The last drink of Agnes's brew had slid down without much pain. If she could have her voice back, she wouldn't let anyone talk about her so. Even if she couldn't remember who she was, she definitely knew who she wasn't. She wasn't a thief nor a harlot. A thief would covet the pearls Cullen had shown her, and a harlot would be calculating his seduction.

A blush prickled the skin of her exposed neckline, making her pull the shawl closed. Had she been thinking about seducing Cullen Duffie? Admiring a man's rugged form and accepting his arm didn't mean she was seducing him, despite the heated thoughts that kept popping into her mind. As long as she didn't act on them, she was not a seductress.

Although…acting on them was tempting.

But she had other issues with which to deal, namely figuring out who and what she was. It was difficult to know how to act without a base from which to start, a title or family name to act as a keel while traversing these tricky waters. Who was she without a past or title?

They walked down the narrow bricked pathway, while Errol led Beatrice to another part of the garden. "Here." Cullen released Rose so she could sit on a stone bench. She ran her hand along the chiseled vines that bordered the seat and let the breeze cool her cheeks. Winter twigs showed evidence of a rich and vast array of herbs growing in bunches and patterns amongst the bricks.

Rose cleared her throat as he sat next to her. "Is your voice coming back?" he asked. She nodded and met his gaze. She watched the deep gold of his irises and had the overwhelming urge to talk with him, show him that she had thoughts and could be quite clever. *You know now how to speak on a variety of subjects. Use your mind but remain entertaining.*

Rose took a deep breath, her voice coming out soft, like a breeze through cattails. "*Merci, monsieur. Vous avez été gentil.*"

She watched his face for the surprise. Maybe a joyful shock. But instead of a smile, Cullen's mouth froze. Like ice forming on the surface of a lake, his features hardened into a mix of open disturbance and something worse—abomination.

"My God," he murmured. "Ye're French."

Chapter Five

"Cull." Broc jogged into the gardens, and Cullen stood, turning away from Rose. He had to think, and looking at her tangled his mind.

French? She was bloody French, not English, not someone who might turn King Henry's gaze from Islay. Quite the contrary. Bloody hell, he was harboring a Frenchwoman.

Broc stopped before Cullen, his usual grin missing. "Captain Taylor and Captain Thompson are here."

The English captains from Oban. "Damnation." Cullen volleyed a look between Broc and Rose, struggling against the insane urge to stuff her under the bench. One word before the English captains and Islay might be invaded, the people he'd sworn to protect, fighting for their lives and freedom. Power surged through Cullen's limbs as if he waited for the battle charge.

"It's only the two of them with three men. They landed and asked to inspect Dunyvaig for suspicious activity." He rolled his eyes at the ludicrous notion.

"Bloody hell." Cullen cupped his chin, rubbing a hand

down his throat as he pushed the brutal scenes from his mind.

Rose sat, her brows pinched. Did she know what trouble her presence could bring to Dunyvaig? All Farlan's and William's paranoid predictions wormed into his mind. War on Islay. Because of Cullen and his oath to protect Rose. He'd be judged more rash than his father. His uncles would be justified in calling for a new chief.

Errol and Beatrice strode over. "What has Cull cursing?" Errol asked.

"English captain's here to inspect," Broc answered, but he watched Cullen closely. "Or is there something more?" He glanced to Rose.

God's ballocks. "I will meet the captains in the great hall, not here. I don't want them to see Rose."

"Why not?" Beatrice asked, curiosity evident in the *V* of her brows.

"I think he doesn't wish me to speak," Rose answered, her thick French accent obvious.

"Ye can talk," Broc said, but Beatrice's gasp overrode his words.

"Good God, she's French," Errol ground out. "We are harboring a Fr—"

"I bloody know that," Cullen cut him off, his words full of grit. He looked at Rose and realized that she was staring at him, her face closed, emotionless. But right now he couldn't jeopardize his clan by worrying about the woman's feelings.

Slowly Rose stood, her slender frame seeming to grow with the strength of her look. "So what the *bloody hell* do you want me to do?" she asked, his favorite curse sounding absurd in her French accent.

"Disappear," Beatrice spit out.

Rose's voice was still soft. Did the effort hurt her throat? "I am French, *mademoiselle*. Not a witch."

"At the moment, we'd rather ye be a witch," Beatrice

said. "Good Lord." She gasped, turning toward the door of the keep.

"I believe The MacDonald is out here," William's voice called as he stepped into the garden, Captains Taylor and Thompson filing behind him with their armed men. Why the hell hadn't the man sent for him instead?

"As ye can see," William said. "The MacDonald is enjoying a walk in the gardens with the ladies, not planning an attack on England with a French battalion." He gestured for the captains to continue on the path, while he turned to stride purposefully back into the keep. Captain Taylor's glance at the man's rapid departure clearly said he thought that William was running inside to hide the French battalion he mentioned. He turned toward their small group.

Cullen leveled his gaze on Rose. "Whatever happens don't say a word."

"Or a sound," Broc added softly. He tapped his nose. "French make a French noise through their nose, even when they grunt." His cousin turned too quickly to see the daggers in Rose's gaze.

Errol rubbed a hand down his face. "How would ye ever know what a French grunt sounds like?"

"Cease," Cullen ordered under his breath and stepped forward, hoping to stop the English advancement in his kitchen gardens. Otherwise Cook may need to wash blood off her blasted rosemary and tansy.

"Captain Taylor," Cullen said about halfway up the brick pathway. "Captain Thompson." They stopped and nodded in greeting, but Captain Taylor's gaze surveyed the rest of the group.

"Having a little gathering in your herb gardens?" he asked.

"Ladies like to walk the paths. We can return to the great hall to discuss this unexpected visit."

"There was a sighting of a French ship off the coast," Captain Taylor said, even though his gaze remained on Rose. "Has anyone come ashore on Islay?" Finally, he tore his eyes from her.

"Nay," Cullen said. "We patrol the vast shoreline continuously and have seen no evidence of a landing. I doubt a Frenchman would desire anything on Islay unless he's looking to thieve our fine whisky." He gave a wry grin.

"Or to find a welcoming place for his sovereign to house troops off the coast of Britain," the other captain, Thompson, offered and scrunched up his lips in a beak-like grimace.

"Ye may ride the isle with us to look," Cullen said.

Captain Thompson nodded. "After we inspect your keep."

Cullen fought against his growing fury. Until swords were drawn, he would do his part to keep the peace. "Aye," he said slowly. He extended his arm. "Here is the herb garden. Shall we view the kitchens next, to search the ovens for French patriots?"

"You haven't introduced us to these fine ladies," Captain Taylor said and sidestepped around Cullen.

Blast! How could Cullen keep the English from advancing on Islay if he couldn't even halt their advancement in his bloody herb garden? He followed Captain Taylor, with Thompson bringing up the rear. Cullen's glance met Rose's serene expression, her beautiful greenish eyes hard with a slight sheen. *Och*. How quickly this day had become a disaster.

As Captain Taylor approached, Rose sank into a becoming curtsy. Not too low as one would bow to royalty and not a quick bob like a country lass. She floated down and up with grace. Beatrice mimicked Rose, bowing her head much deeper.

"This is Beatrice MacDonald and Rose…Maclean," Cullen said, stepping closer. He didn't like the way Captain Taylor's gaze rested on Rose's breasts.

Taylor held out his hand to Rose, and she touched her fingertips to his palm. "Have we met, Mistress Maclean? Perhaps on Mull?"

Rose shook her head.

"Speak up now," Captain Thompson said next to Taylor.

"She cannot speak," Cullen answered for her. "And no, she is visiting from a northern branch of the Maclean clan."

"Cannot speak?" Captain Thompson said. "How so?"

"An injury," Cullen said and felt very much like he was digging a bigger hole with each utterance. But there was no going back. He only hoped his explanations came across as genuine.

Captain Thompson stepped closer, his gaze narrowing in on Rose's neck where the shawl slipped to reveal the scabs. "God's teeth, Duffie, what have you done to the girl?"

Rose's hand went immediately to the shawl, tucking it higher around her throat. Beatrice stood completely still beside Errol. He and Broc both wore frowns and rested their hands on the hilts of their swords.

"Mistress?" Captain Taylor said, his hand tugging on her shawl until it slipped away, showing the dark ring around her neck. "You were being hanged?"

Broc made a noise through his teeth. "Of course not. We don't hang *Scot* visitors." He left the rest of the boast, about hanging English visitors, unsaid.

"An accident," Errol said.

During the exchange Rose kept a calm expression, her head held high, as she rearranged the shawl around her abused neck. Was she really as brave as she looked or could he add actor to his uncles' lists of Rose's possible sins?

Captain Thompson looked between Errol and Rose. "What type of accident leaves that sort of mark about a woman's neck?"

The whole exchange was twisting out of control. He

needed to cut the conversation and guide the captains out of the garden. "'Tis of a personal nature," Cullen said. "Now, if you would like that tour, we can start in the kitchens." He held out his arm to indicate the pathway.

Captain Taylor refused to take his scrutiny from Rose. Even though she cast her eyes to the bricks, she stood firm, transforming to stone like a maiden in Medusa's garden. "I am not leaving this spot until you or Mistress Maclean tells me how she came by the rope burn around her neck," Captain Taylor said.

"Aye, what is this *personal* injury?" Captain Thompson asked, thick lips jutted out.

Cullen exhaled and glanced at Rose. "Forgive me." She did not move. Did she think he'd give her away, throw her to the English captains? The thought made his fists clench. He looked to Captain Taylor, who'd finally pulled his gaze from her to Cullen, demanding the truth with his stare. "The rope burn was obtained in my bedchamber," Cullen said.

Broc choked and began to cough into his fist. Beatrice held her fingers pressed to her lips while Errol's eyes went wide.

"Aye. We were but playing, and the rope caught around her neck," Cullen finished.

"Playing?" Captain Thompson said, the idiot not catching on. Did he require a sketch drawn?

"In a carnal fashion," Cullen explained for his benefit.

"He likes to tie the lasses up," Broc added. "It's something we don't tell his mother."

Cullen cut a glare toward his cousin. The look on his face was a mix of uproarious mirth and an ardent wish to help.

"Good God," Captain Thompson breathed, his paunchy face flushing red.

How was Rose faring? She stood exactly how she had before, but her gaze had risen from the bricks. Despite a light blush to her cheeks, giving them a lovely glow, her mouth pursed and one eyebrow rose, challenging the captains to ask for more detail. Nay. Rose was no fainting flower. Silent and weakened by her ordeal, but as strong as steel in spirit.

"Now if ye will follow me, we can check the ovens," Cullen said. "Errol, see that Rose returns to my mother for some more of her salve."

"We should have one of our surgeons look at the injury in Oban," Captain Taylor said, but followed Cullen's prompt to turn. He looked back over his shoulder at Rose and wiped the tip of his tongue over his bottom lip. "I will care for her personally. She can return with us today."

"Don't ye think that would be best?" Beatrice said from her spot near Errol.

"Nay," Cullen responded quickly.

"If she has no family here, it would seem the civil thing to do," Captain Taylor pressed.

Cullen turned, ready to grab the man by the throat. Rose would hardly be safe in the captain's hands. He was English, to begin with, and the idea of her being tied up while tupping had piqued the captain's interest, even if he sought to hide it. "She is a Scot, and she has her family here."

"I thought she was from the Maclean clan," Captain Thompson said, his embarrassment fading to suspicion. The two were itching to uncover lies on Islay.

Cullen held Captain Taylor's gaze and looked back at Rose where she stood alone, stripped of her pride but still strong and determined. "She is my betrothed. We will be her family as soon as the banns run three weeks."

Chapter Six

Rose watched the Englishmen, Broc and Cullen, walk away, a sick twisting in her stomach. She kept her gaze on Cullen's back. His betrothed? Had he sought to give her back a *petite* parcel of her honor? Tie her up in bed? *Mon Dieu.*

Beatrice and Errol stared at her. "*Quelle*?" she whispered. "You know Cullen lied."

"Of course," Errol said.

"Not the being French part," Beatrice blurted out.

"God's teeth, Bea," Errol whispered. "Keep quiet. Do ye want to bring Captain Taylor's regiment down on Islay?"

"I wouldn't be the one responsible," she said, looking down her nose at Rose.

They watched as the Englishmen followed Cullen out of the kitchen toward the keep. Captain Taylor stared Rose's way, his guarded leer making her skin crawl. Apparently this unsought attraction was nothing new to her. She had evaded lustful, powerful men before, bulging members pressed to her skirts. She rubbed at a sudden throbbing at the back of her neck. *Mon Dieu.* Who was she?

"Rather telling how we feel about the French," Beatrice whispered. "That Cullen would rather say ye're a fornicating strumpet who likes to be tied up."

Rose turned her gaze on her enemy. "A Frenchwoman to whom he said he was betrothed."

Beatrice's mouth pinched tight as her eyes narrowed. "Ye know that was part of the lie, or are ye a French idiot?"

"Bea," Errol warned. "Shouldn't we go inside?" He shifted, his gaze flipping warily between them.

"I am not the *Scottish* idiot who pants after him like a bitch begging for his bone," Rose said softly, letting her French accent lay thick along the words.

Beatrice gasped and raised her arm to strike. Rose gripped her hands before her, fingers intertwined. *Slap*.

Errol grabbed Beatrice, nearly picking the wild woman off the ground as he wrestled her away from Rose. Rose let a smug smile touch her lips. Her cheek stung, bringing moisture to her eyes, but she wouldn't let tears fall. She never had before.

I've been slapped. Numerous times. The realization made her turn away from the scene of Errol hissing for Beatrice to calm down. Only when they couldn't see her face did she let her mouth pinch with worry. From what horrible life was she running?

Rose walked evenly away from the lunatic shrew, who still hissed and spit like a demon as Errol tried to contain her. *Beatrice MacDonald wouldn't last a day at court.* Rose paused, her feet suddenly rooted to the bricks where green moss outlined the pattern of rectangles. At court? *Oui*. She'd been at court, the French court. A vision of papered walls, golden urns, large portraits, daintily curved couches… She squeezed her eyes shut, trying to press into more memories, but any other images looked faded like inked parchment in a puddle. *Zut*.

The potent tang of rosemary, growing beside the path, revived her, and she continued to the back door, swinging it inward. She stepped into the dark corridor and halted. Cullen, his large frame taking up the space from floor to low ceiling, strode toward her. The scene from the gardens fanned her anger and hurt. Not what he had said, but how he looked when he realized that she was French. He made it clear that he despised the core of who she was. Was he coming to retrieve her for the captains? No matter what, she wouldn't beg, wouldn't cower.

He stopped in front of her. "*Och*, Rose," he started and dipped his head with a small shake of it. "I'm sorry about the…rope explanation. And Broc sought only to help."

"He would help the French?" she whispered.

"Aye," Cullen said and shot fingers through his hair, raking them out to cup the back of his head. "Nay, not the French, but aye, a lass we found battered and in need of healing and maybe sanctuary." He lowered his arms. "Do ye remember anything else?"

She stared hard at him. Should she tell him of the court memories, the knowledge that she'd been slapped often and suffered the unwanted attention from lechers like Captain Taylor? How would he look at her then? Rose's heart thumped behind her borrowed lace bodice. She shook her head, the lie coming easily. "No."

Cullen exhaled through his nose. "It will come in time, like your voice."

A breeze blew in against Rose's skirts as the door behind her opened.

"Errol," Cullen said. "I asked ye to see Rose to my mother."

Rose turned as Errol walked in alone, his hair in disarray. What had he done with the lunatic shrew?

Cullen's cousin straightened his sash. "I had a bit of a

problem with Bea. Sent her to eat a tart or two in the kitchen. I was coming to find Rose," he said, looking at her. "I'm sorry she struck ye."

"Beatrice hit Rose?" Cullen asked, his voice hard. He tipped his head to examine Rose's face in the dim light, but as his palm came closer, Rose backed up.

"A slap." She shrugged.

Cullen dropped his hand and frowned at Errol. "Ye let Beatrice slap her?"

"I wasn't expecting it," Errol said, his hand open.

"I was," Rose said, causing them both to look her way, twin confounded expressions. "I baited her." She shrugged and looked at Cullen. "The woman has very little control."

"Ye wanted her to hit ye?" Errol asked.

It had been worth the sting to watch Beatrice lose all composure, flying apart. "A worthy risk for the outcome."

"But ye lost," Errol said. "Ye didn't even react to her."

Did he jest? "Who lost all control?" Rose asked. "Who became an animal that had to be lifted from the ground and subdued?"

"Uh…Beatrice," Errol answered.

"Bloody hell," Cullen swore. "Lifted from the ground? Are those scratches on the side of your face?"

Errol swiped at a thin line of blood near his temple.

"And who had the last calm words that didn't include incoherent rage and unbecoming cursing?"

"I am guessing that was ye," Cullen said, his frown relaxing.

Rose nodded, turning to Errol. "And who walked away with dignity?"

Errol's lips pinched and curled upward. He nodded while still dabbing at his bleeding cheek. "Aye, ye won."

Rose turned back to Cullen. "Your bedmate is quite passionate. Perhaps *she* would like to be tied up. *Excusez-*

moi." She purposely slid to the other side of the narrow corridor to step around Cullen's large frame, though her arm still brushed his. He caught it, halting her.

"Beatrice MacDonald is not my bedmate."

A lie, but she was not ready to jump immediately into another battle. "I would retire now to rest. Am I permitted to use the bedroom I've been sleeping in these past days or will you escort me to the dungeons instead?"

"*Och,* lass," Errol said, but didn't answer.

Cullen's hard gaze met hers. "She is *not* my bedmate."

Rose ignored his statement. "Where shall I sleep tonight?" Her eyebrow rose as she pointedly looked to his hand manacled around her upper arm.

"Not in a dungeon," Cullen said and released her.

"Cull, what's keeping ye?" Broc yelled down the corridor toward them. "The captains are mounted and ready to ride."

He turned to Errol. "Do ye think ye can handle walking Rose to her room?"

"Humph. Aye."

Cullen's gaze touched her, powerful, arresting. Without another word, he strode back toward the great hall, his boots clipping on the stone.

· · ·

"I knew she was a spy," Farlan called out, standing from his seat at the long table.

Cullen strode in through the entryway, having spent the last six hours riding along a small portion of Islay's massive shoreline, plenty of time for him to mull over the horrendous scene in the garden. He'd left Garrick and four other MacDonald warriors with the captains and their men to stay with a fisherman overnight.

They would continue the next day and most likely give

up the search by horseback and return to Oban. Captain Thompson didn't look like he appreciated traditional Scottish fare and would be grumbling by tomorrow. And Captain Taylor, with his scar across his face, looked like he'd rather be commanding his legions than searching a rocky coastline for weeks. Cullen had suggested they return to Oban and sail around the island to search from the water.

"Did ye hear me?" Farlan asked, his deep voice cracking like thunder.

"Unfortunately," Cullen said. He grabbed a quaff of ale from the sideboard.

"A French spy." William followed his brother to stand. So Bea had filled them in on Rose's recovered voice.

"She was not a simple passenger on that French ship," Charlotte said from her spot at the hearth. She set aside her needlepoint. "She was tied up and escaped during the storm," she continued. "That certainly doesn't make her a spy."

"I'd wager she remembers who she is," Farlan said, puffing up his already round chest. "Keeping secrets, probably about how she came by her rich clothes and those pearls."

Charlotte rolled her eyes. "Why are ye determined to see only evil in the lass?" She strode closer to her brothers and jabbed her finger at each of them. "The both of ye. Our country has always kept ties with France, and yet ye act like the woman is speaking the Devil's language."

William looked down his bulbous nose at his sister and then turned to Cullen. "If the English find her here, ye will bring war to Islay. Ruin us."

"She is still an injured, lost lass who happens to have been born in France," Charlotte said.

It was true. Rose couldn't help where she'd been born or what accent curled off her tongue. Yet his uncles' dire predictions about him destroying the peace on Islay, throwing away his duty to his clan like his father threw away his mother's money, twisted inside him, making Cullen's head ache. He rubbed at the back of his skull. Despite all of that, the fact remained that he would never surrender Rose to Captain Taylor. Never. Cullen crossed his arms over his chest, his gaze shifting between both of his scowling uncles. "If ye two would stop being so frightened of the bloody English, ye might see reason."

Farlan's face turned red, his breath coming out with blustering force. William opened his mouth to speak, but Cullen beat him to it. "If ye wish to continue to yell and puff up like ornery cocks because I won't throw an injured lass to the English dogs, ye can do it elsewhere. I've heard enough."

"Heard enough?" William asked, his mouth snapping with his words.

"Frightened of the English?" Farlan sputtered at the same time.

Cullen turned away from the two men while they decided if they wanted to push him further or leave off for now. His hand itched for his sword, but his very tired patience still held him in check. They were his mother's brothers, after all. He looked to her. "Where is she?"

"Upstairs. I brought her some food when she wouldn't come down for the evening meal."

"Did she tell ye anything?" Had she cursed him? Told his mother that he was bedding Beatrice and had forbidden her to speak with her French accent?

Charlotte shook her head. "Nothing except *merci*. She only stared into the fireplace from her perch on a chair."

The lass was brave enough not to hide her language. Or proud enough. Although the gardens proved her to be exceedingly brave. Behind him, he heard his uncles stomp out, probably to plan Rose's interrogation.

Rose. A beautiful, frustrating mystery. Her stalwart courage showed through every graceful movement. Even before she could utter a word, he'd realized how different Rose was from the manipulative, eyelash-flapping lasses around him. Everything about her lured him in. Her lush curves and expressive eyes. Her silken, wavy tresses. But it was the strength of her character, her challenging spirit, and her refusal to meekly hide away that drew him. *Och*. She'd wanted to know where she should sleep for the night. "My chambers" had been on the tip of Cullen's tongue, but luckily stayed put after her accusation of him sharing a bed with Beatrice.

His mother bid him good night, and he threw himself into a chair before the hearth, reveling in the silence of the empty hall. The fire crackled and warmed his damp hair after he'd washed off the day's grime in the soldiers' quarters.

English soldiers were sleeping on Islay, and his uncles were likely planning a mutiny. His gaze turned toward the stairs, and all he could bloody do was think about the French woman sitting above.

• • •

The fire danced in the tiled hearth. Rose watched the shapes in the flames, ladies with their partners, hopping and turning around in the light galliard dance. She could almost hear the strains of a viola, the caress of a harp, and the soft trill of a flute. Her blood thumped in her ears, and she laid one hand over her exposed neckline where her heart beat.

Mon Dieu. The memories tried to surface. Trapped under ice that seemed to encase her past, she could almost make them out. Squeezing her eyes shut, she tried to catch the colors and movements. Dancing, the changing cadence of music, deep laughter, and clinking sounds. A *fête*? Layers of damask and brocade with birds and flowers embroidered in gold threads. The fabrics whispered with movement, sliding together to complement the tinkling chirps of women laughing, the mirth as fake as the birds on their dresses.

In her mind, Rose turned in a circle, the feel of her skirts brushing her legs. A deep voice boomed from a corner, drawing all attention. Her heart thundered as his black eyes pierced her with his gaze.

Knock. Knock.

Rose blinked, her eyes opening to rest on the dancing flames in the hearth, and the images submerged back under the ice. She breathed deeply and ran a hand up her forehead to her bare head.

Knock. Knock.

She glanced over her shoulder to the door that she'd bolted. She pushed out of her chair and tied the belt of the robe tighter around her waist as she walked.

"Who is it?" she asked, her lips hovering near the firm oak of the door. Why was her pulse so rapid? No one could get through the thick plank that she'd lowered. Much safer than a lock that could be opened with a key.

"Cullen Duffie." The mellow timbre caught her inhale. "I wish to talk to ye if ye're still up."

Her stomach tightened, her wounds still raw from his disapproval in the garden. She rested her palms on the door. "'Tis not proper. I am undone."

There was a pause. "I hoped to talk. About the garden today. It was...bloody awful. I was bloody awful."

An apology? Even though being hoisted and thrown in Dunyvaig's dungeon didn't seem forthcoming, she hadn't expected to hear an apology from the lips that had twisted in shock and repulsion.

Rose lifted the bar, letting it scrape in a controlled fall to the floor. She backed up, anticipating his push inward, but he waited. She wrapped her fingers around the curved iron handle and pulled.

The narrow corridor was painted in darkness. Cullen stood, framed by black, a picture of restrained power with his hands braced on the sides of her doorframe. Serious and full of masculine strength, his handsome features were drawn tight. He didn't try to enter until she stepped back, a little motion with her hand.

He shut the door behind him and stood, his hands tucked in opposite armpits. Rose leaned her rigid back against one of the four posters surrounding the bed. Quiet and shadows fell like a veil between them. Did he expect her to say something? She'd learned, from somewhere, that it was best to hold her tongue, especially now that she knew it was distasteful to him. The thought soured in her mouth.

"So, ye are French," he said, his voice breaking the thin web of silence.

"*Oui*," she answered and raised her chin. "Apparently the kind who speaks through her nose."

Cullen dropped his hands and rubbed a fist across his forehead. "Broc didn't mean anything cruel by the observation." He shook his head. "Or his comment about tying ye up."

A blush prickled up Rose's neck, but she ignored it and kept her expression firm. "We can move on from Broc's attempts to help and onto your bloody awfulness. That is what you mentioned outside my door." She let contempt lace each succinct word.

He exhaled, his gaze connecting with hers. "It was the best story I could come up with at the last second. I didn't mean to insinuate that ye…desire or would ever allow me to tie ye up in my bedchamber. I apologize for the embarrassment and the taint against ye. Broc and Errol will make certain that no one who might hear the details believes them to be true."

So the "bloody awful" in Cullen's mind had to do with the ruse about her bedchamber theatrics. Not the expression on his face when he realized she was French. Disappointment saturated Rose like a sponge left out in a cold, driving rain. She wrapped her arms around herself to fend off the chill.

Pushing away from the bed, she walked toward the hearth and held her hands out to the flames. Disappointment was something she had dealt with previously, the ache in her chest pressing against old scars. Even if she couldn't remember the details, she knew she'd survived before. The knowledge gave her strength. "Do you think that I am a French spy?" Her words came out harsh with her anger. "Hoping to bargain with you about allowing a French battalion to land on Islay, creating it into a post for attack on England?"

The silence stretched for long enough to carry Cullen's answer, and Rose's hands curled into fists at her sides.

Cullen walked up behind her. "I had not. Are ye remembering things?"

She turned to him without bothering to hide the ferocity in her stance. He hadn't believed that tale before, but now he could. She narrowed her eyes. "Not anything as broad as being a ringleader for a French invasion." Her lips pinched tightly together. She turned back to the flames and breathed to release some of her anger. Unchecked rage made one foolish, like Beatrice in the garden.

She collected her composure to give him a taste of her memories, else it would look like she truly was hiding everything. Despite her anger, she needed allies. "I lived somewhere very different from Dunyvaig Castle, more lavish and cultured, definitely more beautiful." Somehow attacking his castle and home with her insulting description didn't make her feel any better. She watched the flames dance lower in the grate. "Yet…" She let the word trail away.

"Yet?" Cullen touched her shoulder, turning her around to face him.

She clutched his arm that tethered him to her, ready to

strain away if need be, and inhaled through her nose. "Yet dangerous."

• • •

Dangerous? Cullen looked down into Rose's lovely face, her almond-shaped eyes dark with shadow. Smooth, pale skin lay across her cheekbones like moonlight on the flawless surface of a frozen pond. "Ye were in danger there?"

"*Oui*, but I can't remember from what or from whom. A man, I think." A slight wrinkle appeared between her brows. "That is all."

"For now," he said. "That is all for now, but it will come back."

Some of the anger dimmed from her gaze. "What if… what if I don't want it to come back?"

Cullen's muscles tightened as he glimpsed Rose's fear, the first he'd seen in her. She'd bravely baited Beatrice, had fought him off when she'd woken drenched and broken, and had acted with grace and dignity when confronted by the English captains. Rose was strong and courageous, but whatever was in her past was enough to bring fear to the surface when she didn't even know what it was.

Strength and conviction rushed through Cullen, readying him for battle. He might not know the extent of Rose's past, but one thing was certain. She did not deserve to live in fear, and he wouldn't allow it. The thought of her gentle body being tortured or her courage plundered until she was bereft of all but terror, struck at him like a sword point through the gut. Nay. He wouldn't allow it.

His voice was low as he stared into her gaze. "I give ye my oath. No harm will come to ye again as long as there is breath in my body and strength in my arm."

His damned body was responding to her nearness and

the light scent of flowers she gave off, but he didn't pull her in to him. She didn't trust anyone, so he relaxed his hold and stepped back. "I will let ye sleep." He shoved away the images of Rose's dangerous past to allow a smile to spread across his lips. He bowed his head slightly, keeping his gaze on hers, and turned to the door.

"Cullen Duffie," she called out as he opened it, and he looked back at her. The flames behind her cast her like a mythical goddess in her robes, hair flowing free and darkly golden in the light. "*Merci*," she whispered.

He nodded one more time. Shutting the door, he leaned against the rough wall in the pitch-dark corridor until he heard the scratch of the bar fall. He traipsed to the stairs leading to the rooftop where a cold, brisk wind would cool his blood and untangle his thoughts.

Cullen climbed the stone steps to emerge on the roofline of the keep. The moon hid behind clouds that raced toward the mainland where the rest of Captain Taylor's regiments watched and waited for a reason to invade Islay.

"So, the thick, round captain—" Broc's voice shot toward Cullen from the far wall.

"Thompson," Errol finished.

"Aye, the sot, he asked if all Scottish ladies liked to be tied to the bed."

"Rose doesn't," Cullen said as he strode close, frowning. "Make sure everyone at Dunyvaig knows that."

Broc cocked an eyebrow. "Ye know that for certain?"

"'Tis not something I'm ever going to ask her, but make sure it doesn't circulate as truth," Cullen said. "What did ye say to Thompson?"

Broc's grin grew until his white teeth showed. "I said that Scotsmen's yards are so large, that the lasses like to have a rope for some leverage. Ye know, something to hold on to while we pound into them." Broc thumped his fist into his palm. "'Tis why we can't wear trews like the English." He finished by adjusting himself through his plaid.

Errol choked, coughing into his fist while he shook his head. "And he believed ye?"

Broc shrugged. "Couldn't say, but I did catch him spying on me when I was taking a piss."

"Bloody hell, Broc," Errol said. "The first thing he's going to do, if his men attack Dunyvaig, is to strip us all naked."

Broc stood tall, fists set on his hips, legs braced apart. "Let him. He'll see I speak the truth."

Errol laughed, a curse floating up into the night. Cullen leaned out against the wall, watching the patch of black over the trees to the east where the tip of Jura Isle and the ocean buffered them against the English. Could more be rowing across even now? Bloody hell, he was becoming Uncle William with his worry.

"Not even a chuckle," Errol said, leaning, his arms crossed. He met Cullen's gaze. "Must be bad."

Broc took up the other side of Cullen. "The lass furious? Did ye tell her I am sorry?"

"Aye," Cullen said. "And she is still furious, though I can tell only by the sharpness of her gaze."

"She holds her emotions in check," Errol said, his fingers absently running down the scabbed scratches from Beatrice. "Not like the usual lass."

Cullen watched the moon shine out for a moment before another cloud tried to erase its glow from the sky. "She's like a warrior in battle," he murmured. "I think she's been in many."

"Battles?" Broc asked. "Doubtful."

"Not the ones we fight out in the open," Cullen explained.

Errol sniffed, wiping a knuckle under his nose. "More like the battle she won against Beatrice in the gardens."

Cullen let his gaze scan the edge of Islay until it disappeared to the southwest. The smell of hearth fires floated upward, reminding him of the people who slept below in the village, the people he had sworn to protect. Who depended on him to keep the English from destroying their world. Would his oath to Rose chip away at the one he'd made when he'd accepted his grandfather's blessing to be chief?

"What do ye think happened to her?" Broc asked.

Cullen rubbed his face and turned from the view. "Something I will not let happen again."

The wind blew around the edge of the keep, bringing a whispered wail. "Even if it causes England to invade Islay?" Errol asked, sounding nothing like his father, yet representing him well.

"It will not come to that," Cullen answered with finality, but Errol didn't pick up on his tone or ignored it.

"It very well could if they find out she's French, and we are harboring her," Errol said. "They won't believe that we didn't know from where she came. The English captains are tasked with finding reasons for King Henry to take our lands. If they think the MacDonalds of Islay favor the French and are willing to give them an outpost for attack, they will invade us, kill our people, take our lands, at the very least throw us off our island." He paused, and his gaze sought Cullen's. "Despite her beauty and probable innocence, Rose is a danger to our clan."

Errol had just spelled out Cullen's biggest fear, fear that he would fail as a leader and bring his clan to ruin. "I will take her away from here before any of that happens," Cullen threw out.

"*Och*," Broc said. "Ye best think that through, for if ye leave, William and Farlan will likely take over the clan, William as chief. And except for Errol coming from the old man's seed, I don't think William will do anything good for Islay. Ye better think long on that. The clan needs ye. Ye can't act on what Cullen wants to do. Ye must act on what The

MacDonald, Chief of Islay, should do."

Errol exhaled a long breath. "Ye should stay away from Rose. A lass as bonny as she will turn your own soul against ye. Ye need clarity, Cull, to figure out what's best."

"Aye, stay away from her for a bit," Broc said. "The less ye see *la mademoiselle*," Broc said in a poor French accent, "the less she'll affect your head. Maybe visit the twins for a couple nights, or even Beatrice."

"Bea is like a sister," Cullen said. There were quite a few lasses on Islay who had welcomed him between their lovely legs before. His charm smoothed over would-be broken hearts, making them each feel special. But somehow the thought of touching another woman felt lacking. He frowned. Rose's sweet, full lips and curves, displayed so beautifully through her dress today, were the only things that stirred his blood tonight.

His mother's words came back to him. *My father thought ye to be the best leader for the clan. The one to guard us against unneeded war.* Unneeded war. Bloody hell.

"Maybe ye're right," Cullen said. Was he letting Rose's beauty affect his reasoning? He wouldn't be the fool his father had been, irresponsible and selfish. Where the cost of his father's shortcomings was kept within their small family, any of Cullen's shortcomings could have widespread consequences to the whole clan, now that he was chief. "I'll keep away from her." He looked at them both, resting his gaze on Broc. "But so will the two of ye."

Broc's eyes opened wide. "Ballocks. I thought I'd finally have a chance to beat Cullen Duffie into a lass's bed."

Cullen punched him in the upper arm, and Broc grunted, rubbing it. "God's balls, Duffie." Damnation, he was becoming more of a rogue than him. Or was Cullen being tamed by a pair of hazel eyes?

Chapter Seven

Beatrice MacDonald was a *lichieres pautonnier,* wicked and evil. Rose watched her hang on Cullen's arm as he walked across the bailey toward the open gate. Beatrice tossed a smug grin over her shoulder toward Rose. What did the shrew need up at the castle every day anyway? Her mother had stopped visiting since Rose's throat had healed. She touched the pink line that ringed her neck and frowned as the woman's trilling laughter floated on the brisk wind.

Zut! It had been four days since Cullen had sworn to protect her before the hearth of her bedroom, and he'd barely spoken a word to her. The morning afterward, Rose had descended to breakfast only to find Charlotte and her grumbling brothers. "Riding the coastline," Cullen's mother had said. Up before dawn and back after dark. Rose knew when a man was avoiding her, and Cullen Duffie certainly was. Had he decided that he'd spoken in folly about protecting her? That she didn't deserve his defense?

Errol and Broc strode out of the barn toward the steps where she stood. Looking up, Broc offered her a smile, and the two warriors changed direction to walk out of the bailey gates. Rose's face flamed. They were all avoiding the Frenchwoman.

She rattled off a curse in French. Pivoting on the thin heel of her slipper, Rose used both hands to push in through the doors, catching it with her foot so it wouldn't slam. Slamming doors showed loss of control, and she still possessed plenty of control. Silence, avoidance, and frowns wouldn't break her. She stepped through the dim entryway toward the great hall.

"We can't ship her over to the English," William said, his words making Rose sink into the shadows. "They will know Cullen lied about her."

"She'll be the ruin of Dunyvaig," Farlan hissed.

"Pish," Charlotte's voice came from around the corner toward the hearth. "Cull knows what he's doing. He'll keep the English away. And she's definitely not some spy or French general trying to pull us further into war against England. She's an abandoned lass in need of a home."

"And Cullen told Captain Taylor that he was going to marry her," William said, thumping his fist on the table where he sat. "They'll probably return in three weeks to see if he spoke the truth."

"Cullen could take her to wife," Charlotte said. Rose flattened her palm against her rapidly beating heart. *Mon Dieu.* "She seems to like him." Humph. That was before he started ignoring her to parade around with Beatrice MacDonald on his arm. Not that Rose cared where he slept, but he'd lied to her about the woman being his bedmate. Obviously, deceit was what plagued her and not the thought of him lying naked with the lunatic shrew.

Farlan choked on his own spittle. "Marry a Frenchwoman who will bring the English to storm Islay. Bloody hell, no. I'm sure our father would rather see him dead."

Rose had had enough of their rudeness and stepped into the room. Farlan saw her and started coughing again, his face turning crimson. She walked straight toward him and controlled her grin when he pressed back in his chair. Leaning down toward his ear, she spoke slowly. "Take care, *monsieur*. The words that come from a black heart taste bitter on the tongue. *Oui*?"

Without another utterance, she walked evenly toward the hearth to pick up a needlepoint hoop, which Charlotte had given her. She wasn't about to run to her bedroom so they could keep speaking ill of her. *Keep close to your enemies.* The words floated to the surface of Rose's mind, words she'd heard recited like a lesson.

The hearth fire kept her warm where she sat, listening to the soft pass of her needle pulling thick, colorful thread. A whip of wind shot in as the front doors opened, heavy boot-falls coming into the hall. Cullen strode in, reading an open missive.

"Is it the English?" William stood as if he'd been waiting for a letter from King Henry himself.

"Nay," Cullen said without looking up. "'Tis from Tor Maclean of Aros. He requests to come visit for Christmastide."

"Here?" Charlotte asked and shot out of her seat, her gaze taking in the stark hall. "They wish to come here?" She walked to the hearth to pace before Rose, stopping to *tsk* her tongue at some dried flowers forgotten on the mantel, which she plucked off and threw in the fire.

"Aye," Cullen answered. His gaze settled on Rose but moved back to the missive in his hand. "Tor Maclean and his wife, her companion, and his mother—"

"Joan Maclean is coming?" Charlotte asked and wrung her hands.

"Aye."

"We need to clean this tomb out." She flapped her arm toward the dusty tapestries and cobwebs up high along the rafters, their strings swooping across to the unused globed chandelier hanging in the middle. "Decorate it for Christmastide."

"Why are they coming?" Farlan asked.

Cullen turned toward his uncles, something Rose had noticed he rarely did. Was he avoiding the sight of her as well? "Tor says there's been a mishap at Aros and asks to visit Islay for the festivities."

"The English have invaded Mull," William said.

"He would have summoned aid," Cullen countered. "Not asked to come make merry." He turned away, his eyes going to the ceiling, beseeching patience.

"God's teeth," Charlotte swore, but the excitement across her face tempered it. "When will they be here?"

It was a couple days before Christmas Eve, and the winds off the Atlantic never seemed to cease, pushing clouds through the gray sky that matched the dull gray stone of Dunyvaig keep. Rose hadn't seen anything done to prepare for the holiday.

"They will be here within a few days and stay through twelfth night," Cullen said.

"Few days?" Charlotte turned in a circle. "Tell Broc and Errol that we need ladders and a Yule log. Farlan, tell Maggie Duffie to tap into her best whisky." Her eyes widened. "Rose will need a new gown. Heavens! I will need a new gown."

Charlotte thumped one of the tapestries, sending a puff of dust to filter down through the air. Rose walked to another tapestry, which showed the biblical serpent tempting Eve. She ran a hand down the dust-muted colors. "I can help." It would keep her mind from devising hateful ways to torture Cullen for lying to her about Beatrice and probably breaking his oath to protect her.

Rose tipped her gaze to the arched ceiling. "We will definitely need ladders to catch the dust webs. And to string up garland." She lowered her line of sight and caught Cullen watching her. Immediately he found something interesting to stare at in the hearth.

"Aye," Charlotte said with a groan. She turned in a tight circle. "My father had a taste for the drab and bloody."

"Serious and noble," William countered.

Charlotte snorted. "Gray and ugly, neither of which make for an inviting home. I need to talk to Ellen and Jillian." She tossed a look back at her son where he stood by the desk. "She will need more fresh meat for the feasts."

Charlotte hustled off, and Cullen turned to trudge at an angle toward the doors. Before Rose could reconsider, she grabbed her shawl and strode forward herself. She was several steps ahead of him. Would he turn back or brave walking out through the entryway with her?

Rose didn't stop to look but pushed once more into the brisk December air. Without hesitation, she descended the steps like she knew exactly where she was headed. The horse stables, where Cullen housed his charger, were off to the left. It would be more comfortable inside out of the wind.

Flecks of white fell from the heavy clouds, dropping to melt in the puddles she avoided. Rose paused to look up and blinked as several fell on her eyelashes. Clutching her arms, she turned in a circle, watching the pattern of falling snow filter down. Snow. She knew snow.

"Ye will fall down if ye keep spinning." Cullen's voice jolted through her. Had he followed her? Her foolish heart leaped at the possibility. Or had he truly needed to venture out? She leveled her chin, giving no hint of the ridiculous hope warring against the ire within her. He stood at the bottom of the steps, probably on his way in the opposite direction. She'd save him the trouble of turning away from her.

Without a word, she lifted her shawl to place over her head and continued her short journey toward the stables.

"Where are ye going?" he asked, but she walked on.

"Rose."

No matter how ruggedly handsome he was or how he made heat flow through her disloyal body, she wouldn't reward his treason with a dutiful answer. Blast his muscular arms and powerful stride. To hell with his perfect, sensuous mouth. Damn his deep, accented voice as it formed the name he'd given her.

The stable door whisper-creaked as she yanked it open and slid inside, closing it behind her. The smell of hay permeated the cozy interior, made warm by the heat from the horses in their stalls and a pen of wooly sheep at the far end. Small mews came from a loft, no doubt where a mother cat minded her offspring. The dirt floor was packed and free of dung. Polished leather riding tack hung on the wall with curry brushes, iron shoes, and various horse care implements, and a large sled for traversing over snow stood polished and ready off to the right.

Rose stood for a moment and shook her hands to dispel the tremors that revealed just how much Cullen affected her. She flexed her fingers, stretching and balling them into fists. Breathing deeply of the sweet, hay-filled air, she walked the length toward the large black horse who eyed her curiously, his head over the stall door. "*Bonjour*," she whispered and watched his ears twitch. She forced a smile. It helped her regain control of her temper. "You are as big as your master," she said in French. "Are you as infuriating?"

Rose's calming heart leaped at the sound of the barn door sliding open. Her eyes darted about the interior. *Never become trapped by a man who is not your master.* The words caught at her. Master?

Cullen leaned inside, his arms spread between two beams framing the closed door. "I asked ye where ye were going."

She looked up at the ceiling where the beams slanted to a point. Several birds had made their nests up high, bits of hay woven to rest in the sharp angles of timber. "I thought it rather obvious." She lowered her gaze to his, her chin tipped higher in challenge. *Mon Dieu.* Why did he have to look so damn desirable? The muscles in his biceps strained against the fabric of his sleeves as he held on to the beams. She kept her features bored.

"Am I hindering your retreat?" She gestured toward his horse.

He crossed his arms with a frown. "I don't retreat."

She laughed, her palm going to her mouth for a moment before lowering. "Perhaps not on the battlefield, *monsieur*, but surely that is what you have been doing these past days whenever I come close." She tipped her head to the side. "Do you fear I will draw blood like your lady?" She held her fingers up, curled like a claw, and showed her teeth as if hissing.

He remained at the doors, his eyes narrowing. "I did not lie to ye; Beatrice is not my lady, bedmate, or anything. There is nothing between us."

And yet the shrew paraded around on his arm and flashed her smug smile whenever Rose saw them together. *Everybody lies.* It was up to her to guard herself against them. She flipped her hand, brushing off his comment. "Very well," she said, both her voice and her gaze flat. She turned toward his curious horse who nuzzled her hand. She should have brought a treat.

"Very well? Bloody hell, Rose." His boots thudded with his weight as he neared. She stroked his horse's nose without turning to him.

"What the *bloody hell* have I done now?" she asked, imitating him. "Am I corrupting your mount with my French touch?" She peered closely at the horse, searching his long-lashed eyes. "We French damsels are known to turn horses from their masters."

Cullen's hand closed around her upper arm, and he

turned her, not roughly, but firmly.

"I apologized for the garden. What has ye so furious now?"

She looked up at him, her face defiant. "A lady is never furious."

"God's balls," Cullen swore, his arms going wide. "Ye're seething. If ye had a dirk, my heart would surely bleed."

Rose's lips tipped upward at the corners with dark mirth. "And yet you risk backing me into a corner." And she risked baiting a mountain lion. But somehow, despite his lie, despite his shock over her accent, deep down she didn't think he would harm her, at least not physically. A woman's instincts were one of her most powerful defenses, and she trusted hers.

He withdrew a step and raised his arms to cup the back of his head, his mouth pinched. The door behind him opened, letting in a swirl of snow. "Get the hell out!" Cullen yelled without turning to see who the intruder was, and the door slid quickly shut on their retreat.

"And you accuse *me* of being furious," she said quietly, her gaze direct.

"Ye drive me there, woman." He lowered his arms to cross his chest, his shoulders wide and strong. Arms as solid as trees. *Merde*.

She swallowed against the dryness in her mouth, her stomach fluttering in girlish foolishness at his proximity. She was supposed to be sparring with him, not noticing how tall and warrior-like he was. "You've barely seen me over the last four days," she said, covering her reaction with a cool face. "How could I drive you to fury?"

He exhaled long and studied her. "I've been busy," he said.

Busy? Too busy to eat a meal inside or stop by her room. *Non*, he'd realized his folly in swearing to protect her. Her lips parted and then shut. She took a deep breath, tipping her head slightly. "I relieve you of your oath."

His brows drew low. "My oath? To protect ye?"

"You obviously wish I hadn't washed up on your shore, a Frenchwoman, a barb in your family peace, a harbinger of English retaliation."

"I have never said any of that," he said. "My vow stands."

She broke away from his gaze and moved down to the next stall where a gray horse munched. The mare eyed her suspiciously but continued to wrestle hay from its feeding trough. "You didn't have to say those things. They were painted all over your face in the garden."

"When the captains were here?"

"Before that, when you heard my voice for the first time, my French voice." She turned to lean her back on the stall door and widened her eyes. "Shock, horror, regret." She punctuated each word with a flick of her hand before crossing her arms to mimic his stance. "Don't deny it."

The words were out, and somehow their release weakened her. She'd shown her hand. *Mon Dieu.* The released truth cut through the tightness in her chest, making her eyes ache. She blinked, her features stiff. "Don't deny it," she repeated, her voice soft.

"Even not speaking to me for days, I can read your actions, Cullen Duffie. I am a danger to your clan, and you do not want me here. I release you from your oath." With that she turned, walking to the sled where the lowering sun didn't reach. It was harnessed, ready for two horses to be tethered. She stepped up on the runner to climb inside, sitting on a sheepskin throw in the shadows. Should she leave Islay? How could she run when she didn't know from what she was running? Alone, in the dark, Rose's body stiffened with silent worry.

After a long pause, Rose heard Cullen walk over. In one fluid motion, he grasped the sled's curved wooden rail and climbed aboard. Rose slid farther across the seat with a little gasp as he nearly squashed her. The wooden bench was made for two, but one of the current occupants was huge.

"What are you doing?" she asked, pressing over the side of the seat where the wall held her from toppling out.

Cullen turned to her, giving her a little more room. His face was dark with shadows as the daylight surrendered incrementally beyond the walls of the barn. "Ye say ye can read my actions? Can know what is in my mind merely by watching what I do?"

He was going to deny his repulsion of her. Rose tipped her chin up. "I certainly can. You've made it clear you wish me gone, that you do not want to be anywhere near me." Which sounded ludicrous with him sitting so close. She cleared her voice to strengthen it. "Your actions speak louder than your silence on the matter, *monsieur*."

"Well, then," he said, and she watched his mouth form a smile. "If ye're so damn good at reading actions…" He leaned across the chasm between them, his warm arms circling behind her back. "Read this." Rose's breath tangled with her pounding heart as he lowered his face to hers.

Chapter Eight

Pressing his mouth against her softly parted lips, Cullen held on to his last scrap of discipline. For days he'd thought of kissing her. His cousins' advice to stay away had only fueled his thoughts of Rose, the fire he sensed under her composure, the strength of her spirit, the warmth and softness of her skin.

Her hand came up to his chest. If she beat against him, he'd retreat immediately despite the marvelous feel of her lips. But her palms rested flat. With gentle guidance, he tipped her face to deepen the kiss.

"Cullen," she whispered. Her breathy voice was the spark to Cullen's brittle kindling, torching his discipline. Cullen's arms crushed around her, drawing her across the small seat of the sled into his lap. He cupped her cheek, in awe of the smoothness.

With a small noise somewhere in the back of her throat, Rose opened her mouth farther, inviting a taste of her sweetness. All thoughts of staying away, even the constant press to be the opposite of his gambling, irresponsible father, burned to ash in the inferno rushing through Cullen's blood.

Rose lifted higher in his lap to wrap her arms around his neck. They slanted across each other's mouths, delving and exploring, hands wandering in the darkness. Without sight, Cullen's other senses sharpened, memorizing the brush of her loose curls against his cheek, the fresh scent of her hair, the sound of her rapid breathing mixing with his, the taste of her building passion. If her actions revealed her mind, Rose hungered for him as much as he did for her. Had she, too, spent the last four days imagining this kiss and more?

Cullen shot fingers through the silk of her hair, raking her hairpins free to fall on the sheepskin under them. She tipped back, giving him access to her sweet-smelling throat, and he trailed hot kisses down the slender column. Her fingers curled into his shoulders as she arched.

He moved back up to claim her mouth again, cradling her head. For the moment, there was no English army camped across the strait, no judging uncles or oaths to protect the clan above all else. There was only the warm lass in his arms. "*Och,* Rose," he murmured against her lips.

Cool fingers slid along his jawline to rest on his exposed neck. He groaned low in his throat as she ran her hand down his chest and wiggled her backside in his lap. Could she feel how much he wanted her? Reason was gone. The only two beings who remained in the world were Rose and him.

Behind him, the door of the barn opened again, and someone cleared his throat. *Bloody hell and damnation.* "Cull?" Broc's voice cut through, and Cullen pulled back, letting Rose slide off his lap. "Your ma's looking for ye. Something to do with hauling down the tapestries."

Cullen held on to Rose's hands and turned, putting her behind him so that Broc couldn't see her. "Thought I better get ye before she comes out here herself," Broc continued, trying to peer into the shadows. "Sorry, lass," he said. "I'm sure he can finish with ye later tonight."

"Leave." Cullen's voice came more like a growl, but the arse just stood there, grinning.

"Glad to see ye getting your mind off your *petit* bit of trouble," he said and turned, sliding the barn door closed behind him.

If Cullen could throw his cousin into an icy lake right now, he would. Even without looking, he could feel Rose withdraw. He exhaled long. "Ye are not my *petit* bit of trouble," he said. It was difficult to see her in the shadows, but she'd pressed her back against the far edge of the seat.

"No," she said. "I am your *grand* mountain of trouble." With unexpected agility, she hoisted herself up to stand on the sled's seat.

"Rose?" He stood as she raised her skirts to step over the front of the curved dash, her slippers finding purchase on the sloped iron breeching shaft. "Ye'll fall," he said, jumping down to dodge to the front.

"I will do well on my own," she snapped. She continued to inch her way down the front where it let off in a dark corner.

"Ye're liable to step down into a rat's den or into horse dung," he warned and reached up for her.

She evaded his hand. "The barn is kept immaculate, and there are cats everywhere."

"Damnation, Rose," he said and caught her around the waist to set her on the dirt floor.

"I was fine," she huffed, straightening her gown. She wrapped her shawl tightly around her shoulders. "You better find your mother."

"Broc didn't know it was ye in here."

"I assumed that," she said, the *T* being quite succinct. "But apparently, this is something you do regularly with other women."

"Bloody hell." This was ending terribly. He ran a hand through his hair. Indeed, chasing a pretty lass for a kiss had been his habit before he became chief…after as well, but not now. "Blast," he cursed again.

"Go on." She shooed him with a flick of her fingers. "Neither of us would want to be seen leaving together. You go out first and take Broc with you, since we both know he's standing out there waiting to see which lass ye were dallying with in here."

He frowned at her words. "Your imitation of our Scot's tongue is lacking."

"And you don't have enough *nose* in your speech when you say *petit* bit of trouble," she countered, her teeth clenched.

The shadows hid the details of her rage, but her gestures flitted with graceful fury. "We were enjoying each other," he said. "And all that changed because Broc thought I might be with another woman?"

"Go."

"Ye are jealous," he said, eyebrows rising. "That I might love another."

"You are a rogue. I would never be jealous of a woman who's made the unfortunate decision to give her heart to a rogue." She flapped her hand. "And love is only a child's tale. There is no such thing."

"No such thing as love?" he asked, surprised by her rejection of the feeling he thought all lasses longed for.

She pointed toward the door. When he didn't move, she huffed, dropping her arm, and traipsed down the stalls past his steed, Jasper. "There must be another way out, even if I have to muck past the horses," she murmured with bite. She continued in whispered French, her words sputtering.

"Even though I don't understand ye," he called quietly, "I can tell ye're swearing. Very unladylike."

"*Tais toi*," she hissed and pushed through the narrow corridor beside the sheep pen.

Cullen couldn't help his grin. He turned and slid the barn

door open and then closed, striding toward Broc on the keep stairs. Broc looked at Cullen and back at the barn. "Aren't ye forgetting someone?" he asked.

"Get inside, ye arse," Cullen said and dragged him by the arm into the entryway. "And keep your mouth shut. Every time ye say something, I get in trouble."

Broc chuckled. "Trouble? If it's trouble that's brought back your good cheer, I'll find ye more."

"Bloody hell," Cullen said, but smiled broadly. He'd had a taste of *grand* trouble, and he wanted more. She may have fled cursing and denying that love existed, but that didn't change the fact that Rose was jealous.

. . .

His hands trailed down over her breasts, sending jolts of sensation deep into her pelvis. Wet kisses seared her neck. "Mon Dieu," she breathed, clawing at Cullen's naked back. Sleek muscles under hot skin, she slid her fingers across the expanse as he kissed down her body. Her clothes faded away, leaving her nude. Skin against skin, his mouth clamped down over—

Knock. Knock. "Rose? Are ye awake, dear?"

Rose's eyes snapped open, her parted lips framing rapid breaths. The thin bedsheets coiled around her legs, and she kicked at them to loosen herself. "*Oui*," she called. "Yes."

"Good," Charlotte called through the barred door. "I am in need of your help below, stringing holly. The Macleans could show up any day."

Rose glanced at the window where the frosty glass looked gray. *Mon Dieu.* It was barely dawn. "Of course, I will be down soon." As soon as her traitorous body stopped aching for that blasted man's touch. She raised a hand to her peaked breasts and felt a clenching below. Closing her eyes, she flopped back onto the mangled bedclothes.

After the barn incident, she'd taken her meal alone in her room, barred the door, and forced herself to forget the feel of Cullen's hot mouth on her throat and lips. She'd suspected that he was a charmer from the start, but the giggling women and Broc's words last night, not to mention Cullen's acceptance of her accusation, all proved him to be a rogue.

Don't lose your heart to les coquins. *Don't believe their words of love. There is no such thing as love.* Someone had warned her about scoundrels and their lies. Rose didn't like the feeling of anticipated betrayal. *Once a rogue, always a rogue.* It was better never to start something that was doomed.

She could guard her unwanted thoughts while awake, but her dreams continued to betray her. "*Zut*," she cursed. With such detailed imaginings each night, it was no wonder she'd opened under his skillful hands in the barn. She huffed and rolled onto her stomach, but the bunched blanket rubbed against the *V* of her legs, reminding her of the hardness she'd felt yesterday through her skirts when sitting on Cullen's lap.

Rose punched her fist into the mattress and continued to the far side of the bed, sliding her legs out. Cold water. That's what she needed to combat Cullen's heat. "Damn Scot," she hissed and hurried to slam her arms through the sleeves of the robe Charlotte had found for her. With the door barred, no one had been up to tend the fire, and it had grown cold overnight. The chill in the room gave her something else to focus on, and slowly the ache in her body released its hold. *Oui.* Ice, snow, and frozen feet would help keep her body in line.

A quarter hour later, Rose stepped lightly down the steps to the great hall. She'd quickly braided her hair, letting it fall down her back, and wore one of the dresses Ellen had found for her to work in. It was gray and without adornment, so Cullen would hardly notice her.

"We must air the castle and string up garlands of holly and some mistletoe," Charlotte instructed Broc and Errol as Rose rounded the corner out of the alcove. "Errol, help Cullen lower the tapestries, so we can beat them outside."

Cullen balanced on a ladder at the far end of the room, his upper half lifting under the ponderous tapestry. Only his muscular legs showed above the lip of his leather boots. The strength in them made Rose's stomach flutter, and she turned away.

Broc yawned. "It's hardly light out."

Errol jogged over to help Cullen as the ties gave way.

"'Tis best to roll it to carry outside," Charlotte advised. "Broc, help them."

"Ye know it's snowing," Errol said. The heavy tapestry collapsed over his head, muffling his words. Cullen stood above his cousins, hair in disarray after having been raked by the dust-filled depiction of a dragonfly-encircled lady and unicorn.

"The snow will freshen them," Charlotte said, propping hands on her hips.

Footsteps pattered from the corridor with the sound of wooden wheels on the floorboards. "There now," Charlotte called and waved Ellen, Dunyvaig's head maid, over to the table. "Rose can help me dust these extra candles to put on the mantel."

"My mother never let anyone decorate before Christmas Eve," Broc called, his words strained as he rolled the tapestry. "Said it was unlucky."

"We will cut holly and string it," Charlotte said, "but won't put it up until day after tomorrow, which *is* Christmas Eve."

"Bloody," Broc said. "She's right."

"Stop yer gabbing," Errol chided.

Cullen jumped down from the ladder. He looked Rose's way, but she pretended to be already turning toward the table. Would he start ignoring her again, walk past her since his cousins were there? Or would his cousins wonder why he wasn't ignoring her? *It barely matters,* she told herself.

Charlotte wiped her hands. "I need to get some girls from the village to clean the extra rooms today. My father never had visitors after Mother died. They're probably thick with dust."

Rose pulled a large pillar candle out of the crate. From the corner of her eye, she noticed Cullen moving the ladder to the next tapestry, depicting courtly ladies. Errol and Broc stomped toward her, carrying the rolled unicorn tapestry between them. Broc yawned again, his eyes red and his skin dull.

"If you didn't stay up so late drinking whisky," Rose said, "mornings wouldn't be such torture."

He frowned sourly. "Have ye been spying on me?" he asked and stumbled, almost dropping his end.

"Bloody hell," Errol cursed, but Broc ignored him, his sleep-filled eyes opening wider.

"Not that I think ye've been spying on me," Broc said. "Or anyone…here. Or anywhere, that is."

Rose graced him with a grin. "Good to know."

The men spent the rest of the morning outdoors, thumping the massive tapestries that Cullen's grandfather had brought from Edinburgh decades ago. Rose felt Cullen's gaze on her nearly a dozen times as he traipsed in and out. He desired her, that was obvious. At least for now. *Men want what they can't easily acquire.* And she wasn't planning on falling into his embrace again like in the barn. Despite his actions, she couldn't erase the memory of his face in the garden.

He walked past her twice, close enough to brush her skirts. The sound of his voice, and the strength of his stride, made her stomach flutter until she was slightly nauseous, like consuming too much wine and sugared fruits. *Non.* She would not submit to the pull she felt and kept her gaze from following him, though she still knew exactly where he was, as if he were a lodestone, pulling her.

Rose dusted and set the candles in small groups on the mantel. Beatrice and her friends wafted inside with a few other girls from the village, brooms in hand. When she saw Rose, Beatrice sniffed condescendingly. Would she be so triumphant if she knew that Rose and Cullen had nearly set the hay ablaze in the barn with their passion? Was there really nothing between Cullen and Beatrice?

This was maddening. The imprint of Cullen's warm, hard body pressed to hers was still fresh, the lure of his kiss still strong. *Mon Dieu.* But she was French, and he was the leader of a Scottish clan that didn't want her on their island.

· · ·

Rose sat before the tiled hearth in her room. Supper had been a stilted affair with haphazard frowns from Cullen, mumbles from his uncles, and a worrisome diatribe from Charlotte about the state of the keep. As soon as polite, Rose retired to her room without even a glance in Cullen's direction.

Would he come to her door? If he did, would she let him in? Her head shouted "absolutely not," which only made her loins demand a beheading. Rose let her face fall into her hands. She ran fingers through her hair, releasing little knots that her natural curls bred. The soft mass mimicked her predicament. Every time she raked through one knot, more threads wound around each other into a new knot, making a glorious mess.

She needed to consider her future. Whether remembered or not, she would never voluntarily return to France. Where, then, should she go? The thought of climbing aboard a ship made her stomach roll. Could she stay in the village at Dunyvaig, hiding the fact she was French, ignoring

Cullen when he lived so close? Watching him hop from woman to woman as rogues were wont to do?

Her stomach twisted painfully at the thought. Had she been stricken by the foolish emotion that Cullen had mentioned in the barn? "Love," she murmured and snorted. She'd been warned about the weakness that came with it. That love was used only to control someone. That it was best to keep clear of it altogether. Certainly, she was angered only by the thought of Cullen with another woman because it would mean he lied. It had nothing to do with love.

"*Zut*," she cursed and stood up, turning to the door. She rested her ear against the solid wood. Nothing stirred. He must be asleep. "Good," she whispered and turned to her own bed. She huffed, knowing her traitorous dreams would likely torture her.

A door opened and shut farther down the hall, kicking her heart into a race as she spun around. Cullen? But no boots clipped toward her door. Rose hadn't placed the bar yet, so it was easy to tug her door open. First an inch, and then six, until she could glance out and down toward Cullen's room.

In the dim light of a taper, a woman hurried toward the stairs, a woman in a white chemise and robe. Beatrice MacDonald.

Chapter Nine

Cullen stood before his hearth, a cup of ale in hand. He was tired. Not physically. After so much training for war, a day of lifting and beating tapestries couldn't exhaust him. It was the mental games of chess he played daily with his uncles—proving to them that he was responsible—that wore on him, and, of course, dodging Bea. The woman was relentless.

He heard his door open again and sighed heavily. "I said," he started and turned. But it wasn't Beatrice returning. "Rose?"

She stood there in her robe, hair flowing down around her shoulders like a fallen angel. Her gaze dipped to his naked chest. She swallowed, raising her eyes back to his. "If you lie about something as simple as inviting Beatrice to your bed, your oath to me is as worthless as…as…as a lily to a starving peasant." Her face pinched as if she weren't happy with the metaphor she'd chosen, but then firmed her glare at him. She waved her hand in the air. "Or a fur coat to someone burning under the summer sun." She closed her eyes, both her hands going to her forehead. "Or…something…" She huffed as if angry over her strange retorts.

"Starving peasant?" he asked.

She dropped her arms to her sides. "Never mind. And never mind your worthless vow to see me safe." She turned on her heel, but he beat her to the door, shutting it with a soft *whump*.

He turned and leaned against the escape. "Inviting Beatrice to my bed?"

"*Oui*, Beatrice," she said, a quiet disdain in her words. "Or do you have another tied up in here? One of her giggling friends?" She turned in a tight circle as if searching the dark corners.

He stopped before her, and she straightened, hands fisted at her sides. Her lips were bent into a frown, but still looked so incredibly luscious that he had to breathe deeply to gain control. He'd never kissed a woman who didn't want him to, and he was fairly certain, after she'd risked life and limb last night to escape the sled, that she didn't want his kiss.

"Would ye have some whisky?" he asked.

"Absurd," she muttered and glared at him.

He *tsk*ed. "Such jealousy from a rumor."

"I just watched her leave your room in her chemise."

He snorted. "Of course ye did," he said, his mouth tight with sarcasm. He stepped forward and encircled her fragile wrist with his hand. "Come here."

"*Non.*"

As gently as he could, he dragged her along behind him across the room. "I'm not going to do anything but show ye something. After, ye can decide if I'm a lecherous pig. Or a flower seller to peasants."

Before the door to the secret steps, he let her snatch her hand away. Cullen handed her a taper from the mantel and lifted the bar across the door. "Have a look," he said and ushered her toward the gaping maw.

"Is this your dungeon?"

He rubbed his chin. "That's not a bad idea. I could put some bars at the top of the stairs."

Rose brandished the taper before her and peeked around the doorway, all the while keeping Cullen in her periphery. Damnation but Rose was gorgeous. Her robe and gown flowed loosely around her, showing and then hiding the lush form underneath. *Och*, but to see and touch her. He sipped at his ale and tried to think of something to cool his blood. Rotten teeth. Spoiled cabbages. His dead grandmother's toenails.

She stepped inside the small room and backed out quickly. "It's a staircase," she said.

"It's a bloody annoyance," Cullen answered. "Beatrice sneaks up them almost every night, or one of the others hoping to be the next Lady MacDonald of Islay."

Rose set the taper back on the mantel. "This proves nothing except that you have a secret way to sneak women up to your bedchamber. What a convenience for a rogue."

He cursed. "It was a hidden passageway for the chief to use, and I inherited the room. And it surely isn't a secret."

Rose looked back and forth between the black chasm of the stairway and Cullen. "The morning you found me, Beatrice was coming out of your room. I remember seeing her."

"Aye, she'd snuck up here, got drunk on Duffie whisky," he said, setting his ale cup down near the decanter. "I left her here to sleep it off, while I stayed in the room I put ye in next door."

Rose studied him, and he met her gaze without looking away. Slices of flame light and shadow cut against her high cheekbones and slender nose. Could she read the truth in his words?

"Hmmm," she said in the back of her throat and walked

over to the decanter where he stood. She leaned over and sniffed. "Duffie whisky?"

"Aye, my father's sister distills it." He poured some into his empty cup and held it out to her with a nod. "A peace offering."

Rose stared at the cup, her hand rising slowly to take it. Scrunching her nose, she moved it over the top and inhaled the oaky fumes.

"'Tis very smooth," he said with a nod. She touched the cup to her full lips and tipped it. Cullen watched her throat as she swallowed, his mouth going dry. *Och*, he'd tent out the front of his kilt before long if he kept watching her. He walked away, squatting before the fire to stir up the embers and add more peat.

"*Oui*. Smooth," she said behind him. He adjusted his growing erection before he stood and turned back to her.

She took a second taste of the cup and set it down near the decanter. "So, you really are not bedding Beatrice," she said. Her beautiful eyes reflected the flames, making them shine.

"Nay, no matter how much she insinuates that I am." He shook his head. "She grew up acting like an annoying sister, and I certainly wouldn't take a sister to my bed."

"And the others?" she asked. "Do they climb your secret stairs?"

Cullen leaned against the mantel, watching her. She was like a doe, ready to flee at the hint of danger or the suggestion of a lie. The fire was hot on the bare skin of his back, and he breathed in the cool air in the room. "I'm not a liar, Rose. If ye want to know about my past conquests, I will tell ye. I was not chaste, but since I've become chief, I know that the consequences to bedding a lass could be dire. Therefore, I do not take the act lightly. And I do not invite lasses to visit me, up those stairs or through my door. At least not for months now." He crossed his arms, making sure to meet her gaze.

"Before that, aye." He tipped his chin forward, a slight tilt to his head. "I hadn't grown into my years." He shrugged. "Rogue probably was an accurate name for me. We all have things in our past we'd rather not flaunt before people whom we want to impress."

Rose moved closer to the fire, on the other side of the mantel from him. She reached her hands out toward the flames. "You shouldn't have kissed me last night."

"I was showing ye that I don't despise ye for being French, since ye believe actions, not words."

She nodded slowly. "*Oui*. Words are like the clothes we cover ourselves with. Actions show what is inside a person, what is in their heart." She looked at him and crossed her arms, which only propped her breasts higher. He raised his gaze to her eyes. "Then you don't despise the French," she said, her voice breathy, like deep velvet.

He cleared his throat. "I don't know the French. I know only a lass who washed up on my shores who has a face of an angel and a voice like a purring wildcat."

The hint of a smile tugged at her mouth. "You haven't heard me purr, *monsieur*."

Her words flowed like clear, strong whisky straight into his rushing blood. No amount of putrid thoughts could hide the desire growing in him. "Ah now, lass," he replied, giving a slow shake of his head. "I would surely love to hear ye purr."

She lowered her arms, and he saw the faint tips of her nipples brush against her smock where her robe fell open. "And how exactly would you make me purr?" she asked.

He stood straight, the muscles in his arms contracting as his hands clenched into fists. He barely dared to breathe. Was this really happening? Surely, she couldn't be intoxicated by two sips of whisky. "I would kiss ye, Rose, from each of your beautiful eyes to the underside of each of your naked feet."

Rose glanced down to where her toes clenched on top of each other on the warm tiles before the hearth. "A wildcat doesn't tame easily," she volleyed back. "Kissing my feet would not elicit a purr."

Cullen stepped closer so that they faced each other. His heart pounded with the effort to control his movements. "Ye will purr, lass, when I kiss ye here." As slow as fog wafting in around the islands, he slid his hand up around her neck, his thumb resting lightly on the throbbing of her pulse. It beat hard, and she swallowed. He leaned in with painstaking control, and touched a slow kiss under her ear. He trailed lower along the underside of her jaw and the column of her throat, just the whisper of a kiss. His fingers warmed under the weight of her unbound hair.

Absolutely, intoxicatingly beautiful. Her eyes were closed, lips open like she was already begging for him. Long lashes blinked as she focused on his face. "No purring yet," she whispered.

If she knew what her gentle words were doing to him, how they strung him so tight he might fly apart and grab her to him… He set a kiss upon her collarbone, the flesh exposed above the lace-edged dip of fabric. Her skin was fragrant and smooth. "How about here?" With each kiss, he trailed his fingers over the spots, reveling in the silkiness of her flesh. Chill bumps rose along her, making her nipples jut forward.

He inhaled low on her neckline. "Lass, ye smell delicious."

Her fingers touched the back of his head, holding him to her chest, so he could nuzzle the warmth between her breasts. She wound fingers in his hair, and he let a groan escape.

"Do fierce Highland chiefs purr?" she asked, and he felt his control waver with the intoxicating flow of her accent.

He lifted his gaze to hers and grinned. "Nay, we growl."

He looked down at her peaks straining against the white fabric of her smock, and pushed the heavy robe from her shoulders. It dropped to pool around her bare feet. Slowly Cullen lowered his face. When she didn't move away, he opened his lips and kissed her nipple through the fabric. She gasped softly, and he sucked inward, tugging on the sensitive peak to flick it with his tongue. He bent over her, and she arched her back, lifting her breasts to him. He growled low in his throat as she reached forward to pinch one of his nipples. The sensation shot right down to his groin.

Rose's breath came faster, and she pressed her body in to him, accepting his mouth and hands fully. Reaching behind, he cupped her luscious arse, molding her to his massive erection. *Och*, she was round and soft in every womanly place possible. When she rubbed herself against him, the floodgates he'd held so tightly opened on a groan. He nearly lifted her from the floor, wrapping her in his arms, and loved her with his mouth. Rose clung to his shoulders as he sucked and kissed. She rubbed her pelvis against him, spurring him to shore up the back of her smock, exposing her naked legs and arse.

"*Mon Dieu*," she whispered.

He stilled his hands on the soft globes of her backside. "Was that a purr, wildcat?" His breath came hard.

She shook her head. "Not a purr," she whispered. "A humble prayer for my legs not to buckle."

He gave her a wicked grin. "I'll catch ye if they do." He lowered his mouth back to hers, tasting her deeply, meeting her tongue as they breathed and strained against each other. She tasted of honey, whisky, and raw passion. He could feast on her forever.

Rose clung to his shoulders as she pressed back into his plundering kiss. His hands explored the smooth skin of her bare backside. When her legs relaxed, his fingers dove lower between them, touching her hot, wet core from behind. She gasped, arching back against his hand, parting her legs to give him better access to her heat. He moved his hand in front to find her most sensitive spot, rubbing until she whimpered softly.

With small steps, he guided her before the fire, pressing her down into the cushioned chair. Her eyes fell to his kilt which jutted out proudly. Cullen lowered to his knees and grabbed one of her feet, rubbing the arch. "Relax back, lass," he said. "And prepare to purr."

He kissed the bottom of her small foot and set it down, grabbing the second one for a rub and small kiss. He looked expectantly at her, his brows raised.

A whispered chuckle came from her. "No purring."

It was a tease, a flirtatious challenge. And he was certainly more than ready to take it on. "Yet."

Dark lashes fluttered against her rosy skin, watching him gather the edge of her smock. She breathed smoothly, in and out. He rolled the hem slowly upward, and his gaze dipped to her wet breasts, pebbled behind the now-transparent white material. Full and pert, he ached to cup them.

When he looked back to her heart-shaped face, she wet her bottom lip. Her slender fingers reached up and plucked apart the ribbon tying the neckline of her smock. He stopped breathing, stopped moving at all, and watched.

With a dip of each shoulder and tug, she lowered the neckline until it rested under her full breasts, exposing the beautiful globes to his view. The firelight played across her skin. "*Och…* Rose, ye are lovely."

Slowly Rose scooped under her breasts, pinching her own nipples, her gaze trained on him. He groaned loudly and slid the white material up her legs until the roll sat at the bend of her hips, all the while watching her pull and plump her breasts.

She wiggled slightly in the seat. "You like?" she asked, her voice a velvety whisper.

"Aye, bloody hell, aye, lass," he answered. He inhaled, searching deep for control, and slid up her chemise until the dark *V* of her legs was exposed.

Rose's lips parted as he stroked her silky inner thighs, brushing her sensitive folds. Circling until she surged forward into his hand, he pressed a finger inside her wet channel and stopped. She moaned, moving against him. Everything about her invited him in, but… He hesitated.

"What's wrong?" she asked, her breath coming in quiet pants.

Cullen shook his head. "Ye are perfect." He worked another finger inside until her head rolled back against the chair. "Aye, an angel dropped to earth." Lowering, he kissed her open thighs, the creamy flesh begging him to feast. He licked and teased higher until he covered her heat with his mouth.

She cried out above him as he loved her, delving in and out with fingers and tongue, working her most sensitive flesh. The rhythm, forged between them, grew faster. He glanced up at the wonder of her, straddled open in the chair, head thrown back, pale breasts raised and swollen, her white gown bunched around her narrow waist to expose the beauty of her most intimate parts.

Rose gripped the arms of the chair as he played her deftly, bringing her higher with each thrust of his finger and each lick of his tongue. She pressed upward, following his mouth, and he dug farther into her, nibbling and teasing until the pressure was too much. With an upward thrust, Rose moaned loudly. Cullen continued to kiss her intimately as wave after wave washed through her.

Sliding up her body, he kissed her breasts, rising and falling with her heavy breaths. He lifted their weight in his palms. "*Brèagha,* beautiful." He flicked his thumbs gently against the still-hard nipples.

"*Mon Dieu,*" she whispered, her breath whooshing out of her.

The weight of desire roughened his voice. "I believe ye purred."

Rose's lips turned up seductively. "I believe I growled."

She was a passionate lass. He chuckled and stood, knowing she'd instantly see that he could do so much more to her. Instead, though, he lifted her smock back onto her shoulders to cover what he'd rather feast upon all night. But he shouldn't. No, he couldn't.

He helped her stand and hugged her close, his aching member between them. He kissed her sweet mouth. When she slid her hand down to his kilt, his inhale caught. "Rose," he said in warning as she lifted the edge and wrapped her hand around his length.

"I would do the same for you," she said. She stroked him, picking a steady rhythm, and his eyes shut for a moment. He swallowed hard as the pounding in his blood overtook his reason.

"Nay, Rose," he managed to say, his words slipping past clenched teeth.

She rubbed harder. "I think *he* is arguing, *oui*."

Cullen's groan came up through his gut, breaching his lips loudly. He stilled her hand with his. "I would not have ye on your knees before me."

She turned the hand that he had stilled, intertwining her fingers with his, and tugged him toward his bed. "Lie upon your back."

He watched in torture as Rose crawled slowly onto the bed, her round arse showing as she hiked up her smock. Turning, she patted the thick mattress. His jaw worked as he fought an internal battle. He couldn't sleep with her. Not when she didn't know who she was. Not when—

"Come here," she said. "I won't bite." A spritelike grin tugged at her lips as she shrugged. "Or I will."

There was only so much a man could withstand. With a

flip of his buckle, Cullen let his kilt drop, exposing his hard body. Rose's eyes widened slightly. He was large, which had never been a problem before.

"Are you waiting for me to run away screaming?" she asked, her gaze moving slowly up him to his eyes.

An appreciative grin spread across his face. "A wildcat never retreats." He climbed onto the bed, leaning over her for a long, wet kiss. When she began to stroke his bare skin, he nearly took over. But she pressed a hand to his chest, prompting him to recline in the pillows. She leaned over him, kissing him soundly. She trailed nips and licks to his ear.

"I cannot wait to taste you," she whispered. He shuddered beneath her stroking hand. Aye, actually shuddered. Never in his life before had Cullen been so hard and ready to explode.

"Lass, ye are playing with an inferno."

"I'm not afraid of fire," she said, gripping the base. He growled low as she moved, seeming to know exactly how he would like it. Rose leaned forward, letting her breasts sway as she lowered the top of her smock again, her fullness bursting out of the confines. He groaned.

His mind fought against the surge of need within him. How did Rose know such deliciously wicked play? His wildcat's past was blank to both of them, and her reactions had been honest and fresh. But all questions blew to mist when, with a saucy smile, Rose lowered her mouth.

Chapter Ten

Cullen wrapped his kilt around his middle while watching Rose breathe in and out. She slept, and the dawn light, filtering through the warped windowpanes, cast a warm glow over her bare arms. Her dark brown hair, painted with flashes of gold, lay in tussled curls over his pillow. He'd inhaled its floral scent all night and explored every inch of Rose's silky skin until he was certain he'd memorized all of her.

Och, but she was passionate and brazen and full of adventure. Beautiful and mysterious. The things they'd done to each other were certainly not innocent.

He tied the neckhole of his shirt closed, better to hide the lass's nibbles and scratches. His delectable wildcat, well versed in the art of love, was a mystery. Cullen stared down at the long, dark lashes against smooth pale skin. He'd loved her in nearly every way, as she did to him, exploring, tasting, bringing each other to shattering completions over and over. They needed to talk when their minds were free of need. Until she remembered her past, he wouldn't claim her with his body. There were too many questions to do so with honor.

He would wait despite both of their obvious desires.

With a hearty spring in his step, Cullen left the room and descended to the great hall.

"Good morning to ye," he called to William and Farlan. They stared at him like he'd just said that cows were pissing from the turrets.

Cullen broke off a chunk of the dense, aromatic bread sitting on the table and topped it with a slice of yellow cheese.

"So, what of the Frenchwoman?" William asked.

"Her name is Rose," Cullen replied.

"Her name is *not* Rose," William countered. "And ye'd do well to remember that we know nothing about her except that she is French and therefore a traitorous beacon to the English across the strait."

Bloody hell, the man could ruin a perfectly beautiful morning like a crusty, black-toothed crone could ruin a lad's wedding night.

"Rose," Cullen stressed, "is our guest." His mouth hardened into a frown. "I will not throw her to the wolves, so ye can stop asking."

Farlan sucked on his teeth. "Have ye told Tor Maclean about her? He is bringing his family here. He might not want to risk them associating with a Frenchwoman with bloody England hunting for a way to mark us as traitors."

Cullen knew better than to write about Rose in a letter that could be intercepted. "I will alert him when they arrive. They can return immediately if it doesn't sit well with him."

His mother bustled down the steps and into the hall. She grabbed some cheese. "I'm off with Agnes to find mistletoe. Someone told her there's bunches hanging on the other side of the loch, not too high up in some birch." She tied her cloak before her and found a basket near the hearth. "When we return, Rose can help us string it. I don't suppose ye've seen her up yet?" Charlotte looked expectantly at Cullen.

He shook his head. "Nay, just these two…" He was goin to add "cod droppers" but thought better of it.

A slice of cheese in hand, Cullen strode out of the ha into the crisp winter air, puffs of white breath coming from hi mouth. It was invigorating, and he inhaled deeply. He glance back at the windows lining the top floor of the keep. How would Rose act today? Would his wildcat blush or taunt hir more?

"It should be a crime to smile this early in the morning, Broc said, walking up to him. He followed Cullen's gaz upward with a frown. "Aye, 'tis a lovely castle, but no need t cast cow eyes at it, Cull."

Cullen slapped him on the back as he strode toward th gates that were opening. "Come now, Broc. The air is fresl the sun is golden, and Christmastide is nearly here. The worl is merry."

Broc cursed and caught up as he reached the gates wher Errol spoke with one of the younger warriors. "Ye told hir about keeping the warning fires ready if needed?" Culle asked Errol and nodded to the youth.

"Aye, I'm going over it again before he rides out to th farms along the western shore."

"Fresh air? Golden sun? Christmastide? The world i merry?" Broc asked as he scratched his neck. "Somethin has ye spouting poetic." He stopped, lowering his arm as on eyebrow rose slowly. "Or is it some*one*? The lass in the barn?

"I'm a jovial sort. Ye've said that yourself." Cullen me Errol's watchful stare. "What?"

Errol rubbed a spot on his own neck. "Got a bit of nibble there."

"Bloody hell," Broc said, circling him. "And here another." He tugged on Cullen's shirt collar, pulling it down

Cullen shoved Broc's hand away and nodded to th youth. "Kenneth, ye have your orders." The young warrio jogged off to the stables while Cullen strode out through the gates. The heavy crunch of pebbles told him Errol and Broc followed.

"Did ye sleep with Bea?" Errol asked, his voice rough.

Cullen exhaled. "Nay, Errol. She's all yours." He looked at his friend who walked beside him. "But bed her soon so she stops sneaking into my room at night."

"The twins?" Broc asked. "I hear they climb the secret stairs weekly when ye're home." They walked toward the smithy. "Lucky bastard."

Cullen snorted, but Broc didn't seem to notice his dark look and went on. "I hear the first lass to get done with her chores, who makes it to the door in the bushes at the bottom of the stairs, ties her ribbon to the handle to let the rest of the lasses in the village know not to bother the two of ye. That she's won ye for the night."

"Ye hear a bloody lot," Errol said and kicked a rock in the path, sending it flying up to hit the stone wall around a cottage.

Cullen spoke low. "The twins are not climbing those steps, at least not since Bea's been doing it, and Bea's trying to get me to sleep with her only so she can be the next Lady MacDonald."

Broc slapped Errol on his back. "Bea's being a saddle-goose where Cull's concerned. Ye know he thinks of her only as a friend."

Errol cursed softly. "I wager it's her mother."

"Agnes?" Cullen asked, bowing his head politely to three elderly ladies who were whispering in the doorway of a large thatched cottage.

"Aye," Errol said. "I heard her saying to Bea that she best not get with child, unless that child be yours."

His words sank into Cullen as Broc clicked his tongue. "Really?" Broc said. "Agnes is plotting to get a bed up at the keep."

It certainly explained why Bea kept throwing herself at him. Otherwise, if her mother had found her sneaking out to bed a man, the Agnes MacDonald of old would tie her daughter to her own headboard at night.

"Ye need to marry, Cull," Errol said. "Then she'll let Beatrice choose her own man."

"If ye weren't with Bea," Broc said as they turned down a path toward the edge of the village. "And ye weren't with the twins." He tapped his chin with two fingers in exaggerated thoughtfulness. "Who put the merry in your step?"

Errol's eyes narrowed. "Someone ye're supposed to be staying away from?"

Broc dodged before Cullen, turning to walk backward in front of him. "Aye, instead of sneaking up the stairs, all she'd have to do is walk down the hall. *Très* convenient," he said in a poor French accent.

"I do not talk about lasses," Cullen said as they stopped at the smithy where the fires were already burning, the tang of hot metal on the breeze.

Broc laughed. "Bald-faced lie. Ye always talk of the lasses."

Errol caught Cullen's arm. "There will be consequences, Cull, if ye keep a Frenchwoman at Dunyvaig. Unless ye hide her away, ye can't keep her mute before the English forever. They will know ye lied about her being a Maclean." He dropped his hold. "Ye are The MacDonald now, not just Cullen Duffie."

Errol and his damned clear reasoning could suck the joy from the morning more effectively than his father. He met Errol's gaze with strength. "As second-in-command, 'tis your duty to advise. Thank ye." He gave one brief nod. "As a cousin and friend, 'tis none of yer bloody business."

"Ballocks, Cull," Broc said, always one to break the

tension. "Meddling about meddling with a lass is what family does." He grinned, though he stood tense as if he might be called upon to dodge among fists.

Aye, protecting Rose on Islay was not an easy course of action, but throwing her to the English or sending her away... The thought was a punch to the gut. If there was a way to protect both Rose and his clan, he had to find it.

Cullen broke the staring contest with Errol and turned to the open-air smithy. "Donald?" he called, his voice gruff. He stepped in, his gaze searching past the stone hearth, billows, and water barrels.

"Aye, back here," came the rough voice of the old blacksmith who kept Dunyvaig armed with the strongest swords found on the isles, as well as lethally pointed maces, arrow tips, and spears.

"Here to see if the crown is ready." Cullen flexed his jaw and heard his cousins step up on either side of him.

Errol's hand came down on his shoulder, making Cullen meet his gaze. His cousin's scowl softened, and he splayed his elbows out to grab the back of his head, glancing toward the sky. "Cull, do ye remember when my ma died?"

How could Cullen forget the anguish in Errol's face when they'd carried Elizabeth MacDonald from her death bed to ready her for burial? William had turned from everyone, too sorrow-filled at the loss of his wife to comfort his son. Cullen had taken Errol away to a cottage mid-island where he could, in private, lament and wail and drink until some of the pain bled out of him. Cullen had stayed with him for days, keeping him company, lending an ear and a shoulder until he was ready to return to Dunyvaig.

"Aye," Cullen said.

Errol nodded. "As The MacDonald ye have my fealty as your second-in-command, but as the man who stayed by my side at my worst, ye have my life and my support," Errol said.

"Even if it goes against your father?"

Errol's mouth turned upward in a wry grin. "Especially if it goes against my father."

"Hear, hear," Broc said.

Cullen's fists relaxed at his sides, and he nodded, glancing between his two best friends. They had faith in him. "Thank ye, but I'm not talking about any lasses, French or Scots." He turned toward a sleek steel blade Donald had set out, awaiting the binding of a leather hilt. He should have Donald check the balance and sharpness of his grandfather's sword since his grandfather hadn't used it for a score of years.

A young apprentice ran around to the fires, loading more peat and working the billows. Donald shuffled from the back, his decade-old battle wound stealing his once strong stride. He held the polished iron circle out to Cullen. "I was shining it up along with the headpieces for the lasses to use in their Christmas pageant."

Cullen took the simple, hammered crown that his grandfather had made long ago for crowning the Christmastide fool in charge of the festivities. Now it was Cullen's turn to choose the Abbot of Unreason to rule from Christmas morning through Twelfth Night on January fifth.

"Ye better be careful whose head ye put that on," Errol said. "Or he may not give it up." He spoke of his father, no doubt.

"Wise lad," Donald said, his mouth twisted up on one side in a smirk, confirming what Cullen had already discerned. All of Islay knew that William and Farlan MacDonald wanted their nephew out of the chief's seat. They would surely use his desire for a Frenchwoman as leverage against him, if they knew.

"Thank ye, Donald," Cullen said, nodding to the man. "Make sure to come up to the keep for some of my aunt's fine whisky and wassail."

Donald's grin grew, showing more gaps than teeth. "I wouldn't miss Maggie's fine whisky for all King Henry's gold."

"How about his head?" Broc jested. "Would ye pass on Maggie's finest for that?"

Donald laughed. "I'd miss me own turn at Heaven's pearly gates to see King Henry's head cut from his bloody neck."

They thanked Donald and strode back to the bailey. Cullen searched the heavy clouds for snow. "My mother would like ye two to find a suitable Yule log for the keep."

"So ye really aren't going to talk, are ye?" Broc asked.

Cullen flipped the circle of polished steel between his hands. "Ye both read too much into simple morning cheer."

"And love bites around your neck," Errol said.

Broc elbowed Errol. "Watch to see if any of the lasses have a hard time walking this morning."

"Or a blush and a satisfied smile," Errol added.

The two of them were as bad as…well, as bad as Cullen had been before his grandfather had died and left the burden of the entire clan on his shoulders.

• • •

The warmth around her seduced Rose to snuggle deeper into the sheets. They smelled of Cullen. They smelled of her. They smelled of the two of them intertwined. Memories of their passion-drenched night surfaced, making Rose's heartbeat quicken and a rush of sensation to spread through her. She blinked, turning her head on the pillow. Gone. She was alone in his large bed, the dark curtains hanging around the four posts of carved, heavy wood.

Pushing up on her elbows, Rose looked about the room. A cheery fire danced in the hearth. When she spotted her chemise draped over a chair by the fire, she peeked under the covers, but of course she knew that she was completely nude.

"*Mon Dieu*," she whispered and touched her tender flesh tha
was beginning to ache anew from the memories alone.

A door down the hall closed, and she gasped, eyes wide
To be found naked in Cullen's bed… What would Charlott
think? A French wanton, seducing her son.

Rose slid from under the blankets, as silent as a specte
and padded over to the chemise. With a quick yank over he
head, it floated down into place. Should she go down th
secret stairs? *Non.* Getting back into the keep unseen woul
be impossible. She grabbed her robe, pooled in a heap by th
hearth, and shrugged into it.

Her toes curled upward, away from the cold floorboard
as she stood for a long while with her ear pressed to Cullen'
bedroom door. Nothing. Holding her breath, Rose cracke
it, cringing at the spark of sound in the silence. She peeke
around the edge. No one. With a quick prayer to God, wh
was most likely damning her for her licentiousness, sh
stepped out, shutting the door with a soft click.

Barefoot and swift, she raced to her own room, yankin
the door open and shutting it quickly behind her. The har
wood braced her back as she leaned against it. Her hearth wa
cold, *Dieu merci.* No one had come to stir it, only to find he
gone, her bed still made.

Rose took deep breaths and walked to the fire. She use
the poker to tap the embers, blowing underneath until a ribbo
of smoke curled up. She tossed on some of the brittle strav
and a chunk of peat to burn, brushing her hands together.

The fire caught, warming her face, and she walked t
the water pitcher where the surface was edged with ice. Th
cold in the room was both torture and balm to the heat sti
threatening to pluck at her body every time she thought c
Cullen's delicious skills.

Washing and dressing quickly in a green day gown, Ros
sat before the polished metal mirror. She touched her tende

lips, slightly bruised from their passion. When the erotic ache started to spread again in her pelvis, she pushed away the images and picked up the bone-white comb.

Rose teased through a snarl, one of many in her curls, and her mind drifted. She breathed, relaxing, and the stone walls of the bedroom seemed to fade to flowered wall coverings. Tinkling laughter echoed in her thoughts. The sounds were joyless, hiding pain and desperation in forced merriment, stringed poppets dancing on a gilt stage.

Rose stared at the reflection of her wide eyes, green and gray, long lashes curling upward. She touched her cheeks with light fingertips, confused at the brief memories of her past, which had already faded. "Who are you?" she asked the image, but her face looked as frustratingly blank as she felt.

She exhaled with force. She might not know who she was, but she absolutely knew whom she wanted. Cullen Duffie. The desires he had kindled in her last night were beyond anything she could imagine having practiced before. And even though the motions of some of their play seemed familiar, the feelings she'd experienced with Cullen were new and intense, as if the world before had simply been black and white, and now he'd painted the details in vibrant jewel hues.

Such passion, raw and honest. They'd touched each other everywhere, learned the contours of each other's bodies. She'd memorized every one of his scars, nicks, and jagged lines showing past battles. He was exquisite, full of strength from his rock-hard calves to his mounding biceps and broad shoulders. And the things he had done to her...that she had done to him... The thought made a flutter thrill through her belly. *Mon Dieu.*

Rose dropped her face gingerly into her hands, resting. *Never be needy for a male's attention. Always leave them wanting more yet totally enraptured with what you have given.*

The words clipped through her mind like familiar

recitations. Somehow, she knew these things, yet her heart wanted to throw them all away in front of Cullen. Such physical power and obvious discipline and control made her tremble. He'd brought her to fulfillment over and over, and yet…he hadn't joined with her last night despite her openness and desire. Was it because she couldn't remember her past? Was he worried she was married or worse, a loose woman?

Rose shot up off the dainty bench, the thought too much to bear sitting down. She paced across the room on her borrowed slippers, wearing the borrowed day dress, in the temporary bedroom. Nothing was hers, except for her body. And what if she'd used that body before, given it away?

She wrapped her arms around herself, glad she'd left her hair down to warm her neck. Was she unaccustomed to the cold? Kept and pampered in a palace with printed walls? She'd arrived richly dressed, with a lady's unmarred hands, and a necklace of rare pearls. She would guess that she was a young aristocrat waiting to marry, stolen away from her life of innocent leisure, yet the things she'd done with Cullen… They suggested something much more scandalous. Rose ran her hands down her curvy body. *Mon Dieu.* Maybe it was shame that wouldn't allow her to remember her past life. Who was she?

Knock. Knock. Rose pivoted, hand to her chest. "Are ye coming down to breakfast?" It was Charlotte. With a soft exhale that she could feel nearly to her tingling toes, Rose crossed to the door, opening it.

"*Oui*," she said. "I am up. Even had time to make my bed."

Charlotte looped her arm through hers, and they chatted about Agnes and her gathering mistletoe as they walked down to the great hall. The vaulted room smelled of freshly baked bread and roast pig that steamed from a platter on the center of the table. Fire danced cheerfully in the hearth, chasing off the morning cold. The thumped tapestries had been rehung, their colors more vivacious and the details sharp. Extra candles lined the mantel in varying heights. But what drew Rose's immediate attention stood beside the mantel, tall and broad, dripping with sensual appeal. He practically made her mouth water, thinking how delicious he smelled when she nibbled around his neck.

"I know," Charlotte said beside her. "'Tis a stunning sight."

"*Excusez?*" Rose asked and felt the blush creep upward past her lace-edged neckline.

"The holly and candles. It makes the mantel look so fresh."

"*Oui.*" She nodded vigorously. "Yes. The room has a lovely appeal now, inviting."

Charlotte let go, her brow creasing at Broc, who stomped his boots just inside the great hall, speckling the polished wood with bits of mud. "Trying to maintain a home with men about is as maddening as sweeping a dirt floor," she mumbled and strode across the room, leaving Rose alone.

Stand straight and tall, gaze level and always assessing. Walk with purpose even if you have none other than looking grand. Speak to someone close to your target, but do not approach the man you desire straight on.

More words tumbled through Rose's mind, advice, buoys in a turbulent sea of fog and unease. She began to follow Charlotte, but when Agnes walked in and pulled her into the alcove, Rose veered toward the only other person close by. William MacDonald. *Mon Dieu.*

With the weight of Cullen's eyes on her, she took the empty seat opposite William at the chess table. It was set for a new game. "Good morning," she said in her best English and moved a pawn forward from its starting position.

He looked up at her, his eyes narrowed, but said nothing.

"Do you play?" she asked. When he refused to answer, she

sighed. "Fear of losing to a woman." She nodded, pretending to understand why he wouldn't move a piece. "And a *French* woman at that."

He muttered something in Gaelic and moved his pawn. She lifted another, the tactics suddenly clear in her mind. Rose knew this game, knew it well. How to move the bishop, the rook. How to protect the queen and use her to guard the king. Strategies ghosted across the squares, but unlike the tiny memories that popped inside only to blink away like distant stars on a cloudy night, the game seemed etched in her mind. She'd been taught how to challenge an opponent.

They played in silence, each one moving their pieces quickly. "You are skilled," she said to William as he stole her knight. She'd seen the vulnerability several moves back, but thought to give it to him. *Let the man win, no matter how clever you are.* The words filled her head until she wanted to plug her ears. Ignoring them, she moved decisively, offensively, until she had William cornered. Her stomach flipped as she placed her queen where the king could take her, kill or be killed. But William also saw the small pawn waiting behind the queen on the diagonal.

Rose watched William stare, his eyes wide. "Checkmate," she said, her voice low. "Thank you for the game." He hadn't said a word the entire time.

"Could Dale see if the ship was French or English?" Cullen's voice carried across the room. He strode toward them, his gaze on her as he spoke.

Broc walked beside him. "Possibly French, but it's remaining far off, near Colonsay Isle."

"Hunting our shoreline," William said, standing. Rose followed.

"Send word for the beacon to be lit if the ship or crew come close to land," Cullen said.

Land? Would the monster who tied the rope about her

neck risk landing to hunt her? A scattering of chill bumps prickled over her head and down her back.

"Ye are to stay here at Dunyvaig," Cullen said, his gaze fastened to her. Where else did he think she could go? She nodded anyway.

"They could be coming to take her back," Agnes said, having reentered the great hall with Charlotte.

Farlan added something in Gaelic that made Cullen's frown darken. "She stays here," Cullen said, his words as stony as the walls surrounding them.

"For the love of God, Farlan," Charlotte chimed in. "The lass had a rope tied about her neck."

Cullen rounded on his uncles, taking in both with a stare. "And if your bloody love for God isn't as strong as your fear of the English, I hope ye have a love for your own lives." He let the rest of his threat seep into the silence of the hushed room. Even Charlotte had saucer-like eyes. Cullen was choosing Rose over kin, maybe even over clan. Rose fought to control her flush, but the more she tried, the hotter her skin felt. What if she wasn't worthy of Cullen's choice?

Chapter Eleven

Their horses clipped over the hard-packed dirt of the mai
road up to the gates. Broc, Errol, and Cullen had spent th
morning hunting for the upcoming feasts. With the Maclean
attending, more venison and a roasted boar would be adde
to the menu. But even with the concentration required for
straight and power-filled arrow shot, Cullen hadn't been ab
to drag his mind from Rose. She'd floated across the floor th
morning, as graceful as when she'd walked naked before th
fire last night, smiling softly when he'd finally caught her gaz

Broc rode beside him and nodded to several villagers wh
peeked out of their doorways. "Ye've been quiet all morning
he said to Cullen. "Thinking about the one who nibbled a
your neck?"

"Too bad ye haven't a lass to keep your mind busy an
tongue still," Cullen said, his frown in place, as they cloppe
through the gates.

"She seems to have thieved your good cheer," Broc sai
while Errol studied Cullen. The two were as prying as hi
mother. They'd thrown out the names of other lasses in th

village, trying to bait Cullen into revealing the nibbling lass, but he'd remained quiet.

After tossing reins to stableboys and instructing some older lads to gut the deer and boar, Cullen jogged up the steps to the keep, Broc and Errol behind him. Damn but his heart began to pound when he spotted Rose. Head bowed, she worked with the housemaid, Ellen, stringing clusters of holly at the table. Rose's simple day dress of deep green molded beautifully to her soft curves. Even bent, her back remained straight, her arms working fluidly.

Cullen picked up one of the cups on the sideboard and took a drink of the cool ale. Rose looked up from her work, a small grin on her red lips. Oh, those lips. Looking at them, knowing where they'd been, made him harden beneath his kilt. "*Bonjour*," she said, nodding to Cullen and his cousins. Unlike other lasses, who giggled and preened after an evening of sport, she met his gaze directly, bold and beautiful. All other lasses faded from Cullen's mind. There was no comparison.

"I see my mother still has ye working," he said.

Charlotte walked in from the back. "One can never have too much holly at Christmastide."

Ellen yelped and stuck a pricked finger in her mouth. "Treacherous work," she said. "Mistress Rose has nimble fingers." Ellen rubbed her abused fingertip on her apron. "I'm the one who keeps getting jabbed."

"Oh, I've been poked over and over," Rose said with a light voice.

Broc spit his ale back into his cup, coughing, his face blotching as he choked, and Errol whapped his back. Rose looked curiously at the pair. Cullen picked up the crown he'd retrieved earlier to draw her attention. "For the Abbot of Unreason."

"Abbot of Unreason?" she asked, stepping from the table. "Is that like the *Prince des Sots*? A fool to rule over the twelve days of Christmas?"

"Aye. This will be my first year to elect."

Rose glanced at Broc, who had finally stopped coughing. "I think there are a number of fools about from whom to choose."

"Ye have no idea."

Her lips lifted at the corners, and she swallowed, her cheeks turning pink, maybe recalling something wicked.

He leaned forward. "So ye do blush."

She blinked several times, her mouth tight as if she held in her laughter. "I actually blush quite a lot. You don't notice in the shadows," she whispered.

From behind him Broc chuckled, making Cullen turn. There was a look of innocence across his features, his brows rising high on his forehead, as he watched the two of them. He elbowed Errol, who stood next to him. "What was that ye said about blushes and smiles?"

• • •

Before Rose could ask or even wonder what Broc was jesting at, a boy ran into the keep. "The Macleans have come. They're riding across the moor."

The great hall broke into chaos with Charlotte sweeping up the half-strung holly to deposit in a basket. "Ellen, tell Jillian that we will need more of that fish cooked for the evening meal. Rose, take off your apron. Broc, stir up that fire. The air in here is chilled."

Cullen leaned in to Rose's ear. "I must greet my friend."

She nodded. There was no time for words before he turned. Her gaze followed his powerful stride as he walked away, the muscles of his calves flexing over his boots. How could Cullen make so alluring the simple act of walking?

Rose shucked her apron and straightened her skirts.

Should she retreat to the hearth, blending into the stone wall? *Never blend in. Always stand out in a room.* She tucked a few curls back into her modest bun and placed a mask of mild interest across her features. Charlotte flew along the table to straighten the tankards and peeked into the ale jug before wagging a finger at her brothers. "Be cordial and welcoming."

Farlan grunted. "I haven't seen Torquil Maclean since he was a lad, practicing with a wooden sword."

"And now he's chief of the Macleans," William added. "Ye heard about his first wife dying."

"Oh no, ye are not to talk of that," Charlotte exploded and thumped William on the chest. "Cordial and welcoming doesn't include reminding guests of terrible pasts."

They stood in silence, all turned toward the doors, waiting. Charlotte sighed, her hands clasped before her. "They will be here any minute."

Time stretched, and in the lengthening silence Farlan farted, prompting Charlotte to frown at him. "Keep your wind to yourself."

"Better before they walk in," he responded.

"Oh, my word," Charlotte swore, her eyes raised high. She fanned the air to disperse her brother's odors. Rose pressed a hand to her lips to hide her smile.

The doors opened in the entryway, prompting Farlan and William to stand up straight and Charlotte to touch her pinned hair once more. A weave of ladies' voices and deep chuckles broke the silence as the group filled the archway and stepped into the great hall.

"Joan Maclean," Charlotte called, striding up to her friend. "It's been too long. Welcome to Dunyvaig." Charlotte hugged the shorter, comely lady with gray-streaked hair coiled about her head.

"It was a long journey," Joan said. "Two full days with all our trunks."

"Come warm yourself by the hearth," Charlotte said and turned to the tall man escorting a lovely young woman who glanced about the keep. "Welcome, Tor. Ye've certainly grown into your da's brawn."

"Thank ye for letting us intrude on your Christmastide," Tor responded. "There've been some mishaps at Aros. I'll tell ye over a cup of the Duffie's famous honey whisky."

Rose watched the three young ladies. Would they be wasps and serpents like Beatrice and her friends? Charlotte had schooled Rose on their names and stations. The lovely brunette on Tor's arm met Rose's gaze and smiled. Her thick middle and high-waist gown confirmed that Tor's new wife was indeed pregnant. The woman bowed her head to Charlotte with several pleasantries and patted her husband's arm, leaving his side to stride toward Rose. The lady with the lighter hair and merry eyes followed.

"Welcome," Rose said when they stopped before her. She curtsied, bowing her head in greeting.

The woman reached out and squeezed her hand warmly. "*Bonjour*," she said. She continued in English with a refined accent. "I am Ava. And this is my sister, Grace or Lady Grace."

"Grace, please," the other woman said.

"Cullen told us about your plight as we walked through the village," Ava said.

Grace's smile ebbed. "And the farmer who lent us his wagon when we landed last night told us about the mysterious woman who'd washed ashore. What a horrible experience."

Mon Dieu. She was the talk of the island. How had the English not heard of her yet?

"Thank you," Rose answered and relaxed a little. They seemed to accept that she was French, and even though their gazes had dipped briefly to the jagged line encircling her neck, they hadn't gasped or asked about it. "We should find you refreshment."

She led them toward the long table when Agnes and Beatrice strode in with baskets on their arms. They stopped to speak with Charlotte and Tor's mother. Behind them came Broc and Errol.

"We are thankful that you were able to take us in," Ava said as she sat, her hand going to her back where she rubbed.

"Oh yes," Grace continued. "It was dreadful at Aros."

Rose poured watered-down wine from a pitcher. "Dreadful?"

Grace leaned closer to her. "That troublesome old warrior, Duky, accidentally set fire to the hall in the keep. Banked the hearth too full and left it to roll out enough to catch the closest tapestry, which spread to the rest, scorching the walls and leaping to the table and chairs."

"How terrible," Rose said. "I wondered at you risking travel in your condition," she said, looking to Ava.

The woman nodded, a tired expression on her pale face. "With the burned vapors permeating the keep, I've been living with Grace in her sweet cottage, but Tor won't stay in it," Ava said.

"It's where his first wife was found dead," Grace whispered. "But we've since had a resurrection." Grace's eyes widened. "The cottage, not the wife, of course." She gave a nervous half grin.

"And I told Tor I couldn't celebrate our first Christmastide apart, so he wrote to Cullen." Ava squeezed Rose's arm. "Thank you for letting us intrude."

Rose smiled. "You and your family are most welcome at Dunyvaig, although I am not the one to thank. I am also a guest of their generosity."

"Of course." Ava twisted, looking for her husband. With the movement, she gasped, both hands going to her middle.

"What is it?" Grace asked, standing.

"A pain," Ava said.

"Joan," Grace called. "Ava's feeling a pain."

Charlotte's friend scooted around Agnes and Beatric and grabbed her leather satchel, heading toward them. "I wi brew a medicine."

Brew a medicine? The words caught at Rose's memor She knew about brewing medicines. Her gaze shifted to Ava hand resting on her stomach, and a dreadful feeling sank int her.

"What type of medicine?" Rose asked, looking to Av "Some are abortive and very powerful."

"Good Lord," Joan said, pulling a clay jar from her bag. ' wouldn't give her anything like that."

"Joan and Ava are both skilled healers," Grace said, he face still tense.

Ava tipped her head back to look into the frowning fac of her looming husband. "I'm sure it is just from the travel He kissed her forehead gingerly. There was a light in his fac soft and concerned.

"Did you feel ill this morning after that pennyroy brew?" Grace asked, pulling Rose's attention back from th affectionate display.

Pennyroyal? *To create an abortive tonic, combir pennyroyal and tansy, but beware giving too much or tʰ woman will die as well.* "Pennyroyal kills *le bébé*, especiall mixed with tansy, but they can kill the mother, too," Rose sai rising.

All gazes fell on her. "Ye know of abortive brews?" Joa asked, her brows raised.

"Ye're remembering things," Cullen said, stepping close

Rose leaned down to look in Ava's startled face. "Did yc drink pennyroyal?"

"No." She shook her head and peered past Rose to Grac "That was raspberry leaves."

"Drink," Tor ordered and passed her a cup of watere

down wine. She did while Charlotte instructed Ellen to hurry back with a cup of boiled water for Joan's raspberry leaves.

"How do ye know about abortive brews?" Agnes asked, her tone soft but clipped. Beatrice stood beside her, staring with wide eyes and thin lips to match her mother.

Rose shook her head. "I don't know. When she mentioned pennyroyal, I felt…ill." She met Cullen's concerned gaze. "That is all, not really a memory. More of a feeling. Pennyroyal and tansy or…black hellebore and savin boiled in milk. That they are dangerous, poison."

"Ye felt ill, like ye've taken it before?" Agnes asked, making Beatrice gasp, her hand flattened to her breast.

"I…" No definite memories came to Rose. Only the herbs and how to mix them. "I don't think so."

"There now, I already feel better," Ava said and set the cup on the table. "I'm merely tired. Perhaps I could lie down."

Charlotte clasped her hands. "Of course. I have a room one floor up for you and Tor. I thought Joan and your companion could share." She glanced toward the third lady who had golden hair, Mairi, Tor's sister. "I didn't know ye were coming, Mairi. I will need to find another bed for ye."

Guilt plucked at Rose. She was taking up a fairly large room. "You are welcome to share with me," Rose said. "The bed is wide enough for two."

Mairi met her gaze and nodded. "Thank ye."

Maybe with Mairi as a bedmate, she'd have reason enough not to run to Cullen's room at night like a wanton. Despite the pleasant mask she wore, Rose's stomach clenched with disappointment.

Chapter Twelve

Cullen waited in the dark alcove by the twisting stairs, listening to the light cautions given by Rose as she and Mairi came down after changing for dinner. With the Macleans arriving, he hadn't been able to speak with her. Or kiss her. And now she was sharing a room with Tor's sister, so he couldn't come knocking tonight. He exhaled in a gust of frustration.

A small gasp issued from the bottom step. "Who is there?" Rose asked, and he stepped out of the shadows.

"Do ye always hide about in dark corners, Cull?" Mairi asked. "Or were ye specifically trying to scare us into falling down your uneven steps?"

He laughed, still remembering Tor's sister as a freckled young girl who used to tag along after Tor and him. Luckily, they had been able to rescue her from a disastrous predicament when her husband died a month ago. "If I'd wanted to do that, I'd have hidden at the top for a much greater tumble."

Mairi gave a soft snort. "Ye probably would push me, too."

Rose looked back and forth between them, and Mairi

laughed. "Not really," she said. "But growing up, Cull's always been wicked."

"Wicked?" Rose asked.

"Playing tricks, always leading a group of lasses around by the memory of his kisses, breaking hearts to leave them floundering on the ground like gulping fish."

Och, he could kick the woman. Rose's eyes widened. "That is quite the visual illustration," she said.

"Why don't ye find your mother?" Cullen suggested without hiding his terse tone.

Mairi's head snapped between them both. "Hmmm… Interesting." She stared and tucked an errant curl into the bun under a small hood. "Very well." She turned to enter the hall. "But guard your heart, Rose. No need to let it flip-flap around in the rushes." She fluttered her hand this way and that as she walked away, leaving them finally alone.

Cullen turned to Rose who was watching Mairi leave. "I like her," Rose said, her gaze sliding to him. "She hides nothing."

"Oh, she can hide things when she wants to," Cullen said, but let it go. He didn't want to talk about Tor's sister in the short time they had alone. "And she exaggerates about the lasses."

"It seems she has the same opinion about you as Broc."

He stepped closer and inhaled her clean floral scent. It brought back a rush of memories from last night. "I regret my sordid youth, and I aim to prove that I've changed." The heat between them surged a tightness up through his gut.

"So my heart won't be flip-flapping in the rushes?" He watched her dainty hands turn upward and down like Mairi's fish.

He caught one of them, softly kissing her knuckles. "I would never let ye flap in the dirty rushes."

She canted her head to the side. "A clean floor before a

fire?"

An image of Rose, naked and sprawled on a soft fur spread on the floor of his room before the hearth, filled his head. All thoughts of talking with her about their night of play crumbled to ash. He stepped closer, knowing she wouldn't retreat, because her face turned up to meet his kiss.

Her mouth was soft and open under his, tasting him as much as he consumed her. She pressed forward against the hardness of his body, molding herself intimately along his length as much as her heavy skirts would allow. Had she spent the day thinking of last night like he had?

The thorough kiss ended, but they remained entwined, foreheads touching. Cullen kept his breath even despite what Rose did to his pulse.

"I missed you this morn when I woke," Rose said softly.

"*Och*, I had much to do today, but I thought about ye."

She smiled. "Me or my nibbles?"

He cupped her head in his hands and stroked one thumb over a cheek, reveling in the fact that she didn't pull away. "Both." He slid his hands to her shoulders, his lips caressing a spot below her ear. "And much more."

A small sound came from her lips, like a purr heavy with passion. How did she do that? With only a noise, he felt ready to toss his vast responsibilities in order to whisk her away. In every association he'd had before with a lass, he'd been the one leading the dance. But not with Rose.

"We should go in, else Mairi imagine the worst," she whispered.

Muscles tense, Cullen managed to guide her hand to rest on his arm and lead her out of the dark. *Bloody hell,* he'd have to avoid close contact with anyone lest someone notice the rigidness under his kilt. Halfway to the table, where everyone was gathering to eat, he realized he hadn't said or asked Rose anything he'd planned. He ran a free hand down his clipped beard. If he didn't know better, he'd think she were a witch. *You don't know better.* He shoved the thought away and brought her to a seat toward the end of the table by Mairi since the seats in between were already full, except the one waiting at the head for him.

Mairi smirked up at Cullen like she wanted to blab her suspicions to the world and was plotting for the most dramatic timing. He sent her a small frown, hoping the fact that he'd taken them in for Christmastide would tame her tongue.

Ellen and Jillian brought in a cauldron of steaming stew. Broc walked behind them, carrying two platters with filleted fish. Agnes appeared with her tarts on a wooden board and Beatrice brought a woven bowl filled with chunks of herbed bread and crocks of freshly churned butter.

"We will have a much larger feast for Christmas," his mother said.

"This is very gracious," Joan said. "And smells delicious." Murmurs of agreement melted his mother's stiff shoulders.

Broc claimed his seat down the table from William, Farlan, and their guest Hamish, Tor's second-in-command, who had come with the family from Aros.

Agnes and Beatrice, whom his mother must have asked to stay, sat on either side of Errol down from Broc. So both of his cousins and Beatrice sat across from Rose. Beatrice lowered whenever her gaze fell on Rose while Broc grinned and whispered across the table to her. Cullen frowned. Formal table hierarchy was maddening.

Tor lifted his tankard beside Cullen. "Thank ye for your hospitality, Cullen."

"Certainly," Cullen said. Tor continued on, but Cullen barely heard him. What was Broc saying to Rose? Would he hint at his suspicions? Regale her with lurid stories of Cullen's past? He should have warned him not to before dinner, but that would have confirmed that Rose was the one with whom he'd been meddling. Not that what they'd shared was a simple romp. It was delicious and somehow deeper than mere flesh How could he feel so wrapped up in a woman with whom he hadn't thoroughly tupped?

"We should invite the English over for the Christmas feast," Tor said.

Damnation. Was that a blush rising in her cheeks? He should have sat her next to him at the head, to hell with what everyone thought. Then he could be inhaling her sweet floral scent instead of ignoring Farlan's gas. He took a bite of the stew but didn't taste it.

"Toast the captains," Tor said.

"Hmmm…"

Broc was leaning halfway across the table to talk to her.

"In fact, I'm thinking of giving up the chiefdom of Aro and swearing fealty to jolly King Henry," Tor said, leaning so his gaze imitated Cullen's, staring down the table.

Someone laughed, but Cullen watched both Broc and Rose turn their attention toward him. She looked perplexed "Sounds splendid," Cullen answered when the long pause prompted him to respond.

Tor snorted and grabbed Cullen's shoulder, shaking him slightly. "Cull?"

"What?" Cullen dragged his gaze away from Rose.

Humor twitched the corners of his friend's mouth while Ava held a handkerchief to her lips. "Call her down here to sit with ye," Tor said.

"Who?"

Ava lowered her handkerchief and whispered, "Really Cullen? The lovely *mademoiselle* you can't keep from staring at."

"I think this is the first time I've ever seen ye look more than two seconds at a lass," Tor said. "Usually they're chasing ye."

Cullen took a drink of the ale next to his plate. "Rose doesn't chase anyone."

"Ah," Ava said. "The charming rogue has met his match."

Was that why he couldn't stop thinking about Rose? Because she was a challenge? Was he drawn to her mystery instead of her graceful confidence and unflinching courage?

Ava leaned forward to look on the other side of Grace. "Lady Charlotte?" she said.

"Aye."

"I was wondering if your guest from France could come closer to this end of the table so I might practice the language conversing with her. Both Grace and I learned French as girls back in England, but I haven't had a chance to use it since."

"Certainly," Charlotte said, nodding to Rose.

Rose stood with the grace of a regal princess. Her face was a mixture of agreeable interest and gratefulness. Broc stood, too, being the nearest man to her. He'd never shown such manners before Rose came to Dunyvaig.

"There's no room for her up here," William complained. "Ye should go down to that end."

"Nonsense," Charlotte said. "We will make room." She shooed people to slide their chairs down until there was room for another chair beside Ava. Cullen met Rose's gaze as he walked toward her to retrieve her chair, his boots clipping on the wood planks.

"Here, set the chair on this side of me," Tor said, putting Rose right next to Cullen. "I cannot be parted from my bride even for the space of a meal."

"'Tis true," Mairi called from the far end. "They are disgustingly happy." She grinned to soften her words, though a bitterness laced them. "And rarely apart."

Rose lowered into the seat, and Cullen helped her push in. Immediately Ava began to talk to Rose in French, with Rose responding, her smile natural. Occasionally Grace would laugh beside Ava, the only other person able to understand.

Ava said the word *amour* and glanced toward Cullen. What was she saying to Rose about love? Was Ava talking about something as trivial as loving the views or something that Rose said didn't exist?

"Give me that," Beatrice said from her spot and grabbed for the cup Errol held away from her.

"Ye should drink something other than whisky, Bea," Errol said, setting the cup down on the other side of him near her mother. She hissed something back in a quieter voice, her bottom lip protruding in a pout.

Rose ate in between varying discussions with Ava in French. Both of them seemed content. William and Farlan watched the exchange with narrowed eyes, listening for traitorous plans, no doubt. When Tor leaned in to talk to his wife, Cullen took the opportunity to speak near the perfect curve of Rose's ear. "We need to talk in private, lass." He needed to ask her about their night together.

She turned her face to him, and he watched a glimmer of worry tighten her brows. "*Oui*, yes, but now I have a bedfellow," she whispered.

Och, he wanted to be her bedfellow instead of Tor's sister. "Before ye retire."

Beatrice's voice rose up above the polite chatter. "She entices men from their duty, struts around like a harlot, too good to work with her hands, and she knows how to kill a bairn. What else could she be but a wicked courtesan?"

The low cadence of conversation around the table cut off. Beatrice's face reddened, and Errol grabbed her reclaimed whisky cup out of her hand, draining the rest of it himself.

"Agnes," Cullen said. "I think Beatrice needs to find her bed early this eve."

Beatrice snorted softly. "Finding beds," she murmured. "I'm sure she remembers how to find a bed."

Cullen pushed up from the table, as did Agnes and Errol, who grabbed Beatrice under the arm to encourage her to rise. Beatrice's comely face contorted with bitterness.

"Enough, Beatrice," Agnes said, and looked up the table at Cullen. "Although, it would be good to know what type of woman we have welcomed into the heart of Dunyvaig. Having a working knowledge of abortive herbs makes one wonder."

William nodded but seemed to know better than to speak it aloud. Farlan swallowed, wiping his mouth. "Aye," he said. "The scant information we have could indicate a sinful past."

Silence sat along the narrow planks of the table, as if the diners were gathered to pass judgment. Rose perched on the edge of her chair, eyes forward, still as stone. Nothing in her posture denoted a defense against the accusation. Could she possibly worry that Agnes's words were true, when they couldn't be?

Cullen's gaze went first to Farlan, and then farther down the table. "Rose is not a courtesan and has never been one." The flames from the candles in the chandeliers above their heads flickered with the drafts, and the wind whined outside, adding an ominous backdrop to the strain in the room.

"A richly dressed woman, without the rough hands of a midwife or healer, who knows more than one way to kill a fetus within a woman..." Agnes let the rest of the sentence finish in everyone's own minds.

"Precisely," Beatrice added with a nod. "And yet there she sits, surrounded by your honored guests, beside the chief of the clan, making a fool of us." She crossed her arms over her chest, shrugging off Errol's staying hand like a petulant child.

Charlotte stood, her lips tight. "This is not the time or place to discuss such—"

"I repeat," Cullen said, his voice low and full of restrained power. He leaned slightly forward where he stood, his hands fisted and propped on the table before him. "Rose is not, and never has been, a courtesan."

Rose touched the sleeve of his shirt, yet kept her gaze across the table, not connecting with anything but the far stone wall. "Since I have no memory, we do not know that for certain."

"Exactly right," William mumbled beside him, but Cullen kept his focus on Beatrice's face, a sneer of dark jubilation lighting it.

"I know for certain," Cullen said.

"If she herself doesn't know," Beatrice continued the volley. "How could ye?"

Lord forgive him. Rather, Rose forgive him. "Because she was and still is…a virgin."

Chapter Thirteen

"Virgin? She is full of lies," Beatrice said. "Ye can't believe a word from her lips."

Rose leaned back and let the chair hold her up as an icy numbness claimed her body, her breath held captive behind her ribs. *A virgin?* She was a virgin, and Cullen knew? Before she knew herself? But how did she know so much about bed play? What a virile man, such as Cullen, would like? She looked up at him, but he still watched Beatrice, the muscle in his jawline tensing.

Rose's cheeks burned, and her stomach rolled with the stew she'd eaten. When he'd touched her so intimately, he'd known. So he hadn't joined with her despite her obvious desire. Tears pressed at the back of her eyes in a rush of relief. He'd stopped from loving her because of honor, not because he thought a Frenchwoman could become with child and demand he wed her. And *Dieu merci*, she wasn't a courtesan, giving her body to men for money.

Rose kept her gaze fastened to Cullen's strong stance. Hands fisted at his sides, he stared down the woman who still didn't realize she was losing this very public battle for Cullen's affections. Her mother either didn't care or was too shocked to come to her aid.

"Don't ye see, Cull," Beatrice said, unaware that Errol held his arms ready to lift her from the floor. Did he wait for a signal from his chief? "She lied to ye about that. She must be a courtesan, a French whore. It is the only explanation that fits all the pieces."

"God's teeth, Beatrice MacDonald," Charlotte snapped. "That's not the only explanation available. And again, this isn't the place—"

"I know she is a virgin," Cullen said. "Without her saying as much."

Mon Dieu. Rose could see the explanation forming pictures in heads around the table. Grace turned pink, Mair pinched her lips tight, her eyes wide, and Ava wiped her mouth with a handkerchief, her brows rising high. No one ate, not even the uncles, sitting silently in judgment across from her.

"A fumbling kiss or awkward fondling doesn't make one a virgin, Cull," Beatrice said with an exasperated sigh.

Cullen stood tall, his arms crossing his chest. "She is intact. I have verified it physically."

"God's balls," Grace swore on a whisper, making Ava cough into her handkerchief, and Tor clear his throat. Rose couldn't make herself look at Cullen's best friend beside her. What in heavens must he think? What must all of them think?

It took a full two seconds for the information to penetrate Beatrice's sotted mind. Her triumphant smile twisted into a sneer. "Nay." Her eyes shifted to Agnes who walked around Errol to take her daughter's arm.

"To home, Beatrice," she said and bowed her head to Cullen's mother. "A lovely stew, Charlotte."

No one moved. Rose sucked in air through her nose. The

all could picture what she and Cullen had done together. *Could I but inhale enough to shrivel into a tiny husk and blow away on the winter wind.*

As the front doors closed behind them, Charlotte grabbed the basket of bread and handed it across to Hamish. "There's plenty more. Errol, pass the fish this way, please," she said, freeing Errol from his statuesque prison to pass and sit. When Cullen sat, Rose looked down at her plate where a sea trout fillet and cooked turnips stared back. How was she going to eat?

A little hiccup burst from Grace, and she pressed two fingers to her lips. She took a full breath and let it out, her gaze connecting to Rose. "I never thought you were a courtesan, knew you couldn't be, just like Cullen." Her eyes opened wide. "Well, not *just* like Cullen." She flapped her hands and swore again under her breath.

Ava laughed slightly. "Don't mind her. In England we don't talk about a woman's virginity at gatherings, and tension makes Grace swear, at least since we've come to Scotland."

Mairi's laughter burst from her tight lips. She leaned forward. "We don't on Mull either. Talk about a lass's virginity, that is. But we swear plenty."

"Back to eating," Charlotte said, popping a bite of fish into her mouth. But Rose couldn't move, and neither did Cullen. A heavy silence lay about the room. Errol cracked his knuckles, apologizing. Grace hiccupped again. Ava's sip from her cup sounded loud in the silence.

Broc swore and rose, moving himself and his plate up the table to fill in one of the two empty seats. "All this quiet will curdle this good meal in my stomach." He thumped his tankard on the table and raised it high. "To Rose and the fact that she indeed is not a courtesan."

Tor was the first to pick up his own tankard to copy Broc, followed by Errol, Mairi, and Grace. Ava laughed and lifted her cup of wine, while Charlotte *tsk*ed but did the same. Even Tor's second-in-command, Hamish, lifted his tankard in salute. Cullen didn't move, nor did his uncles.

"Hear, hear," Errol agreed, looking down toward Rose.

How should she respond? All she could think to do was smile and nod toward Broc in silent acceptance.

Cullen rubbed his face and answered a question Tor asked him about his aunt's whisky. Everyone began to eat once again. Cullen turned his face to Rose, though she kept her gaze straight ahead, landing on the dragonflies in the tapestry near the hearth. "A private discussion is warranted," Cullen murmured.

"Private?" she asked, as she tried to subdue the defensive feeling rising up within her. "I was starting to think that the Scots revealed everything before the whole clan."

Cullen grumbled something in Gaelic. "Come."

At least she could escape the meal, which stared up from her plate with filmy eyes. When Cullen stood, she rose, too, and rested her hand on his offered arm. Her heart pounded, sending tingles down her fingers and into her numb legs.

"Ye can't leave," Charlotte said in frustration as the dinner fell further apart. "Ye haven't crowned the Abbot of Unreason."

Cullen reached down beside the table and pulled up the crown of hammered iron. He set it before his plate with a clank. "I will let ye all choose. Excuse us."

Rose propelled her legs to keep up with Cullen as they strode past the dark alcove toward the back of the keep that opened into the gardens. He stopped in the corridor, releasing her arm. Two sconces in the hall gave only enough light to keep one from running into the chiseled stone walls that arched the length of the corridor. In the darkness, Cullen's eyes looked black, his face drawn in fierce lines.

They were alone, utterly alone, and she had only her wit for defense. Yet she wasn't frightened. Not of Cullen. He'd shown his honor the other night by not taking her maidenhead. The thought washed a layer of her irritation away, and she exhaled in a sigh. "Why didn't you tell me before?"

Cullen strode across the narrow width and back. "I meant to ask ye in the alcove before dinner if ye knew."

"Like I have said," she whispered. "I cannot remember my life before. Only vague feelings and directions about things like herbs and…" She indicated the two of them with a flip of her hand. "What happened the other night."

His stare stretched long, the silence heavy with the stones surrounding them. Finally he cleared his throat. "Ye have memories about…learning how to do what we did?" he asked, his arms crossing over his chest. "Or doing those things with other men?"

A sinking feeling made it hard to inhale. What type of person had she been? She swallowed and flung her fingers, stretched wide in frustration. "I have no idea." She shook her head, frustrated anger flaring up. "I don't remember where I learned what a man might like, Cullen."

"Yet ye showed no shock or hesitancy."

His words were low, and she could almost pick up condemnation in them. Or was she imagining it? "Neither did you," she pointed out, her voice rising.

"I'm not a virgin."

"Are you upset that I could give you pleasure?" she asked. "Angry for touching you, making you quake and strain and roar?" He stared at her, and she watched his face tense with anger or mounting passion, she wasn't sure which.

A woman's words are her power. She could tip a man from one extreme to the other simply by stringing together the right words. And heaven forbid, Rose knew which way she wanted to tip Cullen.

She took a step toward the middle of the corridor to face

him. "Were you shocked, Cullen Duffie, when my teeth razed along your skin or when my lips closed around your length?" Her voice lowered, a whisper in the shadows. "Did you wish I were a meek lady instead?" She rested her palm on his chest and looked up at his face in the thick shadows, curling her fingers into his shirt front. "Demure and restrained instead of running my tongue along you. Lapping at you," she whispered.

The deep sound of a growl came from the back of his throat, and he reached for her, his mouth covering hers. He pulled her with him to lean back against the wall, his legs braced apart with her between them.

All Rose's thoughts of strategy shattered. Lips slanted against each other, and Cullen's fingers raked through her hair, dislodging her hood and *coiffure*. She raked her nails over his broad shoulders, pressing her pelvis into his erection that she could feel through the many layers separating them. He lowered his hold to grasp her backside, rubbing her deliciously against him until she gasped out a small moan.

Everything about Cullen was tantalizing, and she ached for him. Last night had done nothing to diminish her desire for the Highland chief, the exquisite warrior with soft, laughing eyes. The power he held in check, the muscles beneath his skin, his smell, the way his hands cupped her with urgency, as if she made him lose the civil part of his mind. All of it called to Rose, luring her into a fierce tempest of desire that she had no wish to calm.

With the quickness of lightning, Cullen swung Rose so that her back was to the wall and ripped his mouth from hers, spinning around. She blinked in the darkness at his broad shoulders, her breathing ragged.

"So...I've been elected," came Broc's voice from before them in the corridor. "And the Abbott of Unreason has come to find ye two, as Ava Maclean wishes, in order to give Rose an early Christmas gift."

Rose rested her forehead into Cullen's back as she mentally restitched her composure. She breathed deeply, using Cullen and the wall to keep her standing.

"And…" Broc continued in a slow, apologetic voice. "The length of time ye two are down here is being noted. Thought ye might want to know."

"William and Farlan?" Cullen said, his voice low and jagged.

"One glance from Charlotte and they shut their gobs. I think your mother's going to run swords through anyone threatening to disrupt the festivities further tonight."

Mon Dieu. Poor Charlotte. "Of course," Rose said from behind Cullen's back. "We will be there momentarily." As she peered around Cullen's arm, she blinked at the bright torch Broc raised high, illuminating the whole corridor. Her hood lay on the floor between them.

"And um, Cull…" Broc started and rubbed the tips of his fingers on his chin. "Ye might want to have the lass walk in front of ye." He dipped his gaze to the front of Cullen's kilt. He turned, his boots clipping softly as he strode toward the great hall.

Cullen retrieved her hood and took a deep breath, cursing softly. "I didn't mean to attack ye here."

Rose tried to fix her hood with the few pins she could find scattered at her hem. She shook her head and dropped her hands. He'd kept a step between them, but she could still feel the erotic pull of their unquenched desire. She looked up into his eyes. "Anger feeds into passion, Cullen. It was inevitable."

"We aren't finished," he said, and she couldn't quite tell if it was a threat or a promise. She felt a shiver tickle through her, pearling her nipples under her bodice.

"Absolutely not," she said in agreement and took his offered hand. She glanced down at his kilt as they walked through the pool of firelight from a lit sconce. "And I think

Broc was right about me walking in front of you into the hall, she said.

His hand moved to the erection proudly tenting his kil. At the mouth of the great hall, he shifted behind her, bending to whisper into her ear. "Aye, we are absolutely not finished.

• • •

"Here they come now," Broc stated, standing to the side o the hearth, the crown lopsided on his head. Everyone ha moved away from the table, and Errol was adding more pea and logs to the fire.

Would they notice that Rose's hair was undone? Culle plucked out one pin that dangled as if waving for attention.

"Wonderful," Charlotte said, indicating a chair for Rose When she sat, Cullen moved to stand behind her, much t Broc's merriment. His cousin grinned broadly as Cullen trie to picture his Uncle Farlan naked. *Ballocks*. That vision woul geld any man.

"Even though we don't usually give gifts until the firs of January, Ava wishes to give Rose and Charlotte their gift now," Broc announced.

"They are from both Grace and me," Ava said, lifting tw small wooden boxes topped with dried flowers. She set on in Charlotte's lap while Grace carried the other over to Rose

"I picked this one for whomever might be another lady c Dunyvaig," Grace said. "I had no idea you were French at th time." She giggled.

William coughed into his fist and retreated to the tabl while Farlan crossed his arms and leaned against the wall nex to the hearth. Cullen noticed his mother's murderous loo It must be what was keeping them quiet. Not only was Ros not in a dungeon or tied to a boat sailing her over to Captai Taylor, she was being given a gift as a lady of Dunyvaig.

His mother and Rose untied the ribbons holding the lids on top. "Ye are really so thoughtful," his mother said. She pulled out a glass bottle from a nest of cloth. Rose did the same.

The bottle was made of thick white glass with a liquid inside. "'Tis a sweet balm," Grace said. "We thought you might want to wear some during the holidays."

Rose wiggled off the thick stopper and held it to her slanted little nose. Cullen watched her inhale, a *merci* already on her lips, lips he'd been plundering minutes ago in the dark corridor. Bloody hell, he couldn't keep his head around her. What had happened to his famed control? Her words alone made him wild with want. *Uncle Farlan. Uncle Farlan naked.* He couldn't keep thinking about Rose's perfect lips in polite company.

"It's lovely," Charlotte said. "Thank ye so much."

"We bought the scented oils from a peddler traveling along the isles," Grace said.

Ava gave a wry grin. "Even though Tor and Hamish wanted to kill him."

"He looked suspiciously English," Hamish said from his seat farther back from the fire.

Ava waved her hand. "One can't look English unless he's wearing a red military jacket. Anyway, he had all sorts of these balms, and we picked out a few. I thought the one for you, Lady Charlotte, had a deliciously warm scent."

"It is perfect for me," his mother said as she touched a bit to the pulse point on her wrist.

Grace raised onto her toes and smiled down at Rose. "Even though I had no idea you were French, I chose this floral scent. The peddler said it was directly from France. It's a French flower."

"A lily," Rose said, her face oddly blank, pale even.

"A lily?" Grace continued without notice. "Of course.

Ava, it's a lily. Well, the man said it was a very sought-after fragrance in France, especially among the royals."

When Rose didn't respond, Cullen squatted before her, bringing his face level with hers. "Lass?" He slowly disentangled her cold fingers from the glass bottle and replaced the stopper. "What is it?"

"Oh my," Grace said, taking the gift when Cullen passed it to her. "What's wrong?"

"Rose?" Cullen said and cupped her cheeks to bring her eyes to his. They were dark in the dimness of the room, but the look in them was startling. Brows slightly drawn, her lips cracked open, she looked like she was lost somewhere between shock and weeping. "Rose, lass. Ye've remembered something," he said, searching her eyes.

"The smell," Tor said behind him.

Joan stood. "Smells can be very powerful at bringing forth memories."

"Rose?" Cullen said again, coaxing her back.

She finally took in a breath, her gaze connecting with his. "Not Rose," she said slowly. "Madeleine. Madeleine Renald."

Chapter Fourteen

Rose remained perfectly still as the ghosts of her past swam around her like fish in a pond. She sat in a garden of spring lilies, bright green leaves holding white, fragrant bells while bees and butterflies moved on a breeze. A dark-haired lady paced before her, speaking in French and punctuating most of her sentences with a flipping of her slender hands.

You are naturally beautiful, Madeleine. You have learned grace and manners, languages, the womanly arts of seduction, and everything you need to be a success. The lady was Claire Renald, her mother. She stopped before her and nodded approvingly. *You will be my greatest accomplishment. It is time to return to court.*

"Rose," Cullen's voice called, and she reached past the fading images to focus on his kind, worried eyes.

"Didn't ye hear her?" William said, coming up beside them. "Her name is Madeleine."

Rose blinked, her world settling back to the present. "*Je vais bien,*" she said.

"She says she is well," Ava translated, bending forward so

that her concerned face hovered near Cullen's shoulder.

"Can she speak only French now?" Farlan asked.

"I am well," Rose repeated, this time in English.

"Did everything come back to ye?" Charlotte asked.

"Give her a minute," Cullen said, stroking her cheek. "Ye're very pale."

Rose wet her lips. "I was startled." She looked up to meet Charlotte's eyes. "I was in a garden of lilies." Her brow wrinkled as she looked down at her hands in her lap. "With my mother, I think. She said we were to go to court."

"I knew she was royal," Farlan said.

Rose shook her head. "I do not think I am royal. Possibly well-bred and taken to court."

"Ye can't remember more?" Cullen asked.

"*Non.*"

"That's normal," Joan said, stepping closer. "May I?" Cullen gave her room, and she took Rose's wrist to feel her pulse, touched her head, and looked closely at her eyes, finally standing. "I've had a few patients with memory loss back at Aros. In two of them, their memories trickled back one at a time. After something like a smell that awakened a strong memory, the rest followed within a few weeks, filling in the missing parts. Although the actual accident that caused the memory loss never came back." She patted Rose's hand. "It sounds like you'll start remembering soon."

Rose wasn't certain that she wanted her memories returned. Even the beautiful setting of the lily garden was muted by a dark, anxious feel. Her mother had smiled, but something sharp lurked behind it.

"Do ye know the name?" Farlan asked William.

The bald man stroked his short beard under his perpetual frown. "Nay, but that means very little. If I made it a habit of learning the names at the French court, the English would be sure to hear of it. Like they will probably hear of our French uest."

Cullen stood, shielding her. "Madeleine is still under my
rotection."

Her name in Cullen's mouth made her stomach clench.
Call me Rose," she said, prompting them all to look at her.
Until I have my memories back, I feel much more like Rose
ere."

"Also," Tor said, "if the English hear her real name, it
ight pull their attention to Dunyvaig."

The weight of Rose's memories lay across her like a
et bag. She'd come from a very different world, one filled
ith opulence and shallow morals. It was nothing like the
elatively wholesome life here at Aros. "I think I will retire
or the night."

Mairi came to her side. "That sounds like a wonderful
lea after my journey." Her strong arm clasped Rose's as she
tood.

"I will help ye to your room," Cullen said, but Mairi waved
im off. Rose met his gaze. Could he read her exhaustion?
he wasn't up for the fire of their discussion or argument or
utual seduction, whatever it was.

"Rose knows where it is," Mairi said. "I will make certain
he finds her bed."

Blessedly Tor's sister realized Rose's need for quiet, and
hey climbed the turning stairs in silence. The bed was plenty
ig enough for the two of them, and Rose settled under the
uilts after they'd washed and changed.

"Thank ye for sharing your room with me," Mairi said as
he blew out the candle on the bedside table.

"Thank you for not asking me if I remember anything
ore," Rose said into the inky darkness, her eyes still open
oward the blackened windowpanes.

Mairi laughed softly, the tone more tainted than joyful.
I've been questioned continuously before, and it's tiring."

Tor's sister yawned. "This bed is so comfortable. It must b filled with goose down."

Her words trailed away, and within minutes Rose cou hear the soft, even breathing of sleep coming from the oth side of the bed. She turned slowly so as not to jounce th mattress and stared upward at the underside of the canopy.

The scene in the lily garden played before her in th shadows. Her mother's voice was soft, yet her fingers we sharp and pinching if Madeleine veered at all from the pat Claire Renald had planned for her daughter. Was she Claire only child? The one who would win her a spot at court agai The French court? *Oui*, at *Château de Blois* and anoth castle. *Amboise*. Yes, there was another *chateau* there. The li garden was in the countryside where Rose had been raise but her mother preferred the sophistication of town and cou Yet when Rose thought of the smooth white stone façade the *château* and intricate ironwork around the windows ar roofline, a chill shook through her. Madeleine did not lik court. At all.

• • •

Music played. Haunted chords and laughter echoed with clin of gold plates. Gilt walls tilted oddly, the fleur-de-lis *patter reaching from floor to ceiling. Every corner Madeleine turne gave her pause. Lumbering shadows followed behind her she fled on slippers. She reached a door and turned the golde knob, pushing into the sanctuary of the room she shared wi her mother. Claire wasn't there, wouldn't be until dawn whe the parties ended and she came back to sleep until noon.*

Madeleine loved the feel of the sheets on her legs, so co and smooth compared to homespun weave in their count home. She closed her eyes, the darkness enveloping her in t luxurious bed. The sound of merriment was muted here on t second floor, one of hundreds of bedrooms for those lucky enough to be accepted at court. Exotic foods, silk linens, warm baths whenever requested. Of course her mother wanted them to live here, despite the dangers. "I want only what is best for you, Madeleine. What is best for you is best for both of us."

Footsteps outside the door caused Madeleine to twist in the sheets until her legs felt clasped in them, silken shackles around her ankles, making her struggle. "Be still." Her mother's voice made her blink, and the face of Claire Renald loomed over her. "Be still." She leaned in to whisper at her ear. "Don't say a word." Claire's face pulled back, but candlelight cut through the shadows to show a man standing beside her, a large man. A king.

"She is lovely," the king said and ran a hand down Madeleine's cheek, his palm pressing flat on the exposed skin of her chest, pinning her to the bed. He leered under his long nose and thin, oiled mustache. Could he feel her heart slamming under the skin? Giving away the terror she felt?

"Oui, she is of royal blood, and she has skills," Claire said. "I have tutored her in all manners, your majesty, those of a lady and those of a courtesan."

The king turned toward Claire's voice in the shadows. "But she is a virgin, oui?"

"Bien sûr. I have guarded her for you, your majesty."

Madeleine watched in horror as he climbed over her in the bed, pressing his hardness against her pelvis through the sheets as he sucked and slobbered along the skin of her neck. She couldn't breathe with the weight of his bear-like body crushing her. His fingers were manacles, holding her arms out to the sides. She wanted to scream, but Claire had warned her to stay quiet, and she would be slapped if she made a noise. "Tu es à moi," he whispered against her ear, his breath hot and heavy with wine. "You are mine."

Ma mere? How could she stand back and let the king do

this to her? Betrayal sliced like a hot knife through Madeleine. Hate broke through her fear, bubbling strength into her arms as she snapped them away from his meaty hands. He pulled back, startled, and focused on her face. But instead of anger, Madeleine saw an excitement that sent a chill through her. Slowly he lifted off of her and turned to the darkness.

"Have her at the ball tomorrow night, dressed to enchant." He pulled something from his coat, the sound familiar as the pearls hit against one another, tinkling. "For her to wear." He glanced back at Madeleine, lying flat in the bed where she'd been left. "A gift for my new mistress, in payment for her virginity."

He turned back to Claire, his hand sliding up and down over his erection. "But tonight, you will do quite nicely."

"Of course, your majesty." And the bear attacked.

Madeleine squeezed her eyes shut and slapped her palms to her ears to block out the noise. Non!*" she yelled.* "Non.*"*

"Rose," a woman's voice called, and she felt her wrists grabbed tightly as she fought. "Rose, wake up."

Rose's eyes flew open, her breath catching on a choke as she stared upward at a woman's face. Who was she? Where was she?

"Breathe," the woman said. "That's it. Ye were having one bloody hell of a nightmare." She slowly released Rose's wrists and sat back on her heels, watching her warily.

"I…I'm sorry," Rose murmured as Mairi's name came back to her. "Did I wake you?" Dawn filtered through the windowpanes.

She shrugged and scooted back to her side of the bed. "No matter. I was about to get up anyway." But instead of rising, she leaned against the headboard and frowned at Rose. "I'm fairly experienced with nightmares, having had many myself, but it seemed like ye couldn't breathe, and ye tried to punch me."

"*Mon Dieu*," Rose said, pushing onto her elbows. "I'm sorry. Did I hurt you?"

"Nay," Mairi said. "I'm fast at dodging, after growing up with Tor. He'd wished to turn me into a brother by making me fierce. I woke often to surprise attacks when I was a lass."

Rose rubbed her hands over her face and noticed that they shook.

"Ye're remembering more," Mairi said. "And it doesn't look like it's pleasant." She slid out of the bed and padded across to the small jug of watered wine in the room, pouring out a cup. She returned and handed it to Rose.

"Thank you." Rose let the wetness wash the bitter taste of fear from her mouth. Where normal dreams faded quickly upon waking, horror did not. It seemed to sit within Rose's chest, spreading out to coat her with a slick feel of oily dirt. "I wonder if I could order a warm bath. That might help."

"I'm sure Charlotte could see to it." Mairi sat on the edge of the bed, her face growing serious. "I don't pry because I don't like others to pry into my affairs. But if ye'd like to talk ever, I have two ears and tight lips." She cupped her ears and squeezed her lips hard together.

Rose found her first real smile, and with it came the ability to fully inhale. "Thank you, Mairi." Tor's sister seemed sincere, but the thought of telling her about the horrible dream washed the smile from her lips. What would Mairi think of her if she knew what had played before Madeleine's eyes? What she'd been told she must do? *Non.* She would keep her memories to herself while she figured out what was real and what was only a nightmare.

• • •

Cullen nodded to his mother as he and Tor strode into the great hall, their hair still damp from washing for the Christmas

Eve feast. She stood with Joan near the mantel.

"Your hall looks so festive," Ava said where she sat before the hearth, hands resting on her gently protruding belly.

"And much less scorched than Aros," Grace said beside her.

Tor snorted. Cullen slapped his hand down on his friend's shoulder. "Ye have the rascal responsible restoring the keep while ye're here?"

"Aye, with constant oversight," he said and took the tankard of ale Cullen handed him. They'd been hunting and had brought down several large bucks and another boar that were being gutted and cleaned in the bailey. He surveyed the hall, but Rose was absent, as was Mairi. They had walked arm in arm after breakfast as Rose showed her around Dunyvaig.

"Hold the blasted door," Broc yelled from the entryway, sending Cullen to help him and Errol with the Yule log they'd found, fallen and dry, in the small forest, mid-island. The three of them carried it to the hearth, setting the large end in the gaping stone maw to the side of the fire. They would light the end tonight at midnight with the ashes of last year's log, and keep it burning through the twelve nights of Christmas, as was tradition.

Joan sat on the edge of the stage Hamish, Errol, and Broc had built earlier in the day for the Christmas pageant that Beatrice had organized. She'd stayed clear of the keep since her drunken outburst last night, but the pageant was still planned.

Errol and Broc trudged back out, most likely to wash before the Christmas Eve celebration.

"Have ye seen Rose and Mairi?" Cullen asked, his gaze turning to the dark alcove. He hadn't had a moment alone with Rose since their tryst in the corridor.

"They went above to change for dinner," Ava said.

Grace glanced at Ava with a smirk. "They asked us to

accompany them on their walk around your small lake outside the village, but I don't walk near water with Ava, especially in winter."

Ava huffed. "You'd have everyone thinking that I would push you in."

"No," Grace said, fixing the cuffs of her slim, decorated sleeves. "I'm convinced that the world becomes off-kilter whenever you are around water, making me lose my balance or slip or trip or something of the kind."

"Really?" Ava said. "I tip the world?"

Grace pursed her lips and nodded. "Apparently." They both stared for a moment at each other before breaking into light feminine laughter.

"Has the celebration already started?" Mairi called as she stepped out of the alcove from the stairs. But Cullen's gaze slid right off her to Rose, who followed.

"Good," his mother said. "Rose is wearing the gown we had made for her. Mildred is so talented with the needle. And Ellen helped. It turned out splendid, although anything on her would be stunning." She spoke to Joan, but Cullen couldn't agree more. Rose was stunning.

She walked with poise over the polished wood floors, the edge of her full, steely-blue skirts whispering with each step. The material parted in front to show a pale underskirt with burgundy embroidery of swirls and flowers. The sleeves encased her arms, leading up to her slender, straight shoulders. The bodice came to a V down the front, covered with the same vine-colored embroidery as the underskirt, and the neckline was square and low, showing her creamy skin and the gentle swell of her bosom.

Cullen inhaled, knowing how that warm skin would smell, how it would feel under his fingers, his lips.

Rose's hair was woven onto her head, a circle of matching fabric perched like a crown. A soft smile sat on her lips, her cheeks pink and lashes long and dark. She stopped and bowed to the room before moving closer. He met her gaze and gave a brief, slow nod. The dress brought out the traces of blue in her eyes.

William and Farlan stomped inside alongside Hamish. "How many swords does Aros have in reserve?" William asked.

"More than we have arms to hold them," Hamish replied, heading to the sideboard where tankards stood full and ready for thirsty mouths.

"How many?" Farlan asked. "Fifty, one hundred?"

"Hundreds," Tor called. He walked toward the men. "Enough to equip Dunyvaig if need be."

"Ye would come if the English storm us?" William asked.

"The Beast of Aros," Tor said, speaking of himself, "and my clan, back Cullen Duffie, as do the MacInnes." He'd apparently embraced the name Beast, which used to annoy him.

"Ye back the MacDonalds of Dunyvaig," William repeated.

Tor's grin was wry. "Nay. We back Cullen Duffie. I do not know the MacDonalds. I know Cullen, and he has my oath."

William nodded, his gaze crossing to Cullen.

"Enough talk of swords and English," Charlotte called. "'Tis Christmas Eve, and here is the start of the feast." Ellen pushed in a cart laden with platters, the aroma reminding Cullen that he hadn't eaten for hours.

This time Cullen wouldn't waste his time trying to follow dining propriety. He walked directly to Rose and offered her his arm. A slight uncertainty crossed her forehead, but smoothed quickly. She placed her gloved fingers on his sleeve.

"Ye look lovelier than all of Christmastide," he said.

She canted her head. "Don't let Charlotte hear you disdain her grand decorations." She spoke of the garland that had been draped from rafter to rafter, providing a bright green backdrop for the red berries wherever one looked. Evergreens gave off the fresh tang of pine to blend with the scent of the oil lamps and cloves. Candles glittered in all the chandeliers and sconces, filling the room with gay light.

"I stand by my assessment," he countered and led her to sit next to him at the top of the table. She lowered into her seat as Cullen imagined a princess might, her head held regally straight yet without being stiff.

Agnes joined them, thankfully without her daughter, and she didn't say another word about Rose's knowledge of abortives. Charlotte may have threatened her with the blade she said she always wore.

The venison was tender, as was the goose, and the fish was fresh and seasoned to perfection. Turnips and carrots and freshly baked braids of bread accompanied rabbit stew. His aunt, Maggie, brought another cask of whisky and stayed for wassail.

Donald, the blacksmith, and his wife and apprentice arrived for sugared plums. Laughter and the low hum of conversation wove around the table. With each new guest, Cullen rose to greet them, bringing them to the comfort of the table and warm hall. No one questioned Rose's presence or accent. Perhaps they trusted Cullen more than he thought.

When the quartet of musicians set up, Broc clapped his hands, his iron crown skewed on his head. "A dance, my good men." He nodded to the lead player who strummed his wooden lute. Within minutes they started a lively tune for a pavan dance. The lute, wooden flute, and viola blended together, led by the merry beat of the drums. People formed pairs in the center of the hall between the table and the hearth.

Cullen excused himself from the gatekeeper and walked to where Rose sat. He offered her his hand. "Do ye know how to dance?"

She watched the pairs forming two lines. "The tune sounds familiar."

Cheerfulness loosened his stiff shoulders when she set her hand in his, and he led her to the end of the paired lines. They stood opposite each other. Cullen nodded, his heart feeling light. They stepped together for palms to touch, retreated, and circled, bending knees. They turned together, moving close and then back again. Down the line Farlan cursed low and apologized. Charlotte laughed, as did Grace as she leaped forward to meet Errol's palms in time for the next move.

"Beautiful," Broc shouted as the ladies turned, their skirts belling out.

Cullen couldn't agree more as he watched Rose sway and pivot, the folds of her blue skirts twisting and widening around her narrow waist. She floated more than stepped, her shoulders perfectly still, and her neck tempted him with its bare length. When she raised her arm, it was like a great white swan's curved neck. Even her fingers were expressive.

Cullen and Rose came together, and he smelled summer flowers, not the lily that Ava and Grace had brought, but a lighter scent.

"Ye know these steps," he said.

"*Oui*. It reminds me of the *basse danse*."

They stepped in again, their faces only inches apart for a moment. "How so?"

"Dancing like two lines of proud peacocks," she said, and a small laugh came from her lips. It was authentic, one of her first, and it sounded like a silver bell. He'd been prepared to question her more about her memories, hoping that remembering the dance would tease them out of her shuttered mind, but now all he wanted to do was make her laugh.

Tapping boots and ladies' swooshing skirts complemented the lute. Light laughter, down the line, punctuated the pauses in the dance pattern until the last trill of the flute faded.

Before anyone could escape the floor, Broc called out to the musicians. "Another song, fine gentlemen." Broc strode right up between them to claim Rose for the next dance. He looked over his shoulder at Cullen. "Benefit of being Abbott of Unreason," Broc said. "I get to dance with *all* the lovely lasses."

Cullen watched them line up. Everyone, except for Agnes, found a new partner. Even Maggie danced across from Garrick. Bea's mother would feel slighted if no one asked her. Taking one last swallow of the ale in the tankard he'd left beside the hearth, Cullen turned toward her. But a commotion of high-pitched voices broke out in the entryway, with one overriding the rest. Beatrice.

Chapter Fifteen

The merry beat of the dance brought out the laughter among them all, including Rose. The flute trilled, and the lute player strummed lovely chords. Rose floated through the moves, the basic steps coming back to her without thought. Some of her embellishments seemed unique, and Grace and Ava added to their turns as well, raising more cheer.

Rose smiled at Broc while catching sight of Cullen off to the left. He walked across the room, his face intent. With a quick bow and slide, Rose realized his target, and her breath stuttered.

Beatrice MacDonald walked in from the entryway with the evil twins, Bonnie and Blair. All three of them carried fabric over their arms, Beatrice talking nonstop to her minions. Several young men followed, carrying logs draped in woolskins. One brought forth a cowskin over his shoulders, mooing as he sauntered about. Grace and Ava both laughed at his antics, and Broc left Rose to chase after him for milk. She backed up out of the way of the dancers.

One of the guards, usually stationed by the portcullis,

arried in a manger filled with hay. They set their loads down
on the platform next to the musicians, and the twins came at
once to fix the skins over the logs to look like animals. It was
to be the nativity.

Set free from their loads, the young men came over
to watch the couples. One nodded to Rose. "I'm Garrick
MacDonald. Care to dance?"

"Broc abandoned me for a cow, so thank you."

Garrick produced a wide grin. "Broc's a fool, even without
he fool's crown, if he left ye standing alone."

Rose met Garrick in the center of the line before stepping
back with the ladies. Where was Cullen? She turned in time to
see him with Beatrice. Rose missed a step and quickened her
pace to catch the beat. Beatrice leaned into Cullen, talking
while he stood, a mask of patience on his face. He said nothing
while the woman seemed to talk unendingly.

"My turn," said another young man, taking Garrick's
place. A slower tune started, which required Rose's attention
to copy the steps. When she looked back, Cullen had Beatrice's
hand and was leading her to the end of the increasing line
now that the twins had joined in with their helpers.

Rose caught his gaze for a brief second before she had to
turn away, avoiding Blair's broad sweep, her arm outstretched
to bell her skirt wide.

"Sorry there," Blair said, though her frown didn't hold a
drop of apology.

Up the line, Broc sauntered down the middle as the king
of Christmas, looking down his nose, imitating partners, and
avoiding skirts. Cullen's cousin was born to play the *Prince
les Sots*. The flash of a thin man, crowned with a jester's hat,
points drooping over his face, flashed in Rose's memory. She
blinked to clear the image but missed the next step so that
Blair collided with her, giving her another frown.

"*Excusez moi*," Rose murmured and caught up, her

smile for her new partner forced and stiff. As soon as th
song ended, Rose curtsied and stepped out of line befor
another could claim her hand. Suddenly the laughter, musi
and voluminous skirts seemed overwhelming. She escaped t
the alcove near the stairs that led above. Her fingers clutche
the wall of the arch, a solid hold as she felt awash in mor
memories of the dark brunette with flawless skin and har
blue eyes.

Claire Renald. Her mother. She'd instructed Rose c
dance, manners, flirtation, and ways to manipulate men. Bu
the worst lessons had involved a book Claire owned tha
housed erotic pictures of lovers in various positions. The wa
in which Claire shared personal stories made Rose, or rathe
Madeleine, blush.

Madeleine's past was flying back like a book thrown ope
in the wind, pages flipping quickly, throwing information lik
dust in her eyes.

But I am Rose here, not Madeleine. She looked ou
at the holly and evergreens swept along the walls in gran
dips. Clusters of mistletoe and winter berries accented th
entryways. Candles burned brightly, and the Yule log ha
been covered with dried flowers to be lit at midnight. Th
stage was set for the nativity pageant, and the musicians wor
bright clothes and cheerful expressions.

Dunyvaig was the most beautiful place she'd ever see
No gold or wallpaper. No crystal and silks. Yet, Rose realize
she didn't want to be anywhere else. At the far end of the ha
William and Farlan MacDonald sat at a small table set wit
chess pieces. Farlan was stealing one of William's pawns. Eve
the gruff old men were preferred to the lecherous glance
from the king or vicious whispers from the ladies who sa
her only as a rival.

"Rose?"

She turned at the woman's voice, her inhale stuck but he

spine strong. Beatrice stood before her, face soft. "Yes?" Rose answered, the word even.

Beatrice's chin tipped slightly upward, cocking her head. "I ask ye forgiveness for the other night at dinner. The drink was strong, and I let my worries about Dunyvaig out without sober thought. I did not mean to slander ye." She nodded, her face grave, and tucked an errant curl behind her ear.

Rose stared at the edge of Beatrice's jaw where a shadow lay against the skin. With the direct illumination from the wall sconce, she could see her complexion clearly. "Your face is bruised," Rose said. "Did someone slap you?" Rose had suffered many slaps from her mother, the sting across the skin fading, but the bruise sometimes swelling afterward when delivered with rage. She pushed past the memories to focus on the woman before her.

Beatrice yanked her hair forward to hide the side of her face, obviously knowing exactly what Rose saw. "Do ye accept my apology or not? Because I have work to do for the pageant."

Her tone grated against Rose. She'd probably never have another private chance to put Beatrice MacDonald in her place. The girl was vulnerable, and any number of waspish slights and backhanded insults, meant to peel away her confidence as a woman, curled onto Rose's tongue. From Beatrice's country, slightly shoddy attire, to her wild, unkempt curls and vulgar hopes to snare Cullen, Rose could cut the woman down with a sentence or two. After all, Rose had been trained by the best to slander a woman bloody. The French court was a house of serpents disguised as ladies, and the only weapons women were given were the sharpness of their words and the precision of their cutting gestures.

As Rose opened her mouth to unleash a quiet, yet venomous slice, Beatrice shifted, blinking several times as she held her unbecoming frown. She was nervous, obviously outside of her usual role of Dunyvaig's womanly dictator.

With an even inhale, Rose let her hard smile soften to neutral and swallowed down the lethal responses. "Thank you, Beatrice. I will take no offense."

"I want only Cullen happy and Dunyvaig safe," Beatrice replied, her gaze drifting off to the wall.

"That is noble," Rose said, although she was certain Beatrice left some of her other, more selfish, motives out. "I will try not to injure either of them."

"Very well," Beatrice said. "I must get back to work." She turned away but looked over her shoulder, her confident mask back in place. "Would ye like to play a part in the pageant? I haven't enough actors."

A refusal sprang up in Rose with another wounding remark, which she squelched. She wouldn't let her mother's words rule her thinking. It wasn't honorable to intentionally harm, no matter what she'd been taught. "If you are in need, and it is an easy role, I can help. Is the part difficult?"

Beatrice's face lit with surprise. "Nay, there aren't even any lines for ye. I will find ye garments to wear." She turned and strode toward Charlotte without a thank-you. Good manners were not Beatrice's talent. Had she gained the bruise by insulting someone in the village? Blair and Bonnie seemed as enthralled by their leader as usual. Her mother, maybe? Rose blinked as she felt the sting of Claire's flying hand and leaned against the rough stone wall.

"Did dancing tire ye?" Cullen stepped around the corner, startling Rose. Her open hand flew to her neck. "Sorry for the fright." He remained several steps away, yet Rose felt the attraction spark between them. Darkness and privacy were the kindling, and Cullen was the flint.

She shook her head. "I didn't hear you."

"Did Bea beg your forgiveness?" he asked.

The woman hadn't sought her out to assuage her

conscience but had been directed by Cullen. "I wouldn't go so far as saying she begged," Rose said, catching sight of Beatrice arranging animals.

His hand stretched up the wall where he leaned and balled into a fist as he drew closer to her. She could smell a mix of whisky, leather, and pine coming from him. So familiar after the night they'd shared.

She forced her gaze to stay level. It felt that whenever they were alone, anger and passion fueled them. She took an even breath. "I haven't thanked you for the other night. Your restraint."

His sensuous mouth turned serious. "I would not take your maidenhead without knowing if there was someone ye wish to save it for. Someone ye love."

She tipped her head, looking up sideways from under her lashes. "If I'd not been a virgin…?"

He chuckled low and met her gaze with a look that held no guilt whatsoever. "All thoughts of virtue fled my mind the moment I saw your form before the fire, lass." He leaned toward her. "*Och*, Rose. Ye are like…" He slid the back of his finger gently along her jaw to trail a knuckle down her neck. "Ye're like a finely sculpted goddess made of flames and sin."

Her grin broadened at his poetry. "It was I who seduced you," she said.

"From the moment ye punched me in the face."

He leaned in to kiss her, catching her bubble of laughter.

"Ah, we found it," a man proclaimed from the archway.

"Blast," Cullen murmured and pulled back. The immediate coolness, where the heat of his mouth had been, made Rose blink to stare at the bright archway where Tor and Ava stood. "Found what?" Cullen groused.

"The dark alcove where I can steal kisses from my wife," Tor said, and Ava laughed. They held each other, seeming to fit perfectly together in true comfort. "We started looking for one as soon as your Christmas fool announced we were to play Blind Man's Bluff." Tor's merry look darkened. "I wasn't about to have anyone pawing around the room after my wife." Ava leaned in to him, her smile radiant.

Was this what love looked like? Two people who wished to be together because of the joy they felt in each other's presence, not to rise in status or slate their lust or win a boon or persuade one to act on their behalf? Rose studied the couple, seeking any telltale sign that one of them lied, but there was none. All she saw was true, deep affection.

A feminine shriek and male laughter exploded outward from the room beyond. Charlotte began to fuss. "Sounds like my mother is putting that fire out," Cullen said, taking Rose's hand. The warmth of his touch was an anchor, and she moved easily to his side as he pulled her to look into the room. Errol whipped off his blindfold while apologizing to Grace. She blushed, a hand to her breasts, which must have been groped.

"That game always brings trouble," Ava said, laughing softly.

Tor set his arm across Ava's shoulders. "I believe it used to be one of Cullen's favorites."

"Old, foolish history," Cullen replied, a warning in his low voice.

On the stage, Beatrice clapped her hands. "The Christmas pageant will begin soon. All actors and musicians come forward."

"That would be me," Rose said with a sigh.

"You are in the pageant?" Ava asked.

"Beatrice says they are short on actors and asked me." Rose shrugged and gave Cullen a wide-eyed look. "If she makes me a cow, don't let Broc try to milk me."

"Agreed," Cullen said.

Ava laughed. "You are a brave woman, Rose." She gave a look of sympathy while holding a hand to her bosom. "I will emember you fondly."

"*Merci*," Rose said with a laugh, and Cullen led her
oward the stage.

Beatrice glanced between Rose and Cullen, her features
tiff. "Here is your costume." She held out a long, dark brown
unic and a shepherd's staff. "Don't forget to put on the
beard." Her mouth twitched upward in a smirk as she set a
wooly mass on top of the tunic.

Mon Dieu. Cullen took the costume and followed Rose
behind the screen. His brows rose appreciatively. "Ye'll have
o take off your petticoats or the tunic won't fit."

"At least I'm not a cow," she said, making his shoulders
move with muffled laughter, which made her laugh, too. She
snatched the tunic away. "Ask Mairi to help me change or we
will cause more scandal."

Cullen laid the load down on a chair. "Don't forget the
beard."

Rose pointed for him to leave. Mairi came back and
helped Rose out of her broad skirts and into the long, thin
tunic that fell to cover her slippers. Its draping hid every
womanly feature she possessed.

"I think this costume is made for someone two hundred
pounds heavier than ye," Mairi commented and removed
Rose's fabric crown. Pulling a few pins out to unwind her hair,
she kept the braid, tucking the end down the back of the tunic.
"A lovely veil," Mairi said, as she covered Rose's head with
the shepherd's headscarf, using the hairpins to secure it. Mairi
stepped back. "And one last detail." She held up the ball of
dyed wool and shook it out into a beard with a hole for Rose's
mouth.

"*Mon Dieu.* How will it stick?" Rose asked, eyeing what
looked like vermin from the Paris gutters.

"There are ties for the beard," Beatrice called, her face
peeking around the screen. Of course, she was dressed as the

Virgin Mary in light blue. She pursed her lips to contain he
laughter at Rose's ensemble.

Mairi scrunched her face when Beatrice turned. Ros
chuckled softly. "Well, I said I'd help when she asked," Ros
whispered. "'Tis my own folly."

"Hold it, and I'll tie this hideous thing in place," Mai
said, dodging behind Rose. Beatrice directed her actors abou
the stage. Blair and Bonnie walked by, dressed as angels. Th
three wise men were young men from the village.

"I'm the only shepherd, aren't I?" Rose murmured.

"This should teach ye never to volunteer for anythin
again." Mairi barely held in her mirth as she came around an
separated the fleece better between Rose's lips. Rose puffe
her breath out to blow the wool from her teeth. "I hope ther
aren't any bugs in it," Mairi murmured.

"What?" Rose looked at her with wide eyes.

A harp sang out a chord. "I better find my seat," Mai
said. "Good luck."

Rose looked down at herself, totally enshrouded i
coarse, brown material. With the bushy beard, she couldn
even see the tunic's hem. She'd have to lift it so as not to tri
If Beatrice's hope was to make her ridiculous in this oversize
manly costume, she'd accomplished her goal.

One of the wise men ran behind the screen, carrying
wooden sheep. "Here," he said and chuckled when he saw he
Oui, she looked ridiculous. "Carry it out with you when yo
hear the harp play after they reach Bethlehem."

She tried to thank him, but the wool kept falling betwee
her lips so that she had to spit it out. The music began, an
Beatrice stepped out to a smattering of applause. The oth
two wise men snuck behind the screen, along with Errol wh
seemed dressed like Joseph.

"Rose?" Errol whispered. She nodded, unwilling to ope
her lips.

"Errol." One of the wise men gave him a little shove, and he strode out onto the stage. Someone from the audience whistled, and he began his lines. Blair and Bonnie swooped onto the stage to tell him that the child was of God.

"Ye'll be up soon," said the wise man she recognized as Garrick.

Thhpp. Rose cleared the wool one more time around her mouth. "She won't make me speak? I can't in this."

Garrick grinned and shook his head. "The shepherd should be silent."

Rose held the wool beard back as she peeked around the edge of the screen. Cullen sat with the Macleans and his mother. His features seemed unguarded, the frown that had plagued him having faded. Relaxed, he was even handsomer. Dark brown hair, which she knew was soft and fresh, sat tasseled around his head. A strong jaw gave a solid base for his neat beard and sensuous lips. She sighed softly, realizing that she could watch him smile forever. He laughed as Broc jumped up to be the ass to carry Mary on her holy journey. Rose grinned behind her wooly beard.

A few minutes later, Beatrice moaned. "The babe. It comes."

Garrick handed Rose the wooden sheep. "Be ready," he whispered. "Go when the harp sounds three times."

With much flourish from Beatrice, Errol held up a ball of wool wrapped in linen to represent baby Jesus. Blair and Bonnie flew about, singing so loud, Rose missed the sound of the harp until Garrick tapped her shoulder.

She yanked up her tunic and held the sheep under one arm.

"Your staff," he whispered and thrust it into her other hand. Taking little steps on the tips of her toes so as not to trip, she climbed the two steps onto the stage. Applause and laughter made her look at the onlookers. Mairi clapped and

Tor whistled, but it was the happiness across Cullen's face, at her entrance, that made her heart soar.

Rose tiptoed across the stage and set the sheep down. She was about to draw near to Beatrice and the wool baby when the doors at the back of the keep burst open with a gust of whistling wind. The laughter cut off, and Cullen, Tor, and Broc rose from their seats, hands at their swords. It was one of the MacDonald guards, escorting two rough-looking men. As they strode across the hall, the light fell upon the taller of the pair. His straight nose and long beard plucked a chord of terror inside Rose. Her heart began to hammer so hard behind her ribs, she wondered if she'd be bruised by it.

"I am Captain Henri de Fleur," he said, his French accent thick. His gaze raked across the room, searching amongst the people gathered. "I am here for Madeleine Renald."

Chapter Sixteen

Cullen slid his sword free. "I did not give permission for a Frenchman to land on my shores."

"I am here to retrieve what is mine," de Fleur said. "Where is she?"

"Is this woman your wife?" Cullen asked, stepping closer, his sword focused on the man's throat. Was this the man who'd tied a rope around Rose's neck? "How is it that a woman is yours, exactly?"

The French captain ignored him and turned in a tight circle. "Madeleine," he called and continued in French.

"Shut your bloody mouth," Cullen ordered. Errol and Broc had taken his flank with Tor to his right. Together they blocked the ladies behind them, but Rose remained in plain sight on the stage. *Don't move*, he willed her.

The French captain glared at him. "I questioned a helpful fisherman when I landed, and he told me how a woman had washed ashore in a small boat two weeks ago. That she was taken into Dunyvaig Castle."

"No MacDonald would give a pirate information," Errol

said, his voice strong. "Not without coercion."

The side of the captain's mouth crooked upward. "Your peasant has come to no mortal harm. Now…" he said, glancing around the room. "Where is Madeleine?"

"Who is she?" William asked. Cullen cut his uncle a glance that would have shredded a younger man. "She came through here," William said, his gaze level with the captain's. "We have no desire to bring the wrath of England to our shores, so we sent her away, but who is she?"

The captain stared hard at William, his features drawn like he was attempting to anatomize the old man's words for truth.

Cullen's mother stood beside William. "The girl had a rope tied about her neck." She frowned fiercely. "Were ye the *druisear* who did that?"

Broc made a noise in the back of his throat, and Farlan coughed at his sister's foul Gaelic curse. The Frenchman sniffed, pulling himself up tall. "Madeleine Renald is dangerous. Even bound, she was able to escape my ship in the middle of a storm."

"How is a lass, who weighs hardly nothing, dangerous?" Broc asked. "She might have pointy knuckles for punching, but that's about it. Or are Frenchmen afraid of lasses?"

Captain de Fleur sucked hard on his teeth, the noise loud in the quiet room. "She's been taught to manipulate men of the highest rank, raised from girlhood to seduce and tease and make men bend to her will." He swiped his hands about while he talked. "She can slice any woman with her sharp remarks until the girl bleeds to death from weakness. Taught to observe minute details, she will learn everything she can about you and use your faults and secrets to her advantage. She will lure you in with her clever mind, to maim you politically and possibly physically. Unless that is, you are the king of France."

"Francis," Cullen said, his muscles flexing.

"Of course. Madeleine belongs to him. He gave her a set of pearls, a gift for his new courtesan."

"The woman who washed ashore here was not Madeleine Renald," Cullen said with succinct clips.

"*Non?*"

"Nay. The woman was a virgin."

Captain de Fleur's nostrils flared. "Of course she was. She's the king's virgin. Raised for his pleasure alone, the illegitimate daughter of the dead king, Louis XII. She was kept a virgin for him and trained in the erotic arts. But she ran away like a coward with his gift of pearls the night before she was to be given to him." His voice rose higher with each sentence. "Are you saying that Madeleine is no longer a virgin?"

Heavy silence stuffed the room. Cullen stood on a battlefield, staring into the eyes of his hated enemy. "A woman, alone," Cullen said. "Raised in perverse servitude, who managed to escape from the French court and again from your bloody rope to jump overboard into a storming Atlantic sea, has more courage than your bastard king."

The words tipped the Frenchman and his crew member into pulling their swords. Cullen was ready. With a flick and thrust, Captain de Fleur's sword skittered across the floor, and Cullen pressed the point of his claymore into the man's throat. Errol held the crew member in the same manner. Behind them, Broc and Tor yanked the men's hands.

"Ye have a dungeon below?" Tor asked.

"Aye," Cullen answered.

"There is a reward for her return," de Fleur continued. "The king has sent folios, penned with her likeness, to the nobility of Europe to find her." De Fleur's lips quirked upward, his eyes narrowed. "I will be a rich man for returning her." He shrugged. "Perhaps slightly used." He set the tip of his tongue on his bottom lip, sliding it along as if anticipating the taste of Rose's skin.

Cullen's sword clattered as he dropped it, his fist swinging around to slam into the French bastard's jaw. The sound of bone cracking made one of the ladies behind him gasp, and the Frenchman slumped to the ground. "See that he finds a puddle of rat's piss to rest his aching head in," Cullen said and gestured for Broc to lead the way as Tor lifted de Fleur under his arms to drag him to the Dunyvaig dungeon.

Only when they were gone from the great hall did Cullen turn toward the stage, as did everyone else left in the room. Rose stood hidden in the long brown robes and beard of the shepherd beside the manger. Swathed in the voluminous costume, she sank to her knees with incredible grace, sliding off the beard and headdress so that her thick braid could be seen down her back. Before the Christ child of wool, lying in the straw-filled manger, Madeleine Renald bowed her head in prayer.

· · ·

Rose rested on her knees, head bent. *Mon Dieu.* She whispered a litany she remembered now in French. A prayer for help that she'd murmured over and over back at the *Château d'Ambroise*, back when her mother trained her to be the royal prostitute. It all came back to her now, waves of memories rushing within her mind. Vibrant colors, caustic laughter, gold and pearls, whispers and leers, shadows and the heart-hammering feel of being the prey in an elaborate, richly decorated labyrinth.

Dizziness assaulted her, and she sat back on her heels. She had fled after witnessing her mother pleasuring the king, teaching her what would be expected of her the next night. Madeleine had taken the pearls to pay for her escape. Desperation spurred her out of the palace while everyone slept.

off their debauchery. Slipping within the predawn shadows, like the wraith she nearly was, Madeleine had removed a single pearl from the necklace to pay for passage on a ship. She didn't care where it would take her, as long as it was away from France, her mother, and the king. But once they had set sail, she'd realized her jeopardy with Captain Henri de Fleur. Her only protection from rape was the admittance that she belonged to the king.

She jumped slightly at the feel of a hand on her shoulder. "Rose." Cullen's voice pressed tears into her eyes, and she squeezed them shut tighter. *Please God, let me fade away right now.*

"Lass," he said, his whisper rough like the caress of his battle-worn hand. "Ye are safe now."

But she wasn't. Not from the knowledge of what she was, what she had been trained to be. Not from the stares of a room full of people. Not from the fact that she had no home, and her only family had wanted to sell her to a king for a necklace of pearls and a bed in a palace.

"I think she's in shock," Charlotte said somewhere near. "Joan, we need a brew."

"Certainly. Ava, do ye think lemon balm?"

"Definitely," Ava whispered. "And sleep."

"I don't know what you called that captain, but he's that one hundred times over," Grace said, her tone furious. Her tone dropped. "Poor thing."

"Ye should cut his ballocks off, Cull," Mairi said.

"Mairi," Joan said.

"Do ye not agree?"

"Of course, I agree, but that's not something for ladies to discuss," Joan said.

The hushed conversations wove around Rose as she held herself kneeling on the floor. The words stopped making sense as she let desolation weigh hard over her shoulders. Feeling consciousness start to slip away, she fell forward.

Instead of the jarring impact of hitting the wooden stage, strong arms caught her, lifting her up and pulling her against a hard chest. She floated along as Cullen issued orders to those in the room. "Water…stir the fire in my room…lemon balm… broth…" Words she couldn't latch onto as her mind filled with memories.

"Wake up, Rose," Cullen said, leaning over her, and she realized she now rested on a soft bed. She blinked, staring upward. Worry bent Cullen's brows, his eyes desperate. As she focused on his gaze, he inhaled long and ran a hand up the side of his face to rake through his hair. "Thank God." He cupped the side of her head, pulling her braid from the back of the tunic, working the material up to release her from the heavy costume. He lifted covers over her chemise and bodice

"I am sorry," she whispered. What must these good people think of her? What must Cullen? She was nearly a courtesan, had all but become what her mother told her she must be. Her face pinched as she watched his hands move with purpose. He poured her something and helped her sit up against the headboard.

"No worries about the pageant," he said. "We all know how the story ends." He put a cup up to her lips and tipped it gently. "Only a sip."

The whisky slid down her throat, slaking a smooth trail of fire to her stomach. She took a second sip, and he pulled it away. She exhaled the smooth whisky fumes. "Not the pageant," she said.

He sat on the bed next to her. "I know, Rose." The sound of the name he'd called her made the tears push forward, one pearling out on her lower lid.

Beatrice had been right. She wasn't worthy to be treated like a lady at Dunyvaig. "I am Madeleine Renald, the king's virgin, a whore to the throne."

The shadow of anger captured Cullen's features, and he closed his eyes for a moment, his jaw working. When he opened to look at her, he leaned in, breathing deeply. "Ye became Rose the moment ye decided to escape the palace." His thumb rubbed across her bottom lip. "Brave and strong. Ye are Rose."

He was so handsome, his sensual mouth saying her name. She yearned to kiss him but worried he'd retreat. She would drown in pain if he pulled away. But Cullen leaned forward to kiss her, soft and gentle. Following her slowly as she rested back against the headboard, he stroked her hair, breaking the kiss to lean his forehead in to hers.

"King Francis has made me the hunted," she whispered between them. "I will be found and forced back. If not by Henri de Fleur, then by another. He thinks me too valuable to give up. Of royal blood, a virgin schooled in the arts of passion." She shivered at the memory of the crazed look in the king's eyes that night, how he'd called Madeleine's name as he mounted Claire. He'd hungered for her but waited, not wanting to spoil his fantasy of deflowering her at the ball.

Cullen held her head gently so she couldn't turn away. "I gave ye my oath to protect ye, and that hasn't changed."

Panic still plucked at her heart, making it pound. She clasped his wrists, her fingers circling him. "Cullen," she whispered. "Make me less valuable."

He pulled back to search her gaze. "Less valuable?"

She swallowed. "Take what the king desires. I would choose to whom I give my maidenhead, and I choose you." The words were out. Cullen had heard them. She stared into his eyes, their blue darkened to black in the dim light. "I choose you."

The door behind Cullen opened, causing him to drop his hands from her head, but she continued to hold his wrists and his gaze.

"Lemon balm and some broth," Charlotte said. "Oh goodness, ye're awake. Thank the good Lord. Cullen, out of the way."

Cullen withdrew, and she had to drop her hold on him as Charlotte bustled close. "Ye've had a shock." Rose sipped the warm, tart liquid that Charlotte thrust into her hands. Cullen moved to the hearth, stirring the fire, so she couldn't see his face. What did he think of her? Did his mind wander over all that she'd witnessed, where she'd learned what they'd shared in bed the other night? Even though she was a virgin, she was far from innocent.

"All of it," Charlotte instructed with a nod. She sniffed the other cup. "I don't think whisky will help." She shrugged. "Well, maybe." She took a full swallow herself. "Aye, it could definitely help," she murmured.

"Cull?" Broc appeared in the open doorway. "The bastard's already awake." Broc glanced Rose's way and bobbed a nod to her before looking back to Cullen. He held out a parchment. "He had this on him." Cullen took it, fury hardening his features. "The folios he mentioned."

Charlotte peered over his arm at the missive and at Rose. "'Tis her likeness." She blew air into her cheeks and released it. "With pearls around yer neck," she said to Rose.

"Give back the pearls," Rose said. "I never wanted them, but had no means to pay my way."

"Of course," Charlotte said, rushing to her. She sat on the bed and pulled her into a hug, pressing Rose's face into her ample chest. Charlotte patted her back. "Poor thing." She released her. "Ye've been through so much."

"What should we do with the captain and his man?" Broc asked. "He's yelling up a storm down there. Says that if he doesn't return, his crew will send a missive to the English at Oban, which says the MacDonalds are traitors to the English crown. And if the English don't attack us, his crew will."

"Put everyone on alert," Cullen said. "I want guards along the wall and villagers ready to run to the keep if anyone spotted coming from the water or across the moor." Cullen strode to the door. "Have Donald arm every lad over the age of twelve. And let anyone who wishes to sleep in the castle bring their pallet."

Errol appeared in the doorway. "My father and Farlan want to talk with ye below. Tor and Hamish are planning for war, and Garrick is rounding up his men."

Cullen looked to Rose. "I have to go." Rose's stomach twisted. All of this, because of her. Guilt and shame squeezed together inside her, and she blinked to keep the tears inside. She gave a small nod, and he strode out the door.

Charlotte picked up the folio and brought it to the bed. "It doesn't do ye justice," she said, handing it to Rose. Black lines of ink wove together to form a face and slender neck down to the top of her breasts. Decked in the pearls with an up-braided *coiffeur*, Madeleine Renald held a teasing smile that she'd practiced in her mirror since she'd been a young girl. The artist had taken her likeness from a portrait Claire had commissioned that had won Madeleine an invitation to court. At the time, Madeleine had been excited with the anticipation of making her mother happy and leaving their small country estate for the grandeur of *Le Blois*. One could see it in the tilt of her chin.

The original portrait showed a light in her eyes that added to the enchantment she'd felt at the time. But in this ink rendition, the eyes were empty of emotion, blank, giving her a poppet-like appearance. *Récompense* was listed under the sketch, followed by a sum much larger than the pearls were worth. It made her nauseous.

Charlotte sighed and indicated the picture. "At least we know who Madeleine Renald is now. She is alive and protected by the chief of the MacDonalds." She nodded deeply, obviously trying to make Rose feel better.

"*Merci*," Rose said, her voice sad. "But this woman.. She shook her head and indicated the picture. "Look at h« eyes." Charlotte took the ink drawing from her to study while Rose turned her gaze to the flames eating away at th dry peat in the hearth. Rose breathed deeply against the rap beat of her heart. "That girl is no more. Madeleine Renald dead."

Chapter Seventeen

"What are ye going to do?" William demanded as Cullen trudged into the great hall. Tor's family sat near the hearth, talking softly.

The Yule log lay there, unlit. The musicians and pageant players had left, as well as the young warriors to see about arming the village. Tor and Hamish waited with Cullen's uncles, their stances and frowns indicating a desire to spill blood. It matched Cullen's own fury. Strong emotion warred within him. Fury and a need to protect, both of which were stronger than he'd ever felt before.

"Ye have the Maclean strength behind ye, Cullen," Tor said.

"We can't fight all of France," Farlan said, rubbing his beard. He cursed low and crossed his arms.

"The English could," William said. "They could capture that ship out there waiting for their captain. Ye must hand over de Fleur to Captain Taylor."

"De Fleur will reveal who Rose is," Cullen said. His mind struck out at idea after idea. The only thing he knew for certain was that he wasn't giving Rose up. The very thought of losing her made his blood pump harder through his body, readying him for war. "The man tied a rope around Rose's neck, meant to drag her literally back to hell for a prize." His eyes lifted to Tor. "He cannot talk if he's dead."

"Hear, hear," Broc added. "I think we should cut his ballocks off first like Mairi suggested."

"Hear, hear," Mairi echoed from the hearth while Joan flapped her hand at her.

"Your first duty is to protect Dunyvaig," William said with a sigh and rubbed at his forehead. "Giving a Frenchman over to Captain Taylor will secure Islay's safety. We tell Taylor, like de Fleur, that Madeleine is gone. We can hide her away."

"Would the French king really spend such resources to find a girl?" Farlan asked, his arms opening wide, bushy brows raised. "When she isn't found right away, another girl will catch his eye. 'Tis the way with kings."

"Ye must act quickly," William warned.

"And look past personal desires," Farlan added. "The MacDonald must put his people and their safety before his wants."

Blood lust ran like a deluge through Cullen's body. His uncles' resistance added to the flood. He wanted de Fleur to suffer like Rose had at his hands. He looked to Broc. "Tie a rope around his neck and string him up from the rafters in the dungeon where only his feet can touch. To keep his life he must stand until we figure out what to do with him." Broc nodded and walked away with Hamish by his side.

"Broc," Errol called and tossed him the large cell key. Broc caught it out of the air.

"Cullen," William snapped. "Ye will bring the force of France and England down on us if we don't act before de Fleur's letter reaches Taylor. If the English know the French ship is here, and ye let de Fleur go for fear he will expose your woman, Taylor will think we are in league with them."

Farlan blustered. "I knew ye'd bring the end to Dunyvaig. Ye are exactly like your fa—"

"I will find a solution," Cullen yelled. "I am The MacDonald." He drew his sword. Before him stood his uncles, but he saw only the rope burns that had cut into Rose's slender, fragile neck, her eyes filled with fear. "I have not forgotten my oaths." But at the moment, his oaths to protect Dunyvaig warred with his oath to protect Rose.

William opened his mouth, but Cullen pointed his sword at him. "I will not act rashly, so shut your bloody gob."

William's face turned crimson, and he pivoted, storming out of the hall.

"Ruin of us," Farlan grumbled and followed his brother. Cullen waited the space of several heartbeats, but Errol stayed by his side.

Cullen turned to him and then Tor. "Find out where de Fleur landed and make sure the family that spoke with them is uninjured. See if they saw where the ship sailed if it is not right offshore. And find out if Captain Taylor and Captain Thompson are still on Islay, riding the shoreline."

"I'd wager they've returned to Oban for Christmas," Errol said.

"Avoid them," Cullen said. "But don't say a word about de Fleur if ye run into them."

"So ye will let de Fleur go?" Tor asked.

Cullen gripped the hilt of his sword, a vision of de Fleur, wrapping the rope around Rose's neck, his nasty tongue sliding along her skin, fresh in his mind. "He will have to win his freedom. He can return to his ship..." He watched the blood-red stone catch the firelight as he twisted his blade in the air. "If he can make it past me without his throat slit."

• • •

"After a shock, I find the clean, warm water of an indoor bath to be strengthening," Charlotte called on her way out of the bedroom, the door clicking shut behind her. Rose submerged farther into the soothing water of a wooden tub set before the fire.

Charlotte didn't seem to mind that Rose was naked in her son's room. He'd carried her up to his bed instead of the one she shared with Mairi. Would Charlotte tell him to sleep elsewhere? Did she realize how much safer Rose felt in Cullen's room? She'd have asked but didn't want to risk being moved. The truth was, she longed for Cullen's return. She needed his answer.

Make me less valuable. Without her maidenhead, the king would stop hunting for her. Wouldn't he? She'd been raised as the king's virgin courtesan, a young woman still intact but with all the information to make her the perfect, tantalizing lover. Her mother had been whispering in King Francis's ear about her daughter's erotic education and beauty. From the way he'd brutally pounded into her mother, while calling her Madeleine, the night Rose had escaped the court, the most powerful man in France seemed obsessed with her. No wonder he'd sent her likeness around the continent. No wonder Henri had risked walking into Dunyvaig to demand her back. The king would reward him greatly.

Oui, the only way to make her less interesting to Francis was to ruin the one thing that made her different from the other courtesans. Her virginity. And giving in to the heat that she felt leap within her every time she was alone with Cullen would be something to cherish forever.

Rose ran the fragrant soap along her arms, dipping them under the water. She leaned back, letting her full breasts bob to the surface, her nipples contracting at the chill. She touched them and instantly felt longing ache through her body. Sliding her palms down her stomach, she breathed deeply. Was she

uly wanton, a woman born of courtesan blood, raised to
eep with the highest bidder? For who could outbid a king?
Ierely the thought of the richly bedecked man cooled her
lood.

She now remembered other men at court, most of them
andsome, exceedingly wealthy, and obviously infatuated
ith her. But none of them knew her. They thought of her
nly as Madeleine, untouchable and utterly desirable. Even
 they offered her gold and palaces and comfort, she didn't
ant them, didn't ache for any of them, didn't desire to make
ιy of them happy.

Rose blew against the soap-film surface. *Non.* There was
nly one man who woke desire in her cold body, only one
ιan whom she trusted enough not to hurt her, to whom she
ished to bring joy. Cullen Duffie.

Make me less valuable. Would he come to her? She
aned her head against the tub and rinsed away the soap,
ut she still didn't feel clean. The memories of her past and
ιe embarrassment of this evening lay deeper than skin. She
as valuable to the king, but would the people of Dunyvaig
nd her worthy? By now Beatrice would have spread what
[enri had said about her to everyone in the village. Through
ɛr entire life, Madeleine's worth had been tied to her beauty,
ιrtatious cleverness, and erotic education. At the French
ɔurt, these qualities had brought her fame and acceptance.
[ere on Islay, they brought shame.

Rose breathed deeply and raked the soap through her
esses, freeing the bubbles and dirt. When the water began to
ɔol, she rose, squeezing the thick, wet mass. Stepping out of
ιe tub, she wrapped herself in a linen and hurried to the fire,
ιrowing another square of dried peat on it to burn hotter.
he flames cast light and shadows, its heat luring Rose to sit
own, cross-legged, and pull her hair to the side, spreading it
ith her fingers to dry. Over and over, she combed through

it, the curls returning as the warmth dried them.

A tap sounded on the chamber door, and it opened. Ro⟨
clutched the bathing sheet over her breasts.

"Are ye dressed?" Cullen asked from the crack.

Rose steadied her breath. "I am covered, not dressed."

He hesitated. "Does that mean I can come in or not?"

His question, offered with the hint of humor, turned h⟨
lips up into a grin. After all, he'd loved every inch of her t⟨
other night. "You may come in."

Cullen stepped into his room, shutting the door behi⟨
him. "It's late. I thought ye might be—" His gaze had start⟨
at the bed and turned to see her at the hearth. "Asleep," ⟨
finished. "I can return later, or if ye'd like to return to yo⟨
room, I—"

"I am comfortable here, unless you wish me to go," s⟨
said. She didn't like how her voice faded. She'd been school⟨
against being timid like an easily ignored mouse, but right no⟨
with all the memories and Henri's crassness, her strength h⟨
faded. Rose didn't want to be anything that she was taug⟨
She desired only to be her authentic self, whoever that was⟨

"I wish ye to be comfortable," he answered. "Are ⟨
cold?"

The fire burned hot at her back, and she shook her hea⟨
"Not here."

He crossed to the bed where he sat to brace his toe⟨
heel, ridding himself of his boots and tall socks. He still wo⟨
his dress kilt and white linen shirt. "I have things I need ⟨
say to ye. 'Tis why I asked my mother to keep ye here in m⟨
room. It seems every time I try to speak with ye, someo⟨
interrupts."

She nodded. After Henri's revelations, leaving her alo⟨
in Cullen's room couldn't cause any more scandal. "I am sor⟨
that tonight's festivities were ruined," she said and squar⟨
her hips back toward the fire. "Christmas Eve should be f⟨

of joy. Your guests must be shocked."

She could hear him pad closer. "Well, Mairi is demanding that we cut de Fleur's ballocks off, and Grace has been spouting the most obscene curses that I've ever heard from a lady, while Ava whispers excuses for her."

Rose turned to look at him. Cullen wore a calm smile. He shrugged. "And we are all still reeling from what my mother called de Fleur in Gaelic. So tonight has been full of shock." He bent to his knees next to her and sat, leaning back on his hands to stretch long legs before him as if they sat at a casual summer picnic. "But none of it warrants your apology." He met her gaze, his face growing serious. "None of this is your fault, Rose."

After a long moment, Rose turned back to the fire. Guilt still weighed heavily in her middle.

"Do ye think all of your memories have come back?" he asked.

"I think," she whispered. "When I saw Henri de Fleur…I remembered the ship, his cabin…the rope about my neck." She took a full breath. "And the fear. He desires fear in a woman. Many men do."

"*Och*, Rose," Cullen said behind her, and she looked to him. He sat upright. "It should never be like that. Those men abuse their power instead of using it to protect."

Rose felt the press of tears on the back of her eyelids and blinked. "You are a rare and honorable man, Cullen Duffie."

He reached forward slowly, touching one of her loose waves of hair. "And ye are a rare and fascinating woman, Rose."

Rose turned her face in to his hand, kissing his palm. "Love me, Cullen," she whispered. "Take me tonight." Her heart beat frantically as she braved his answer. One by one, Rose opened her fingers so that the edges of the sheet fell to pool around her waist, exposing her full breasts to his view.

She watched his chest fill with air, making his shoulders broaden. He pulled her onto his lap with slow care, one of her legs on either side of his hips, straddling him. The bathing sheet bunched between them and under her seat, but she could still feel his hardness through his kilt pressing against her sex.

Groaning softly, he slid his hands over her skin and bent forward to capture her mouth with a kiss. Hot and powerful. She wanted to surrender all to Cullen and slanted her face, opening her lips for a thorough taste. She shifted on his lap to rub against him. He stroked the outsides of her breasts and waist, down to her spread hips. Inching the sheet lower, he lifted her to cup the sides of her nude *derriere*. Rough palms stroked against her smooth skin, licking fire through her body. Rose wrapped her arms around Cullen's head and shoulders, rubbing the tips of her breasts across his shirt.

"You have too many clothes on," she said against his mouth and teased him with her tongue.

"There's my wildcat." His hand retreated to untie the knot at his neck. Breaking the kiss to lean back, Rose sat spread upon him as he worked the shirt up over his head, his massive arms flexing as he peeled it off, leaving his chest and stomach bare. From leaning back, ridges of muscle showed from his taut stomach up his torso and chest, making Rose's breath catch. *Magnífique.*

She dragged a fingernail up the center, from his navel to the hollow of his neck, watching chill bumps rise at her touch. Rose wanted to make him groan, make him feel the wonderful things he roused in her. Bending forward, she kissed his nipple and circled it with her tongue. Cullen answered with a primal growl and spread his hands across her back, pressing her forward. She lifted her head and arched upward, her pelvis pressing down onto him. His lips found her nipple and sucked it into his hot mouth. The sensation shot through Rose, making her restless.

She moaned and rubbed rhythmically against him, holding herself to his mouth. He switched breasts, palming the first. The sound of his mouth working against her flesh fed the growing ache inside her. She yanked at the bath sheet until her hands could reach his belt holding his kilt in place. After tugging without budging it, she huffed, pulling his face up to hers for a kiss.

"Why is it so hard to get you naked?" she asked.

He chuckled, but his gaze was still molten as he stared at her, lifting one of her breasts and the other for a kiss. "I definitely have the advantage with ye being in a sheet." Still seated, he yanked the strap of his belt to release the tongue, and it slid to the floor, the buckle knocking heavily against the wood. With a power-filled lurch, he pushed them both upright, catching her to him as he stood.

Rose gasped softly and heard the heavy woven kilt thump the floor with her sheet. The fire gave off its heat, prickling the one side of her bare skin, while Cullen's body warmed her front. He kissed her reverently, his face bent to hers and his hands cupping her cheeks. Cherished. *Oui.* She felt cherished.

She slanted against him as the kiss turned wild. Wet and hot, they breathed against each other as their mouths tasted and seduced. Rose pressed her soft curves against Cullen's hard frame, rising onto her toes to nestle him in the *V* of her legs. His penis, massive and stone-hard, rested hot and heavy against her belly. Knowing what he would do with it made her ache.

Her hands gripped him, sliding the smooth skin up and down, reveling in the groan she won from him. His fingers curved into her *derriere*, seeking. She spread her legs, arching herself to give him access, and he found her wet center.

"*Och,* lass, ye are drenched," he rasped against her ear where he kissed her neck.

She squirmed, rocking against his hand, grabbing his shoulders. "Take me, Cullen. Kill Madeleine Renald, the king's virgin," she breathed as he pressed two fingers into her. "Free me."

Thickly accented words in Gaelic came from his mouth, the passion and heart in them sending another wave of primal need through Rose, and she moaned. Withdrawing his fingers, Cullen lifted Rose. She seemed to float through the air as he carried her to the bed. Cool sheets enveloped her, but Cullen followed, bringing the warmth his large, muscled frame exuded like a bonfire. Her legs shifted restlessly against the sheets as she reached for him, stroking.

"Cullen, now," she said, spreading herself, but still he caressed her with his fingers until she felt the heavy ache build inside. Diving in and out with two fingers, his thumb brushed her most sensitive spot, back and forth.

"Aye, lass," he breathed in her ear as he moved over her. "Give in to the fire, wildcat."

Rose pressed higher into his grasp, her hands fisting the sheets on either side of her. She reached up to grab his shoulders, her nails digging into his flesh. All reason left her. Only sensation existed, the smell of their combined heat, the feel of Cullen's touch. Only his skin sliding against her and his weight upon her mattered. Higher and higher she flew until she shattered.

"Cullen," she yelled as the first waves crashed. And in that instant, Cullen removed his fingers, his knee spreading her farther apart. With a rapid surge he buried himself within her channel. She gasped, and he groaned, holding himself over her, fully embedded.

The sting of his entering was barely noticed as the waves of Rose's pleasure continued to flood her. Rooted to the bed, she pushed upward against him.

"*Och*, lass," he rasped. "If ye do that, I'll move."

"*Oui*. Move," she demanded, her need far more powerful than the sting.

Slowly he withdrew. She watched his eyes close and knew was the pleasure that tortured him. Reaching between them, he grasped him, rubbing until he disappeared back inside her. Pressing against her own sensitive spot, she felt another ache begin to build, her past lessons for self-pleasuring being quite helpful.

He breathed through his teeth as he began to increase his thrusts, and Rose raised her legs to wrap them around his back, hugging him to her as he drove into her. With each deep thrust she panted, feeling him all the way up inside, pressing against her very womb. "*Oui*, Cullen. Fill me," she spoke in French, repeating it in English to drive him mad.

She raked her nails down his back and clung to him, surging into each of his thrusts, wild and completely given over to *joie de vivre*. She knew only heat and pleasure and Cullen. Stroke after stroke, their mouths melded as they kissed, Cullen marking her both inside and out. She felt him all around her, his scent filling her nose, his arms capturing her to him. She felt him moving within her, his taste on her tongue and his hardness plowing up inside her. He was renewing her, bringing her back into life. If love could be touched and seen, it would feel and look like this. This was no longer just passion. This was more.

Rose opened her mouth to scream as the wave of sensation caught her, thrumming through her with such might, stars sparked behind her eyelids. She strained upward, riding the waves, pressing into them as molten fire spread. Still moving, she opened to see Cullen staring into her eyes as his whole body tensed.

"I am yours. *Buin mo chridhe dhuit.*" She felt his words like thunder, shuddering through her as if they were an oath. He growled fiercely and released, the heat of their bodies

combining. Exquisite, his warrior's face tense with passio
powerful and strong, and completely hers.

As he collapsed, he rolled her to the side, their bodi
still joined, legs tangled. He cradled her into his chest. The
clutched each other as their breathing slowed. Cullen kisse
her gently and stroked the side of her face. "*Tha gaol aga*
ort," he said. "*Buin mo chridhe dhuit.*" He repeated the sam
words from before. Deep brown eyes stared into her ow
eyes that mirrored her awe. She touched the side of his fac
too. His words, although spoken in his own language, reveale
the love she saw. Could she return them? Did she even kno
what love was after all the betrayal she'd seen? Never befor
had she witnessed real love.

Rose lowered her face to rest on his chest, feeling th
thudding of his powerful heart under her cheek, and he
on to him with languid arms. Exhaustion, from her emotio
whipping her from despair to satiated bliss, pulled her towar
sleep. In his tumbling language, she was nearly certain he
spoken words of love, but she wasn't sure. Her fear of th
answer stopped her from asking. All she knew right now wa
that she was safe, and for the moment, cherished in Culle
arms. Rose breathed softly, her lips parted and her ey
closing. "Cullen Duffie," she whispered.

"Aye?" The one word grumbled up through his che
under her cheek.

"*Merci.*"

Chapter Eighteen

Merci? Thank you? Cullen buckled his belt around his waist. He watched Rose shift within the nest of rumpled sheets. Like a fallen angel, her hair tangled out from her heart-shaped face, long lashes fanned down above smooth cheeks. Had she understood that he'd said that he loved her last night before she fell asleep? That he'd given her his heart, using the same vows couples spoke at their weddings? Perhaps not. She knew nothing of their language. He hadn't translated his words, realizing the feeling that crowded into him was something completely new. Never had he felt such strength, such power in the knowledge that he loved. Aye, he loved Rose.

A smile crept over his mouth, and he rubbed it, shaking his head in silence. He had a French bastard in his dungeon, a letter calling the MacDonalds of Islay traitors, two uncles who were probably trying to rally a mutiny, and a regiment of English poised to attack at the weakest of reasons. Yet somehow, looking down on Rose, safe and utterly satisfied, all seemed right with the world.

Throwing the sash of his kilt over one shoulder, he grabbed

his scabbard to belt in place. Somehow, he marveled, this passion-filled, courageous woman was giving him strength, even as she slept. He felt like he could take on a horde of English, single-handedly, and win.

Rose stirred, her eyes blinking open. She remained still, curved on her side, and grinned at him from the pillow. "You are up," she whispered, her voice roughened by sleep.

He leaned in and kissed her forehead, inhaling the heady scent of their passion still in the sheets. "I need to make plans below, even though I'd rather remain with ye." He plucked at her chin softly. "And we should talk…about us."

She stretched contentedly. "I prefer action to talk," she said.

His groin twitched as the sheet slipped enough to show her full breasts. He reached below, adjusting himself. "*Och*. If ye keep that up, to hell with France, England, and Scotland."

She chuckled softly, yanking the sheet higher and shooing him with one hand. "Go. I will be down soon."

With another kiss that was meant to be quick but lingered, he tucked her back in the warm bed.

"Cullen," she said and hoisted herself up on her elbows, the sheet clutched before her. "*Joyeux Noël*. Merry Christmas."

She was completely, bewitchingly delectable propped amongst the pillows, quilts, and furs. Like a Christmas gift when he was a boy, Cullen felt the nearly overwhelming desire to pounce on her. He smiled. "*Joyeux Noël*." His simple French words made her smile broader. He ran the back of his finger along her smooth cheek and looked closely into her clear eyes. "We put Madeleine Renald to rest last night. Ye are always welcome here as Rose. Ye can stay with—"

"But I am not welcome here," she whispered, her smile sliding away from her lips. She gave a brief shake to her head, glancing down at the bedclothes. "Your uncles—"

"Can go to hell."

"With the English across the strait—"

"I am not afraid of the English," he said.

She opened her lush lips to respond but closed them slowly, allowing a smile. "I know you aren't." She squeezed his hand in a way that said she was done with the discussion. "Go on, then."

He studied her, but her beautiful face gave nothing away of what might be tumbling inside her head. "I will see ye below."

"*Oui.*"

Cullen shut the door behind him and made his way along the still-dark corridor. Could Rose not wish to stay at Dunyvaig? Stay with him? Despite his oath while loving her last night, she hadn't let him ask her to stay with him. He paused on the steps, glancing back up them, tension pulling at his forehead. It was true that Rose was used to luxuries that weren't practical for life on Islay, but she was happy here. Or, at least, she seemed happy here. Of course, she was.

Throwing off the ridiculous concern, he continued his descent and rounded the corner of the archway into the great hall. Errol stood at the hearth. The Yule log lay unlit, and there was no sign of William or Farlan.

"Merry Christmas. Have ye been here long?" Cullen asked, and Errol leaned the poker against the hearthside.

"Merry Christmas to ye, too." He shrugged. "And I slept here."

"Did he lock ye out or did ye not bother to go home?" Errol still lived in the cottage he'd grown up in with his parents. When his mother died, he'd remained.

"I stayed in case any frightened villagers wanted to unroll their pallets."

When Cullen had left for the night, none of the villagers had come, preferring to stay in their homes on Christmas Eve. Errol's explanation was not the only reason he'd stayed.

Cullen raised one eyebrow at his friend.

Errol shrugged. "And it's better to let him bang around the cottage on his own when he's like that." Errol shook his head and sniffed. "We've always had different ways of looking at things."

Cullen let the weight of his hand fall on his cousin's shoulder. "I thank ye for your support."

Errol grinned. "I wouldn't be much of a second-in-command if I refused it."

Cullen used the poker to move over the burning peat. "Help me light this log," he said, and Errol lifted with him to move the Yule log into place. Cullen set a burning taper to the dried flowers on top that had been sprinkled with last year's ashes. It was Christmas, after all, and the morning after a perfect night.

Cullen brushed his hands. "Any word about the farmer on the coast?"

"Garrick returned an hour ago to say that no beacons have been lit to show boats coming across, and Murdock is well and good. De Fleur must have hidden his ship in one of the coves off Colonsay Isle with instructions to come back for him today."

"Murdock needs a beacon set up at his farm," Cullen said. "He has a good view of the north from his shore."

"Have ye figured out what to do with de Fleur and his man below?" Errol asked as they walked down the corridor toward the kitchens.

"Aye. If de Fleur hasn't hanged himself overnight, cut him down but keep him tethered to the bars with his hands behind his back. Take a flask of water down, and if his crewman wishes to share, so be it. Send the crewman back to his ship later this morning with a message that Madeleine Renald is no longer here, and if their message is sent to the English, de Fleur will die. If de Fleur falls to my sword, we will give his

ody to Captain Taylor and let his English dogs hunt down
nd capture de Fleur's ship."

"What if he doesn't fall?" Errol asked as they paused
efore the kitchen door where the scent of freshly baked
read gave a cheerful smell to their bloody talk.

Cullen met Errol's gaze with the strength of an oath.
Henri de Fleur will definitely fall to my sword. But I wouldn't
loody Christmas by doing it today. Let him get the strength
n his arms back for a day to make it a fair contest."

They ducked into the kitchen and left minutes later with
platter of fluffy scrambled eggs and several tarts. Cullen
icked up the tune Jillian, the cook, was humming and
histled as he and Errol walked back through the corridor
oward the great hall.

"Since when do ye whistle?" Errol asked as the great hall
ame into sight. "Could it be that ye didn't move Rose back to
er own room last night?"

His best friend stood before him. Would he remind
'ullen of his duty to the clan? Rebuke him for falling in love
ith a Frenchwoman? But to hide his happiness would be the
iggest lie he'd ever contrived. Cullen met Errol's gaze and let
satisfied smile spread across his entire face.

Errol chuckled back in his throat and shook his head. "I'd
ay ye found your cheer."

"Bloody hell, yes," Cullen said, once again glad that Errol
asn't his father. He spied Broc dragging his feet as he walked
. Their cousin yawned and raised an arm in greeting.

"Damn," Errol said. "He'll take all the eggs."

Cullen's chuckle cut short at the sight of his uncles
epping up from the entryway. Would the day see them
ccupying another cell in Dunyvaig's dungeon?

"Is he still alive?" William asked without preamble.

"Not sure," Cullen answered and spooned some egg into
s mouth. "Haven't been below yet."

"Ye should be down there questioning him," Farlan said

Cullen swallowed and crossed his arms over his chest. "
I go down there, I'll slit his damned throat." He gestured
the table. "Ye are welcome to eat."

"I'll check on the bastard," Errol said around a mouthf
of egg. "Broc." He waved his cousin over while fishing the k
out of his leather pouch.

Before William could question him further, Tor stroc
out of the archway from the stairs, Ava at his side. It seeme
the castle was waking.

"How is Rose?" Ava asked.

"Very well," Cullen said with a grin he couldn't hid
"Resting."

Tor raised one eyebrow. "From what I could hear when
happened up to your floor to walk the roofline, I'd say she
be resting most of today." He yawned and flinched away
Ava smacked his arm, a look of bewildered innocence on h
face.

Ava looked warmly at Cullen, despite the still-sha
glance she gave Tor. "Let her know that we think only goc
things of her. That she's brave and strong, and we are ve
much in support of her. Heaven knows, I certainly understar
the need to escape a monster."

Tor pulled her closer in to his side and kissed the top
her head, his face darkening at the memory of Ava's sadist
stepbrother.

"Thank ye," Cullen said, ignoring the wide-eyed loc
from his uncles. "I will let her know." He indicated the eg
on the table. "Have some while they're still warm. The coc
will be bringing more soon, and tarts."

"Mmmm..." Ava said. "I love tarts." Tor pulled h
around and kissed her soundly. Their baby, soon to arri
would be raised by a loving family. A memory surfaced
his father pulling Charlotte into his embrace to dance abo

their cottage. Anderson Duffie had given Cullen more than his height; he'd given him an example of a loving marriage. Could he be lucky enough to secure one, too?

Grace and Joan walked together from the back, and Hamish with Garrick came in from the bailey. Ellen rolled a cart in from the kitchens, laden with more eggs, tarts, fresh milk, bread, and bannocks. Cullen took a plate to save some food for Rose. If she didn't come down soon, he'd take it up to her. The thought launched a mischievous grin on his face.

"What about this day is humorous to ye?" William asked from the hearth where he'd retreated, pacing with Farlan. Neither of them had eaten, which was probably making them even more ornery than usual.

Everyone in the hall stopped their chatter. Cullen stood near the table with Rose's plate in hand. "It is Christmas Day, Uncle. A time for forgiveness and a lightness of heart."

"Ye don't intend to forgive de Fleur, do ye?" he yelled, his eyes bulging.

Cullen's look turned lethal. "That bastard sealed his fate the moment he tied a rope around a courageous lass's neck."

William seemed to deflate with relief. He sank into a chair. Did he actually believe Cullen would invite the French captain to dine with them? Cullen looked around the hall. "De Fleur will meet me in a one-to-one battle to the death, but not today. Today is Christmas, and unless attacked, I don't intend to honor the day by spilling blood at Dunyvaig."

Farlan nodded in approval and passed the sign of the cross before him.

"Father Langdon will hold mass at the noon hour in the chapel," Charlotte said, reminding everyone. "It is Christmas despite kings, pirates, and the English army."

"Beautifully put," Grace said, picking up a tart from one of the platters.

Perhaps it was the combination of the holiday and vestiges

of his night with Rose making him feel charitable, but Cullen set Rose's plate down to walk over to William. The man had grown old overnight, his face weathered and pale. Farlan still paced, but William kept his stare centered on the flames.

"Uncle," Cullen said, pulling his gaze. "I have spoken to Errol and Broc. Your son is sound of mind, a good adviser. Ye taught him well." Cullen leaned against the mantel. "Dunyvaig will continue to thrive. The shores are being watched, beacons at the ready. De Fleur is in our dungeon. War does not start today. It can start tomorrow."

William opened his mouth, but Farlan spoke up first "Errol doesn't have the experience that comes with age."

Cullen nodded, willing to give him that. "Ye are right After breakfast we can sit down as a council to discuss my plan for dealing with this threat."

"We must move quickly," William said, finding his voice "Before they send that letter to Captain Taylor."

"His man will be released today, to warn the crew not to send that letter. We will follow him to see which way he rows. If the letter is sent, and the English arrive, we will have the captain of the ship tied up in the dungeon, not sitting at our table."

William stared at him, weighing his words. He neither nodded approval nor glared, but worry continued to tighten his mouth. He apparently still didn't put much faith in Cullen's ability as leader.

Behind Cullen, feminine laughter pulled him around Mairi strode into the hall, and on her arm walked Rose. Head held up, chin even, she wore a neutral face as her beautiful eyes took in the occupants of the room. Her green dress hugged her breasts, sloping to cascade over her hips. She nodded to Charlotte, Ava, and Grace, as well as Ellen. They surrounded her with whispers and smiles. Ava took her hands squeezing them as Grace spoke while waving her arms in broad gestures.

"Excuse me," Cullen said to his uncles and strode across to where he left her plate. The ladies seemed to part as Cullen walked up. "I wasn't sure if ye'd be down so I saved ye some breakfast."

Relief set in the softness of her mouth. "Mairi did not wish to come down alone."

"Aye," Mairi said. "I about dragged her from the bed." She grinned broadly, a teasing glint in her gaze. "It's Christmas, after all."

"Aye, it is," Beatrice called from the entryway. She and her mother traipsed into the hall, shaking their shawls that held a fine covering of snow. "I thought we could redo the pageant today." She looked to Rose. "Ye can watch this time. Garrick volunteered his younger brother to play the shepherd." She turned to Charlotte without waiting for any response. "Edward said he'd bring back the musicians after mass to accompany us."

"Very well," Charlotte said, and looped her arm through Joan's. "We will eat earlier so there is time for dancing again tonight." She looked to Cullen, her brows raised.

"Aye, Christmas should be celebrated," Cullen agreed. "I lit the Yule log."

Broc and Errol returned from the dungeons, their faces grim. Broc went straight to the food. "They are both still alive," Errol said. His nose scrunched up. "Smelling foul and yelling even fouler."

"Luckily, we couldn't understand most of it," Broc said while chewing. He grinned. "We tied the captain to the bars like ye said. The rope rubbed bloody around his neck during the night. He's tethered now, sitting. Put the crewmate into the adjoining cell with a flask, until ye're ready to send him back with a message."

Cullen watched a pallor wash over Rose's face. He leaned

in to her ear. "All will be well, wildcat." He caught her gaze and waited until her lips curved slightly, and she nodded. Before everyone, he kissed her quickly on the lips and walked by. He gestured to Broc, who stood there, mouth hanging open. "'Tis Christmas. Let us talk about foulness away from here."

"He's nothing to fret over," Errol added, looking at Rose as he followed Cullen. "De Fleur is tied tightly, behind iron bars as thick as my forearm. And there are only two keys, one kept by Cullen and one by me."

Tor, Garrick, and Hamish followed them toward the hearth where William still looked shaken and Farlan paced. His uncles might have been Gerard MacDonald's sons, but they certainly didn't have the old chief's steadfast calmness in the face of turmoil. Let them hear the rest of the plan he'd set in motion. With de Fleur in his dungeon, for the first time since discovering that Rose was French, Cullen had a way to protect both Dunyvaig and the woman who had stolen his heart.

• • •

The day dragged by as Rose forced herself to chat with the kind ladies from Aros, even though her mind drifted to the monster tethered in Dunyvaig's dungeon. Mairi had insisted she come down so it would look like they'd left their room together, although Cullen's kiss fairly shouted that they were lovers. With the revelation that she had been raised to be a courtesan, she'd expected coldness or forced politeness from the ladies. On the contrary, Charlotte, Ava, and Grace seemed just as warm. Even Mairi, with her quirked smile to hide what Rose had decided was a secret inclination for Cullen, continued to be welcoming despite finding Rose in his bed that morning.

Joy blew steadily at the embers that had been Rose's cold

eart, stirring it with hope for the first time since her escape om Henri. With his ship so close, a bounty on her head, and lacDonald enemies a boat ride away, it seemed she stood i limbo on a razor's edge between Hell and Heaven. If she ould but fall into Cullen's arms on the side of happiness. But hat would that look like? Cullen's words last night had been damant, and even in a foreign language, Rose had known hat he'd professed to her. He'd said he loved her. Her heart enched, and her stomach rolled. Loved her. He deserved er own in return, but did she even know what love was? Was e truly worthy of love?

Rose's attention snapped forward as the small crowd round her applauded. Beatrice, dressed as the Virgin Mary, rtsied on stage next to Errol, who once again played Joseph. arrick's brother made a much more convincing shepherd an Rose had. She joined in the clapping, brushing off the orry that had crept in despite the Christmas fun around her.

Beatrice took Errol's hand, twining her fingers with his. e looked down, startled, and she whispered something to im. Could she have shifted her sights to Cullen's cousin?

Next to Rose, Cullen's upper arm pressed against hers. he turned her face to him, marveling at his strong profile efore he met her gaze. His warm brown eyes held such rightness, as if all the merriness in the world danced within im. His sensuous lips curved upward, and he leaned in to her ar.

"If ye keep looking at me like that, I will throw ye over y shoulder before all these good people and proclaim to em a good night as I carry ye above to my bed."

Her heart fluttered in her chest, making her feel almost iddy. "Cullen," she whispered with a laugh, glancing to his de to see if Charlotte could have heard her son. But she oke to Ava.

Cullen stretched his arms overhead and yawned loudly

over Edward's strumming as the musicians started a spright
tune. "I'm exhausted," he said. "Think I might retire early."

"What?" Charlotte asked, her chin set back like
perturbed hen. "It's Christmas night. There's dancing an
games."

Cullen's wicked glance told Rose very well that I
had games in mind, but not the kind one played before a
audience.

She raised her hand to her mouth to hide her smile. "I
been such a long day," Rose added. "But I think I can mana;
a dance or two." She stood and held out her hand to Culle
"See if you can recover a bit. For Christmas and your mother
sakes."

"The French are so advanced," Grace said. "A woma
asking a man to dance." She looked at Broc. "I like it." An
she held out her hand to him.

Broc set his crown on his head and boomed out throu;
the hall, "Tonight, the lasses will ask the lads to dance
Laughter floated up around them as Rose led Cullen out
the area before the stage.

Rose let the music and Cullen's presence weave aroun
her until she found herself laughing. She turned and bow
with the lilting notes. Cullen kept her close, his gaze makin
promises that sent shivers over her skin and joy filling h
heart. Was this feeling love? Her chest squeezed with th
possibility. It was the happiest Christmas she'd ever had.

Chapter Nineteen

Rose stretched in the sheets, her well-loved body enjoying the lingering warmth. She pressed her face into Cullen's pillow. It still held his scent, and she hugged it to her chest. Contentment melted her spine, the bliss giving her the unburdened feeling of floating. He hadn't broached the complicated subject of love during their night of passion. They'd lost themselves in each other, and surrendered to sleep wrapped together, until Errol had roused Cullen to ride out to where a lit beacon was spotted on the coast.

There hadn't been time for talk of the future, where she would stay, and what name she would have. Even if she did live on Islay, would he want to wed her? She kept her eyes squeezed shut. *Tha gaol agam ort.* He'd said he loved her, in his language, but hadn't asked her to wed. Perhaps he thought she wasn't the type of woman to wed. She squeezed her eyes tighter and breathed deeply to dispel the worry. Or did he merely wait until she said she loved him?

Her eyes opened to the predawn shadows. Did she love him? He was utterly desirable, handsome, and strong. She lusted for him and felt herself wishing to be near him, even if it was just to see him smile. He was intelligent and kind and kept his vows. The thought of something terrible happening to him made her want to fight and weep at the same time. Was this love?

She breathed deeply, her mind twisting. She should sleep. Clarity came with a full night's rest. The sun wouldn't rise for an hour or more, and Cullen would be away until midday, checking to see if Henri's ship had come out into the open.

Rose reached down the bed, her fingers finding the thin material of her chemise. She warmed it under the covers and slipped it on over her, sighing. *Oui*, they would have to talk. She wanted to be honest with him about the questions churning in her mind.

Knock. Knock. A soft sound tapped through the room but oddly it wasn't coming from the door to the hall.

Knock. Knock. "Cullen? Are ye there?"

Rose sat up in the bed, frowning. The feminine voice came from the door to the secret stairs.

"Cullen?" It was Beatrice. The contentment Rose had started to rekindle inside shattered. Anger seeped up in the shards, and Rose slid from the bed.

"He is not here, and you shouldn't be, either," Rose called back. She found her robe by the hearth and punched her fisted hands through each sleeve, tying the thick wool closed with a belt in the front.

There was a pause. "I saw him leave and wanted to talk with ye, find some peace between us. Could ye let me in? It's cold out here with the wind coming up the steps."

Rose wiggled her toes into her slippers and walked to the door. Unease prickled up her back. "You want to make peace?" Rose repeated, staring at the deep wood grain before her.

"Aye. For the good of Dunyvaig and Cullen, let me in."

It was time to end the woman's obsession with Cullen once and for all. Tell her...tell her what? That she was staying as Cullen's lover? That there was a chance of him wedding her?

"When the sun comes up," Rose answered.

"But he will be back," she said, her voice taking on a desperate whine. "Let us settle this now, between women."

With an irritated huff, Rose lifted the bar. The door swung, opening the black maw of the little room. Didn't the woman even have a taper? Beatrice's face appeared like a moon in the darkest of nights, and she stepped forward into Cullen's room.

Keeping an eye on Beatrice as she walked to the hearth, Rose started to push the door shut. Halfway closed, it caught. In the space of a frantic heartbeat, rough arms yanked her into the blackness. She slammed into a chest, a foul-smelling hand covering her mouth, preventing her scream. Sour breath huffed against her cheek as she was shoved into Cullen's room.

"We meet again, Madeleine," Henri de Fleur hissed into her face. He turned her to pull her back against his front, one hand over her mouth and the other wrapped tightly over her ribs. "And you without my sword in your hands." He inhaled fully along Rose's ear. "I will never let you escape."

Over the man's hand, Rose watched Beatrice with wide eyes, hot betrayal once again slicing through her as if she were formed of butter. "Ye need to hurry," Beatrice said. "Someone may have heard us." She lowered the bar over the main door from the inside.

"Leave the letter," he said. "And we will exit this stone tomb."

Exit? He was stealing her away. Rose sucked air in as her heart pounded blood through her ears. She'd rather die. Rose twisted in Henri's arms, but he squeezed tighter, apparently not weakened by two days tied up in the dungeon.

"Save your strength, *mademoiselle*," he whispered with hot breath in French. "You will need it for my bed." He inhaled against her hair. "So sweet," he murmured. "I should thank Duffie for taking your maidenhead. No longer the virgin, you will belong to me instead of the king." His breathy whispers sent a wave of revulsion washing grime down through Rose. But she was helpless against him. Her heart flew, and she sucked much needed air through her nose.

Beatrice dashed around the room, opening the clothespress and trunk at the end of Cullen's bed. "I don't know where he keeps the pearls."

Henri cursed. "I want them. They are worth more than this whole damn island."

Beatrice flipped open the few drawers in Cullen's desk, her face and neck splotchy, her fear palatable. Could she sense the danger she was in? Rose had learned on the ship that Henri collected pretty girls like bored, cultured women collected pretty threads for their embroidery.

"Here," Beatrice called, raising Cullen's leather pouch high in triumph. She dumped the contents out in her palm; one of the pearls tapped the floorboards, jumping to lodge itself in the fibers of the rug before the hearth.

"Bring it," Henri said. He looked back over his shoulder at the open stairway into blackness. "Let's go. My men will be waiting."

Beatrice poured the pearls back into the bag and grabbed Rose's fur-lined wool cape from a hook. "She will freeze without it. Your king will want her alive, won't he?"

Rose would have laughed if her mouth were free. Would the king even want her after Henri and his men took turns with her on the voyage back to France? If he even took her back to France. More likely Henri would keep her and sell the pearls, letting King Francis think that she'd died at sea, or orse, at the hands of the MacDonalds.

"Fine," he said and gestured to the black descent.

Beatrice handed him the leather bag, which he tucked in is belt. She grabbed a lit candle and hurried to the top of the ecret stairs. Gone was the woman who sauntered, a haughty neer on her face. She was practically panicked. Was she afraid f being caught by Cullen? Or was Beatrice realizing that she ould burn in hell for her betrayal?

Henri shoved Rose into the cold shadows. Maybe she ould knock him off-balance, and they'd both plunge. For s soon as she ascertained that there was no escape, Rose ntended to find the quickest way to death. Her own death as her only weapon at the moment.

Beatrice took the steps swiftly, obviously knowing her ay from the nights of sneaking up to Cullen's room. Henri ullied Rose down the first step and realized he'd have to old on to the damp, jagged wall beside him. He'd have to hoose between holding her mouth or her arm.

He leaned to her ear and spoke in French. "No one ill hear your screams down the throat of this stone beast, Madeleine. And if you scream, I will kill the girl."

Did he actually think she cared about the stupid woman ho was helping him abduct her? Realizing how weak the hreat was, he added to it. "I will also make certain to tie you round the neck on my ship while each of my men has a taste f you. *Oui*? One scream and your voyage will be beyond ell."

The fact that the punishment already churned in his mind ade it very likely to happen anyway, but at the moment, the hreat dampened her natural response. Slowly he took his and away from her mouth. She spit out the taste of him and rew in a full breath.

With a shove, his fingers pinching into her upper arm, Henri forced her to descend. They followed Beatrice's candlelight, which sent shadows across the narrow passage.

"He will kill you," Rose whispered, her French word harsh but controlled.

Henri snorted. "No doubt he hoped I'd fall asleep and ki myself on his damn noose. But *non*, I am alive, and soon ther will be nothing the bastard Scot can do about it."

"Wouldn't you prefer to stay and get your revenge o him?" she said, her toes feeling for the next step.

Henri chuckled low. "I am not foolish enough to remai here, not when I have the prize I sought. Even without yo virginity, your value is beyond measure." His mouth cam down along her neck, leaving a wet mark, and she fought th revulsion that rose from her bubbling stomach. How cou she have ever survived King Francis slobbering over her?

When they emerged through the winter-bare bushes o the outside, Rose saw a jumble of ribbons to the side of th path. Proof that Cullen had been a rogue. But that was before. He'd told her about his past.

Henri laughed. "It seems you will not be missed if tho are tributes from other girls." He switched to English an grinned at Beatrice. "You should leave your ribbon tied her he said. "You've won the war to claim your man."

"He'll know I had a hand in this," she whispered, lookir through the deep shadows. There wasn't even a moon to she light, and the forest was dense, even devoid of leaves.

A twig snapped, and hope teased at Rose's stomach, on to recoil back into near panic as the faces of half a dozen Henri's men appeared to surround them. Familiar, grotesqu leering faces.

Beatrice gasped, but before anything else could con from her, a gag was shoved between her lips, and a pair solid arms wrapped around her.

Henri caught a rag that was tossed through the air. Ro screamed one piercing note, but he jammed the cloth betwee her own lips. Henri *tsk*ed and released her to his second-in-command, a foul-mouthed pirate named John. Rose could see Beatrice struggling as two crewmen wrapped her in rope, taunting her by turning her around and around like a toy top.

Henri uncoiled a rope he had hooked to his belt. "I knew my men would bring rope, but I thought you'd like to share mine from Dunyvaig's dungeon," he hissed and looped the rope, which he'd taken from his own neck, around Rose's.

The rasp of the braid against her newly healed skin tore through her composure. Fighting tears of despair, she couldn't help but tremble. Henri set her cloak around her shoulders, tying it under the coil of rope at her neck.

"Stay warm, my dove." He leaned close to her face. "You will find I'm a merciful master." His lips came around to her ear. "If you cooperate, I won't let the rest touch you. You will be mine, and the woman who betrayed you will become their plaything. Eh? A fitting end for a traitor." Rose watched Beatrice as she struggled in her bindings while the crew grinned.

"To the ship, gentlemen," Henri called. Rope around her wrists and neck, Rose stumbled forward behind him.

• • •

Cullen dismounted his bay, Jasper, and trudged up the stairs to the keep, Broc and Errol striding behind him. Dawn had risen an hour ago while he watched the strait between Islay and the mainland, and he'd seen enough to know he had a traitor in his midst. He slammed through the doors, his boots striking the wood with a sharp cadence.

Several were gathered for breakfast: Tor and his family, Cullen's mother, Ellen, and his two uncles. Even Agnes was present.

Cullen nodded to his mother, keeping his fury in check, as

he grabbed a tankard of ale from the sideboard. Washing the dust from his tongue, he turned.

"What is it?" Tor asked.

Broc and Errol drank, too, and flanked Cullen as he began to speak. "The ship that was spotted is not French, but English. Captain Taylor is sailing over to Islay."

Grace gasped, her wide eyes flying to Ava. "We need to hide you."

"All the women need to be above," Tor said.

"And the traitors who called them here," Cullen said his words hard, "need to be below in Dunyvaig dungeons." He watched Farlan flinch, his eyes blinking rapidly. The man practically yelled that he was a turncoat.

"How do ye know they were called here?" Charlotte asked.

"They come from the east without a glimpse of de Fleur's ship. And they are sailing over on their warship. Somehow they know about the French without seeing a single mast."

"Perhaps they saw something while sailing the coast and just waited until after Christmas to strike," Farlan said.

"The farmers along the shore would have sent word," Cullen said. "And Captain Taylor would choose firing on a French galleon over dancing a Christmas jig without a second of hesitation." His gaze moved to William. "Don't ye agree Uncle?"

William leveled his gaze on Cullen. "It is the better plan for Dunyvaig's safety. To show the English that we've captured a French captain. And they can capture his ship. We don't have a warship."

"William!" Charlotte yelled. "Ye sent word to Captain Taylor?"

"If the French have already sent their missive, and we let de Fleur leave, we'd look like traitors," he yelled back, his face growing red.

"Good God," Agnes said, her nostrils flared. "Ye called the English over to give them de Fleur?" The woman grasped her hands together before her. "Ye imbecile," she hissed.

"Dead or alive, giving de Fleur over is a show of English support," William said.

In that second, Cullen realized that William MacDonald was more irresponsible and dangerous to the clan than Cullen's father ever could have been. No longer would Cullen try to be the leader his uncles demanded. William was a traitor and a coward.

Cullen strode up to his uncle and loomed over him, his face right before William's. "In case ye didn't know, Uncle, I do *not* support England." His words seethed out from between his teeth, each one punctuated with fury. "Your father would be ashamed of ye."

"Do we know if de Fleur survived another night?" Tor asked.

Cullen stared at William until the man wisely stepped back, his face red, lips sucked in. Cullen gestured to Broc to check the dungeon. Now he had Captain Taylor coming, who would most likely demand to speak with Rose. And even if Cullen managed to convince him that she was indisposed, de Fleur would tell Taylor all about Madeleine. Cullen wouldn't get a chance to run the pirate through with his sword, and although Captain Taylor might be an obedient dog to his master king, he wasn't an idiot. He'd guess that Rose was the woman de Fleur sought.

Agnes, the shock on her face turning to outrage, walked up to William and slapped him across his bristled cheek. "I can't believe ye would call the English over here. They will see us only as criminal. Ye've ruined everything."

William took her ranting silently, and Farlan put himself between them.

"Not now, Agnes," Farlan said.

"I'm sure ye're behind this scheme, too," she yelled. "Ye two will destroy Dunyvaig!"

Cullen stared at the woman, her face contorted with rage. He'd known Agnes had a foul temper, but he'd never seen the sharpness of her unchecked fury. Something more than his uncles' stupidity was shattering her composure.

From behind him, he heard Broc yell. Errol and Cullen exchanged glances and took off toward the dungeon, Tor running behind them. As they reached the top of the narrow steps, Broc's voice shot up out of the dank. "He's gone. The bloody bastard's been freed."

Errol stopped, his hand slapping on his leather pouch where he kept the key. He looked at Cullen, his face telling Cullen all he needed to know. Someone had lifted his key. Cullen took the steps three at a time as he ran down to the dungeon where the cell stood empty, the door open.

Cullen stalked inside, his gaze going to the iron loop in the ceiling where the rope had been strung. A stool sat overturned on the floor. Cullen stared at the ceiling as the details around him fisted inside his chest. *Bloody hell*! The rope. The bastard had taken the rope with him when he escaped.

"Rose!"

Chapter Twenty

Rose sat on Henri's rumpled bed, her hands bound and the rope around her neck tied to a hook protruding from the rafters. Next to her, Beatrice sobbed. Henri had left them in his cabin as he worked on deck.

"Crying won't help you," Rose said softly, her head aching from lack of drinking water, cold, and the woman's piercing cries.

Beatrice gasped for breath, sniffing pathetically. "How could ye not be?"

Rose met her red-rimmed eyes. "I've been through all this before."

Beatrice stared at her, her face contorting. "Mother said he'd take ye back to your palace. That he would sail ye away to where ye belong." She looked around the cabin. "Not anything like this."

"And what did your mother say about the rope burns round my neck?" Rose asked. "That someone who would carry me safely home would tie me up? Are you really that senseless?"

Rose turned away from Beatrice's streaked face an heard her sucking in short pants of tortured breath. "You mother let Henri out, didn't she?" Rose said.

"Aye," Beatrice sobbed. "She had me steal the key fro Errol."

"But she didn't know he'd take you, too." Rose snorte softly and shook her head, feeling the rub of the rope on h already chafed neck.

"I don't even love Cullen," Beatrice said, her wor stuttered. "My mother wants me to be the next Lac MacDonald. I prefer Errol. I told her that." She took a fu breath and let it out, trying to subdue her tears. "But whe my mother wants something, if I don't do it…" She let th rest hang.

Rose flinched, closing her eyes at the memory of Claire vicious slaps whenever Madeleine disagreed with her plar There was never a discussion, a compromise, a retraction what Madeleine was required to do. And it had led her her just as Agnes had led Beatrice to this same hell.

Rose opened her eyes on a full exhale and watched th woman. In some ways they were alike. "Can you swim?" Ro: asked.

"Not in winter in the sea. No one could survive that."

Unless she was able to get them to the second small bo tied to the side of the ship, there was no hope in the wate depths surrounding them. "Keep it in mind if you decide yo fate is not to survive," Rose said, solemnly. "For me, it is bett to die than to live at the hands of Henri or the king."

"Oh God," Beatrice whispered. "I…I…" She shook h head slowly. "I am so sorry."

Rose sighed deeply, sorrow heavy in her gut. "It soun like we have similar mothers. I wonder if they would choose different path if they knew the fate of their daughters." Ro had pondered that often in France, but had stopped the nig she escaped the palace, knowing that Claire saw her only as a commodity to be traded for the comfort of court life.

Beatrice rested her forehead on her bent knees, her shoulders shaking in silent grief. Light outside the porthole showed that the sun was up and bright. Henri had risked sailing close to Islay in the moonless night, mooring off the coast and tying up the farmer who was supposed to light the beacon to warn Cullen. Would he dare to sail out of the cove in the light of day?

By now Cullen must know she was gone, even if he didn't know Henri had escaped to his ship. "What was in the letter you left?" Rose asked.

Beatrice peeked up from her knees, wiping her running nose on her muddied skirt. Her forehead wrinkled in a new wave of what looked like regret. "My mother had me write that ye were leaving him to go back to the life of a courtesan. That ye couldn't live at Dunyvaig when ye were accustomed to palace life. And that ye never cared for him. That he should wed within his clan."

Cullen had never seen Rose's handwriting. Had he seen Beatrice's before? Would he know that it was all a lie? Or would he think that was why she didn't return his words of love? Had stopped him from talking about the future? She'd told him that love was a child's tale.

Rose inhaled, her breath shaky, and she lowered her face to her hands, giving in to the pain shattering through her. *Cullen.* A good and honorable man, strong and without deceit. A man who, despite her being a danger to his own clan, had risked his position by swearing to protect her. He was told he must choose his clan above all, and yet, he had risked so much to keep her safe. He must think her worthy, despite her upbringing.

Her heart contracted so hard it was likely to burst into dust. Tears welled out of her eyes, and she let them course down her cheeks for several minutes as she listened to her heart ignore her wish to wither away. Such pain. Would he believe she'd left him? That she was so spoiled and fickle that she would forsake his love for the splendor of court? Nausea swamped her as she cried silently. The thought of losing him, never seeing his smile again, never feeling him pull her to him or hearing him laugh or say her name, the name he'd given her... *Oh Cullen. Cullen, I love you.*

She raised her head. Love? Wiping her wet cheeks against her knees, Rose swallowed, her heart beating harder, hammering away at the numbness that had first enveloped her, pushing back the despair that fisted around her heart. She...loved Cullen. There was no doubt now. Not with this pain at the thought of losing him. "*Je l'aime,*" she whispered just under her breath. "I love him."

The realization that her heart could love after all she'd endured, that it wasn't always just a lie, gave her strength to straighten up. Cullen had called her brave and strong. Perhaps it was time she acted so. Hopelessness loosened its hold on her mind as her gaze searched the dim room for weapons or tools to aid them. Rose wiggled her hands behind her, feeling the slack in the quickly made knot. *I escaped before. I can do it again.* She may have been raised to satiate a man's sexual appetite, but she was so much more. It was time to be brave, strong, and clever. Rose breathed in fully, her tears receding as determination sprouted like a rain-fed seedling. The rope chafed at her twisting wrists, but they had loosened.

"Beatrice," she whispered as one hand finally slid free. "We need to work together."

Beatrice looked up, her face splotchy and wet. "I will do anything ye say."

• • •

Cullen raced up from the dungeons, running across the great hall where everyone waited. He pointed at Agnes. "Keep her here," he yelled without stopping and leaped up the stairs to his room. He slammed against the door, but the bar was lowered on the inside. "Rose!" he yelled, but his heavy breathing was his only answer. "Rose!"

"The secret steps," Errol said and tore back out of the room.

Bloody damn hell. Why hadn't he barred the steps? Cullen slammed his fist against the door, any pain from the impact numbed by his need to see Rose safely behind the door. Beside him Broc and Tor waited silently, all of them ready as soon as Errol lifted the bar.

"The door to the secret stairs was open," Errol said, panting, as Cullen charged into the empty room.

He turned in a circle, searching, but of course she wasn't there. "Nay," he yelled, his voice exploding up to the rafters. "The bastard took her."

Errol pointed to the open wardrobe and the lifted lid of the trunk. "He was looking for something."

Tor went to the desk, picking up a parchment. "She left a letter."

Cullen grabbed it from his hand, his eyes focusing on the unfamiliar script.

Cullen,

I am sorry to leave without saying good-bye, but I cannot stay here surrounded by rock walls and barbaric people. I've been given a chance to return to the French court. It is where I belong, decked in gold and silk, not borrowed wool. You are the leader of a proud people and should look among your own to find a lady to lead by your side. Do not follow me. There is nothing you could offer me that I want.

Thank you for helping me.

Madeleine Renald

Cullen's jaw clenched, his mouth opening to release the breath he'd been holding. "It's not from her," he said, though his chest felt like it was dropping down into his gut. Could he have frightened her away by saying he loved her? No. She would never return to the French court, especially with that dog of a pirate. "Nay." He shook his head, crumpling the thin parchment. "This isn't Rose. He took her."

"What does she say?" Errol asked, picking it up off the ground where Cullen had let it drop.

"He's taken her to his ship," Cullen said, traipsing to the door over the secret stairs. The cold that billowed up from the depths sent a chill through his bones. It was as if the very life of him was balanced on the precipice of finding Rose alive. The bastard had hours lead time. By now he could already be putting to sail, taking Rose anywhere the sea flowed. "Damn," Cullen growled low. He rubbed a hand over his chest where it constricted.

"How do ye know it's not from her?" Errol asked. "It says she wants to go back to France. Could de Fleur have offered to take her back to the French court?"

Cullen swiveled toward him. "Look at the name she signed."

"Madeleine Renald," Tor read.

Cullen met his best friend's troubled eyes. "Madeleine Renald is dead. There is only Rose." The woman he loved the only woman he loved. He should have bound her to him asked her if she loved him. Spoken in English, asked her to wed with him, even if she didn't believe in love.

"I think I know what he was looking for," Broc said near the hearth. He stood, holding up a single pearl. But Cullen could not care less about the valuable necklace, each of its pearls representing an atrocity against Rose.

The men followed Cullen down to the great hall below where William sat deflated and Farlan paced. Agnes stood

er eyes hard and her lips pursed. Grace sniffed into a
andkerchief while Joan stood close to his mother. All eyes
urned to Cullen as he walked in. "The bastard took Rose."

"Did she leave any word?" Agnes asked.

Cullen had never before wished to strangle a woman.
Until now. Striding to halt abruptly before her, he looked
own, forcing his hands to fist at his sides. "We found the
etter that was left."

"What does it say?" she asked.

"Why don't ye tell us, Agnes?"

"How would I know?"

"Because Rose certainly didn't write it."

She walked to Tor, pointing at the wrinkled letter in his
and. "Ye don't know that. She could have simply left when
ne had the opportunity." She grabbed it, reading aloud.

"I've been given a chance to return to the French court. It
where I belong, decked in gold and silk, not borrowed wool.
ou are the leader of a proud people and should look among
our own to find a lady to lead by your side. Do not follow me.
here is nothing you could offer me that I want."

Agnes lowered her hand. "Don't ye see, Cullen? She was
ing about loving you the whole time. It was an act."

But Rose had never told him she loved him, had said love
as a child's tale. She'd never sought to maneuver him with
eclarations of love.

Agnes threw her arms out wide. "She attempted to be
ne lady here, but realized it wasn't what she truly wanted.
emember what the French captain said." She jabbed her
ointed finger at Cullen. "She lies, manipulates men. Lets
nem win and think they have the upper hand when she's
eally scheming inside to undo them."

From the corner, William cleared his throat, his words
oming with a croak. "She won the chess match." He stood
p and took a big breath. "Ye are wrong, Agnes, about Rose."

"How the bloody hell would ye know anything about th[
ye traitor?"

He stepped forward, his gaze moving from Agnes [
Cullen. "She may have been raised to lie and manipula[
but her heart is honest. She could have let me win whe[
we played chess, trying to win my favor, but she chose to [
against her upbringing. She beat me honestly." He turned [
Agnes. "Rose doesn't lie. Ye do."

"Ye sent Beatrice to steal my key," Errol said from whe[
he stood by the table. His face ashen, Errol looked like [
would never believe another female as long as he lived. Agn[
crossed her arms before her and looked away.

Garrick ran in from the entryway. "Captains Taylor an[
Thompson have landed with a group of twelve armed me[
They're marching on Dunyvaig. Do we close the gates?"

Cullen looked between William and Agnes. All [
wanted to do was ride after Rose, bring her back, and mak[
her understand what he should have said last night. That h[
words before were more than passion-filled prattle. *Buin n[
chridhe dhuit*. His oath that she owned his heart and soul, h[
half of their wedding vows. All she needed to do was acce[
him for their union to be complete before the eyes of Go[
He'd pledged himself to her. A few words from her and sl[
would be his wife.

But with the English marching on Dunyvaig, he couldr[
just ride away. None of his light boats or ferries could catch[
galleon under full sail anyway. He needed a plan, a plan th[
would save Clan MacDonald and Rose.

"Nay," he said to Garrick. "Leave the gates open. L[
them come inside and see what havoc three traitors, wh[
don't coordinate their treason, can do within a clan."

"Where is Beatrice?" Charlotte asked, her voice har[
"Ye can add her to the dungeon with these three." His moth[
had apparently disowned William and Farlan.

"Beatrice had nothing to do with this," Agnes said. "She loves ye, Cullen. My daughter is the one ye should marry."

"She loves Cullen?" Errol said, his eyes narrowed at Agnes. "After she attacked me in the barn last night?"

Agnes's lips pursed tight. "A willing sacrifice to free up the man she loves to wed her."

"Oh, shut yer damn mouth, Agnes," Charlotte said. "Ye've done enough damage, releasing a scoundrel to steal away an innocent lass. I wouldn't let Cullen marry your daughter if she were the queen of Scotland."

Cullen turned away from the spiteful old bag to see Bonnie and Blair run into the keep. "There are English marching up the hill," Blair called.

"And we can't find Beatrice," Bonnie said. "She was supposed to meet us at dawn, but we can't find her anywhere. Could the English have taken her?" They both ran toward Broc.

"Ava, ye and Grace go with Mairi upstairs," Tor said, and the three of them ran for the steps.

"Beatrice wasn't back at our cottage?" Agnes asked, her sharp brows pinching closer together.

"Nay," Bonnie answered. "And we've checked every cottage as we ran by. Everyone's locking up their barns and doors, thinking the English are here to steal their livestock and slaughter their children."

Agnes lowered onto the bench behind her. "We need to find her." Her gaze moved about the room, but no one responded. "She...she's innocent. Could the French captain...?"

"The man tied a rope around Rose's neck," Cullen said slowly, staring her down. "He is a brutal devil, who has no honor, and now ye've given him your daughter."

Boot heels cracked up the outer steps, through the entryway, and into the great hall. Captain Taylor at the lead with Captain Thompson following, they marched across and stopped before Cullen. "Duffie," Captain Taylor said "We received a missive stating that you have captured a Frenchman by the name of Henri de Fleur. That you care to surrender him and his ship to England."

Everyone in the great hall remained motionless. Cullen nodded, his arms braced across his chest. "Aye, that is all true But the captain is a slippery bastard and has escaped back to his ship, which I know is moored within a cove around Colonsay Isle." He'd watched the crewman row halfway to Colonsay before the ship came out to intercept him yesterday

"Escaped?" Thompson parroted, his gaze scanning the room. "Or let go?" Did he think they hid de Fleur behind a tapestry?

"Why would we call ye here if we let him go on purpose?" William said. "The man got loose."

Captain Taylor ignored his blustering companion, his focus assessing Cullen. "Which cove? There are dozens big enough to hide a ship."

"I can show ye," Cullen said.

"We have maps," Thompson said. "Just point them out and we will set sail immediately. The *King's Jewel* can outrun any galleon."

Cullen kept his eyes on the shrewd gaze of Captain Taylor "Ye take me with ye or I don't help ye capture a French galleon for King Henry. There's liable to be plenty of treasure on board, too." He raised one eyebrow in an unspoken appeal to the English captain's greed.

Captain Thompson puffed up his chest. "You will tell us where the ship is anchored or you will be arrested for treason against the English crown." He didn't seem to notice Tor Broc, and Errol resting their hands on the hilts of their swords

Taylor held up his hand to stop Thompson from continuing. "What do you gain from this?" he asked Cullen.

"I will guide ye to de Fleur in exchange for one piece of treasure on board," Cullen said.

Captain Thompson came up next to Cullen, but Cullen wouldn't release Captain Taylor's stare. "How dare you—" Thompson huffed, but Captain Taylor interrupted him.

"I could have you hanged for hampering the capture of a French ship. Investigate your people for conspiracy and take your lands."

Cullen's stance didn't waiver. And if William so much as cleared his throat, he would throw his dagger at him.

"Aye, Duffie," Captain Thompson repeated. "What treasure is worth your bloody life and possibly the Isle of Islay?"

Cullen's stare was made of ice despite the fire burning in his gut. "De Fleur stole my wife."

Chapter Twenty-One

Rose stretched to the end of her tether, her back bending to reach her stockinged foot toward Henri's desk drawer. Straining, her chin tipped up to give her the last inch, she grabbed the knob with her toes.

"That's it," Beatrice whispered.

The drawer dropped out with a bang, and both women froze for a long moment, listening. But the tread on the deck above them remained the same, and Rose flipped the contents with her foot.

"*Dieu merci*," she whispered and scooted the knife toward her until she could reach it with her fingers. With only three sawing motions on the rope about her neck, it broke. Heart pounding, she rushed to Beatrice, cutting through the rope around her own neck and hands. Beatrice grabbed her in a hug, squeezing so hard it was uncomfortable. "We are certainly not saved yet," Rose whispered.

Beatrice nodded, eyes wide. "Tell me what to do."

"First we find another blade. And be careful. Henri keeps them all extremely sharp." The first task was easy to ccomplish since Henri slept with one under his mattress. Hide it on you somewhere you can reach easily," Rose said. ose tucked hers in a robe pocket. She scooped the contents f the desk drawer back in so it would look undisturbed.

The glimmer of a needle and thread caught Rose's eyes. he fished them out and hurried to the rope. "Two stitches keep the rope around us, so when they come, they'll think e are still tied tight. If we are to escape, we will need the dvantage of surprise."

"Aye," Beatrice whispered, her fingers moving nimbly to reak the thread and jam the needle point through the thick pe. Soon both of them had ropes strung around their necks nd wrists. "Ye are so clever," Beatrice said.

Madeleine had spent her whole life trying to figure out ays to escape situations, whether it was from her cruel other or drunken courtiers, and when backed into a corner, woman needed surprise to help her succeed. "When he mes for you," Rose said. "I will speak to him in French. 'onvince him to take me, too. If he doesn't, you will have to scape and climb into the one small boat left tied to the side f the ship. There are two ropes keeping it up, one at each end. or it to fall, you need to cut both ends."

Beatrice nodded, her lips parted and her breath coming ist. "I can't do that alone."

"I managed once, but it's not ideal." She couldn't emember how, having been knocked unconscious. Only the and of God had kept her in the boat to live until Cullen und her on the shores of Islay. *Cullen.* She would get back him or die trying.

Footsteps sounded on the rungs of the ladder outside e cabin door. Rose nodded to Beatrice. "Be brave," she hispered and inhaled slowly, fighting off the pangs of panic.

A key turned in the brass lock, and Henri filled the open oorway. Hair windblown and a half grin propping up one

side of his mouth, Rose wondered how she ever could ha
trusted him to sail her away from France. Desperation ma
one rash and foolish.

As anticipated, Henri went straight toward Beatrice. "T
men are anxious to meet you, my dear. Above deck whe
you can feel the sun on your face."

"I would watch her defiled," Rose said in French. "Tal
me up, too."

Henri's grin turned toothy, and he laughed. "*Oui*, n
sweet. You thirst for revenge, *non*." Reaching high, he unti
the intricate knots from the hooks in the ceiling and broug
them along like dogs on leashes. He threw an arm arou
Rose's shoulders. He smelled of sweat and ale. He breath
near her ear. "We can join in, my dove."

The perverse bastard was giddy with excitement a
whistled as he climbed before them up the ladder, the
ropes in his hand. The leers that greeted them above de
threatened to overwhelm Rose with terror. Her valuab
virginity no more, even with Henri wanting to keep her f
himself, he wouldn't be able to deflect all of them if th
turned on her along with Beatrice. Henri's first mate, Joh
was openly stroking himself through his trousers. They thre
lustful taunts at them, but luckily, they were in French
Beatrice couldn't understand all the ways they were planni
to violate her.

Focus. To the boat. Rose narrowed her concentration o
her goal, and shied away from the wall of crewmen so that sl
and Beatrice reached the ends of their tethers with the sm
dinghy hoisted behind them.

"When I say, break through your bindings, jump in
the boat, and slice through the rope on your end," Ro
whispered. "Hold on when we drop." All she needed w
a distraction. *S'il vous plaît, mon Dieu*, she prayed, her li
moving in silence.

"*Navire!*" yelled the lookout from high up in the bare masts. A ship? "*Anglais!*" An English ship?

"What is it?" Beatrice asked as the crewmen turned away from them, running to the bow.

"A distraction," Rose said, breaking through the ropes around her neck and hands with ease. Beatrice followed. "Get in," Rose said. "But don't cut all the way through yet."

Rose sawed apart two of the three threads of the rope on her side, when a cannon boomed. The impact hit the water near the bow, sending a splash high and scattering the crewmen. Henri yelled orders for their cannons to be manned. "Madeleine," he shouted, but she ignored him.

Another explosion blasted, hitting the ship. The impact shoved Beatrice hard into her line, her knife cutting completely through the rope. She screamed as the dinghy listed downward. If Rose didn't cut her side, the girl would be dumped into the frigid water. Without thought, Rose sliced her dagger through the last line of her rope. Beatrice clutched the rails as the small boat plunged straight down into the Atlantic.

Dieu merci, the boat had landed right side up with Beatrice inside. She looked upward. "Jump," she called, waving frantically.

Knife still in hand, Rose propped one foot onto the gunwale. She inhaled, preparing to leap, when two hands dug into her waist, yanking her back. Without knowing who or how many were behind her, Rose lifted the dagger in two hands as she was spun around. Face-to-face with the black-toothed grin of John, she thrust her fisted hands downward, dagger point first. Her aim was true, slicing down through the *V* of his untied shirt, through the dark curling chest hair, and into the hollow at the base of John's throat.

John's hold on her dropped, and he grabbed his neck, blood gurgling up from around the protruding knife. Rose drew his heavy sword as he fell over and looked out at the deck, cluttered with running crewmen.

All of them, including Henri, seemed to have forgotten her as they raised the sails and returned fire. Each cannon release shook the ship beneath Rose, making her stagger. She looked over the side, but Beatrice's boat was halfway to the English ship. Rose squinted at the deck. Was that Tom Maclean? And Errol? Broc? What were they doing on an English vessel?

"Rose." The faint call of Cullen's voice wrapped around Rose's heart, and she spun. Dripping wet, Cullen's head appeared over the bow at the far end of the ship. Hand over hand, he climbed a rope that attached to a long arrow piercing the wooden foremast. His head disappeared as he threw a leg over the side and hoisted himself up onto the deck.

Henri drew his sword, laughing as Cullen reached for his own weapon, only to find it missing. His great-grandfather's sword was probably sinking to the ocean floor. Unarmed, Cullen faced the French captain.

Rose lifted the sword she'd taken from John, the deck length seeming to grow longer like the setting of one of her nightmares. Several crewmen spotted her, turning her way. She couldn't wait any longer to act. With a quick prayer, she inhaled, standing on her toes and leveling the sword tip. *Mon Dieu.* She charged forward.

• • •

Blood pumped through Cullen's freezing body. He curled his fingers, willing the numbness to subside as he faced de Fleur on the deck of his shattering ship. The mightier *King's Jewel* could certainly take this French galleon, but Cullen refused to leave Rose to go down with it. Another cannon struck the hull, throwing both men off-balance, but de Fleur kept his blasted sword. Without his own, the victory would be difficult. But with Rose standing alone on the other end of the ship, there was no choice but victory, for he wouldn't lose her again.

A high-pitched roar shot through the air, and Cullen glanced from de Fleur to see Rose running toward him, sword held out before her. In her white night rail and robe, hair unbound, lips pulled back, she looked like an avenging angel. Dodging two pirates, a third caught her around the waist. But she pitched the sword forward.

Its weight and her thrust sent the sword skidding across the deck, directly toward Cullen. As de Fleur lunged at him, Cullen threw himself on his stomach, rolling to the side to grab the sword. Still warm from Rose's hands, he held it as he sprung up. But instead of attacking de Fleur, he turned, running down the deck toward the bastard who held Rose by the wrist as he lit another cannon.

Cullen slammed his fist into the man's jaw, and the crewman spun away on impact. Rose flew into Cullen's arms. As if taking a breath upon breaking through the surface of the ocean, Cullen inhaled, and for the briefest of moments everything was as it should be. Rose. His Rose, in his arms. "I've got ye," he said. Her scent still clung to her, cutting through the bitter smoke and tang of sweaty bodies and low tide.

"Highlander!"

Cullen pivoted, setting Rose at his back, sword before him. De Fleur spit, stepping over one of his fallen men who had suffered a piece of the splintered mast through the neck. Blood smeared across de Fleur's forehead. "You shall pay for bringing the English here, Scot's dog. Lover of King Henry."

Cullen let him ramble on in mixed English and French. De Fleur defamed Cullen for his lack of manhood, except where it pertained to copulating with livestock and the English monarch. Without another small boat, Cullen needed a plan to get Rose and himself off the ship. But first, he needed to kill the bastard who'd put a rope around Rose's neck. "Stay behind me."

The claimed sword was lighter than his claymore, and despite his climb up the rope, power still radiated through him. He staggered slightly, lowering his shoulders to give the appearance of one who was at the end of his endurance. De Fleur grinned, idiotically taking the cues as truth. With a souring twist of his lips, he lunged. Cullen deflected the blow, pushing de Fleur to the side so as not to expose Rose. She hopped behind Cullen, keeping to his back.

Steel against steel, they struck and deflected. De Fleur threw his muscle into his attacks, grunting and cursing. Cullen let him get close but held him off with weakening grunts of his own. De Fleur laughed with the taste of near victory even though his ship was breaking apart around them under the cannon strikes.

Gasping for breath in the smoke, Cullen lowered his arms to feign exhaustion. De Fleur, spittle on his curled lips, lunged to deal the death blow. At the last second, Cullen raised his sword, bringing the hilt down on de Fleur's wrist. His sword clattered to the deck, and Cullen shoved his heel into the Frenchman's chest. The bastard sprawled backward. With two strides, Cullen stood over him, sword raised.

"She's mine!" de Fleur screamed, crazed fury twisting his face.

"She was *never* yours," Cullen said and thrust the sword down, straight through de Fleur's heart, pinning him to his own deck. The bastard's eyes bulged as blood leaked up around his wound, soaking his once-white shirt. He was surely on his way to Hell.

Another cannon hit, and Cullen ran toward Rose. Arm around her waist, he helped her duck under splintered masts and through the suffocating smoke toward his dangling rope.

hey'd have to brave the winter waters. "Can ye swim?"
ullen asked as he held Rose to him, wrapping the rope
ound their middle.

"Does it matter?" she asked, looking down and back up
meet his gaze. She knew as well as he did that it would be
early impossible for her to survive the swim to the English
lip. He'd made it by sheer desperation to find her and a
etime of swimming in freezing lochs.

Rose curled her fingers into his shirt, her face pinched
ith sorrow. "No matter what, know that…know that I love
u, Cullen Duffie. I would never leave you."

Secluded on the deck where the bowsprit stood splintered
ce a lightning-struck limb, he wrapped his arms around her,
ssing her with all the desperation and fear he'd felt when
e'd found her gone. Raking through her hair to cradle her
ead, he slanted his mouth over hers, reveling in the taste and
eat of his beautiful wildcat.

Rose answered him with her own molten kiss, giving
m as much as she could in that moment before they fought
e cold waves below. Another cannon strike shook them,
amming them, tied together, against the gunwale.

Cullen steadied them. "*Tha gaol agam ort*," he said,
ressing his thumb down her soft cheek. "I love ye, too. Will
marry me?"

Amidst the hell raining down around them, a bubble of
yous laughter broke from her lips. She nodded, in short,
gorous tips of her head, hair blowing around her face. "*Oui,*
ullen. *Je t'aime.* Yes, with all my heart," she replied, her
ay-green eyes the most beautiful color he'd ever seen. The
ords proclaiming their love, spoken in different languages,
anned oceans between their vastly different worlds. It didn't
atter that she was French or that she was meant for a king.
didn't matter that he was the MacDonald chief with a duty
his clan. They were not what they'd been told they must be.

Together, they were more than that.

"*Attrape les*," one of the crewmen yelled, spotting them. rush of filthy, desperate men came running. It was time to jun

Lifting Rose, Cullen stepped onto the gunwale. "Ho the rope, too, if ye can." Rose wrapped her fingers around th line and braced her feet against the side of the ship. Culle straddled her and did the same. Hand over hand, he dropp them closer to the sea. The waves spit up spray as they lapp against the hull. The cannons from the English had stoppe Taylor didn't want to lose his prize to the sea bottom.

The water loomed six feet below them. Above, de Fleu men climbed toward the arrow anchoring them to the sh He began to unloop the rope from their waists. "We ca swim with this rope around us," he yelled.

"I don't intend for ye to swim at all," came a man's strain voice. Cullen kicked against the hull to look around the ed of the ship where a dinghy fought the waves, two people in Beatrice and a half-drowned Errol.

"*Dieu merci*," Rose yelled. "Beatrice!"

"I wasn't leaving ye up there," she yelled toward h "Errol jumped off the English ship to help me."

Errol threw his shoulders into rowing directly under the and Cullen held Rose as he uncoiled her, lowering her into th shifting boat. Cullen followed, sitting quickly to take over f Errol. His cousin breathed heavily. "'Twould have been light to row if the daft woman would have climbed up into the sh instead of deciding to row herself back over here."

"I wasn't leaving her," Beatrice yelled back, tears flowi freely from her eyes as she reached forward to grab Ros hand. Beatrice's gaze rose to the ship, pocked with cann holes in the upper deck, the masts broken, smoke rolling t to the clouds. "Is he dead?" she asked.

"*Oui*," Rose said, meeting Cullen's gaze. "Henri de Fle will never harm another soul again."

Chapter Twenty-Two

"So, your name is Rose Maclean," Captain Taylor said and rubbed a hand down his face. Distrust was evident in his tone, but he seemed less prying since hauling in the French galleon with Cullen's help. Capturing a well-known French pirate's ship would be a huge boon to Captain Taylor's military record.

"Aye," Rose said instead of her usual *oui*.

Cullen rested his warm hands on her shoulders. After risking life and clan to save her, there was no doubt that he supported her in every way possible. And the turnout today showed the clan might feel the same.

They stood in Dunyvaig's great hall before the holly-bedecked hearth. The golden glow of hundreds of candles cast shadows and light over the gathered crowd. MacDonalds, Duffies, as well as others living in Dunyvaig's village had shown up en masse to the night's festivities.

"She is a distant cousin," Tor Maclean said. "From the north."

"She's orphaned," Beatrice said from her spot next to Errol. With her mother exiled, Errol had stepped up to help

Beatrice despite his anger over her trickery. They had much to work through before he trusted her, or any woman, again but he'd begun to help her set up living on her own, and they were talking.

"She has no family to speak of. Only us," Broc said.

"I will swear to it," Joan Maclean added.

All the clan members on the front row, forming a half circle around the hearth, nodded, making Rose feel the press of tears in her eyes. She didn't even know all their names, but they'd heard how she'd risked her life to save Beatrice. In fact, the once-despised shrew wouldn't stop praising Rose for her cunning and bravery onboard Henri's ship.

"Yet you speak with a French accent, and a French pirate stole you from your bedchamber when he escaped Dunyvaig's dungeon."

"The fiend thought she was someone else," Charlotte said, nodding her head. "When he came to ask us to hide his king's ships along Islay."

"But the accent?" Captain Thompson said beside Taylor. "Where did you come by it?"

"I had a French tutor," Rose explained as if it made complete sense. "We spoke so often in his native language that it became natural for me to drop my *H*s and speak a bit through my nose." She tapped the end.

Beside her, Broc coughed into his fist and sniffed loudly. "Sorry," he mumbled when Captain Taylor cut him a glare.

"If ye wish to witness the proceedings, step aside," Cullen said. "If ye would prefer to return to the mainland to continue to unload the treasure from de Fleur's ship, feel free to depart."

"I thought you said she was already your wife." Taylor said, looking between them and Father Langdon.

"In the eyes of God," Cullen said. Rose gazed up into his handsome face, shining with happiness.

A man from the back of the room stood on top of a barrel

"Me arse is tired of sitting on this whisky that ought to be in my cup. On with the wedding." Several grunts of agreement went up through the gathered crowd.

"What happened to the woman the crew said de Fleur was hunting? Madeleine Renald?" Taylor asked, unsatisfied. "The pearls she stole were on his ship."

William stepped forward, his frown severe. "Madeleine Renald, whoever that is, must have been murdered by de Fleur for her pearls. Rose Duffie is the only lass to come upon our shores. She belongs here."

Farlan puffed up his chest, nodding to agree with his brother. "Now let us make this bond official before a bairn rounds out her stomach while we wait for ye to finish with yer questions." A wave of deep chuckles radiated through the crowd.

Rose blushed and blinked back tears. Of all the people, William and Farlan MacDonald had come to her side after Cullen had brought her home. They had immediately sworn allegiance to Cullen and had treated both of them with respect. Trust would have to be rebuilt between them, but it was a promising start.

With another perusal of Rose, Captain Taylor turned, waving Captain Thompson to follow him. Hands behind his back, leaning forward, he strode through the parting people with a regally indifferent bearing. The front doors banged shut behind them.

The crowd gathered back in, and Ava and Grace came out from hiding to join Tor near the hearth. From what Ava said, the English captains thought she was dead, so she couldn't be seen, and they shouldn't be allowed to question Grace since Grace had a tendency of looking guilty whenever questioned about anything.

"We are all here now?" the priest asked.

"Aye, Father," Cullen answered.

Rose turned toward her love, smiling brightly into his beautiful, deep brown eyes. Cullen held her hand in his. "Dearest Rose, *buin mo chridhe dhuit*. My heart belongs to ye."

"Cullen Duffie, *buin mo chridhe dhuit,*" she repeated. "My heart belongs to you." The priest guided them through the rest of their vows and blessed them, causing the room to erupt in cheers.

Cullen pulled her close and leaned in, his lips close to her ear. "From Christmas Day onward, first and foremost…" He backed up so they could gaze into each other's eyes. "I am a man, and ye are a woman. Not a clan chief, not a French royal. We are not what we've been told to be." He lifted his fingers to her cheek, stroking the skin. "We are more than that. We are what is in our hearts."

Rose looked up at her handsome rogue. "And what is in your heart, Cullen Duffie?" She smiled impishly.

His teeth showed with a broad grin. "Love for ye." He leaned forward until his lips brushed her ear. "And a desire to make my wildcat purr."

She laughed, tugging his face around to kiss her. "I love you, too, Cullen." She took one hand down to lay her knuckles against her lips over a very fake yawn. "What an exhausting day, *oui*? I think we should find our bed."

With that, Cullen scooped Rose up, causing a cheer and a wave of laughter to swell into the rafters. The sea of happy faces parted as he carried her toward the steps. Rose's heart beat with joy. She nuzzled into Cullen's neck, inhaling his scent. She was not lusted after for her witty banter or her beauty or her sexual prowess. She was loved, loved for who she was, loved for her heart.

Acknowledgments

A huge "thank you" goes out to my three children, who continue to support me, even though dinner is often late because Mom won't stop clacking away at the computer. You are my most triumphant creations. "Every child is a story yet to be told." And I know you will each have an amazing life story. Love you with all my heart! Mom

• • •

And as always, I please ask that you, my awesome readers, remind yourselves of the whispered symptoms of ovarian cancer. I am now a five-year survivor, one of the lucky ones. Please don't rely on luck. If you experience any of these symptoms, consistently for three weeks or more, go see your GYN.

— Bloating
— Eating less and feeling full faster
— Abdominal pain
— Trouble with your bladder

Other symptoms may include: indigestion, back pain, pain with intercourse, constipation, fatigue, and menstrual irregularities.

About the Author

Heather McCollum is an award-winning historical, paranormal, and YA romance writer. She is a member of Romance Writers of America and the Ruby Slippered Sisterhood of 2009 Golden Heart finalists.

The ancient magic and lush beauty of Great Britain entrances Ms. McCollum's heart and imagination every time she visits. The country's history and landscape have been a backdrop for her writing ever since her first journey across the pond.

When she is not creating vibrant characters and magical adventures on the page, she is roaring her own battle cry in the war against ovarian cancer. Ms. McCollum recently slayed the cancer beast and resides with her very own Highland hero, rescued golden retriever, and three kids in the wilds of suburbia on the mid-Atlantic coast. For more information about Ms. McCollum, please visit www.HeatherMcCollum.com.

URL and Social Media links:
www.HeatherMcCollum.com
https://www.facebook.com/HeatherMcCollumAuthor
https://twitter.com/HMcCollumAuthor
https://www.pinterest.com/hmccollumauthor/
https://www.instagram.com/heathermccollumauthor/

Get Scandalous with these historical reads...

HOW TO LOSE A HIGHLANDER
a *MacGregor Lairds* novel by Michelle McLean

In this Highlander *Taming of the Shrew* meets *How to Lose a Guy in 10 Days* tale, Sorcha Campbell and Laird Malcolm MacGregor are determined to break the bonds of their forced matrimony. To do so, they'll have to keep their hands, and hearts, to themselves, or risk being permanently wed. But there's a thin line between love and hate, and even their feuding clans might not be enough to keep their passion at bay.

UNMASKING THE EARL
a *Wayward in Wessex* novel by Elizabeth Keysian

The Earl of Stranraer is out for revenge. But his enemy has an unlikely protector—an innocent but headstrong miss who's determined to learn the art of seduction...any way she can. Stranraer does his best to protect her from the notorious rake he's bent on destroying, but in the process the earl gets an unexpected lesson of his own—in forgiveness...and love.

THE EARL'S NEW BRIDE
a *Daughters of Amhurst* novel by Frances Fowlkes

The Earl of Amhurst, Simon Devere, has returned to his estate in search of a wife and, more importantly, an heir. But a beautiful woman only brings heartbreak and ruin, and Simon's disfigured visage is proof enough of that. No, he wants a wife who is unattractive and undesirable—and the homelier, the better. But nothing about Lady Henrietta Beauchamp is homely. It's an impossible and unlikely match...unless this awkward beauty can bring hope back into a solitary beast's life.

43486123R00146